THE SURGEON'S APPRENTICE

Recent Titles by Sara Fraser available from Severn House

SPECS' WAR
BEAU SPECS
THE TARGET

THE SURGEON'S APPRENTICE

Sara Fraser

This first world edition published in Great Britain 2001 by
SEVERN HOUSE PUBLISHERS LTD of
9–15 High Street, Sutton, Surrey SM1 1DF.
This first world edition published in the USA 2001 by
SEVERN HOUSE PUBLISHERS INC of
595 Madison Avenue, New York, N.Y. 10022.

British Library Cataloguing in Publication Data

Fraser, Sara, 1937
    The surgeon's apprentice
    1. Surgery - England - History - 19th century - Fiction
    2. Historical fiction
    I. Title
    823.9'14 [F]

    ISBN 0-7278-5758-4

Typeset by Hewer Text Ltd,
Edinburgh Scotland.
Printed and bound in Great Britain by
MPG Books Ltd, Bodmin, Cornwall.

One

Birmingham, Warwickshire
January 1841

J ames Kerr followed his uncle's cloaked, top-hatted figure through the bustling, smoky streets, his boots squelching upon the thick layering of mud and filth which carpeted the ground. They soon reached their destination, the tall-gabled collection of large Georgian buildings that comprised the Birmingham General Hospital.

The uniformed porter at the main entrance saluted respectfully as he pocketed the shilling Septimus Nairn passed to him.

'Does Dr Barnes operate today?' Nairn asked.

'Indeed he does, sir. Within the next half hour I should think.'

'Come, Nephew.'

Nairn walked on into the building with James close at his heels.

James Kerr would never forget his first encounter with the tumult of noise and myriad smells of a great hospital. His nostrils were assailed with the stench of human waste, sweat, excreta, acidic carbolics. The corridors were thronged with hucksters carrying baskets laden with drinks and foodstuffs, pedlars offering their wares, sick and wasted wrecks of humanity crouching against walls, huddling on benches surrounded by fearful-eyed kinfolk. People talking, laughing, vociferously disputing. Distressed men and weeping women. Children shrieking in mirth as they played, or wailing with fright and

1

pain. Stretcher-bearing porters roughly pushing their way, buffeting aside those who stood in their path while their burden of suffering writhed and moaned in agony.

James stared in amazement through the open doors of wards when he glimpsed two, sometimes even three patients sharing the same bed.

He followed his uncle up several flights of stairs until the ceiling above them became the steep slanted gabling of the topmost floor. The long gloomy corridor was empty, but from behind the closed door at its far end a hubbub of noise resounded.

Septimus Nairn came to a standstill and turned.

'That room at the end of the corridor is the operating theatre, Nephew.' There was a hint of challenge in his voice. 'Are you sure that you wish to watch this operation? It can be a disturbing experience for those unaccustomed to the procedure.'

James was dismayed by his own rapidly increasing apprehension. But he hid his feelings and told the older man firmly, 'I'm sure, sir.'

'Very well. On your own head be it.' Nairn led the way onwards, his booted feet thumping hollowly on the bare wooden floorboards, and pushed open the door to enter the room beyond.

It was a Roman amphitheatre in minature. A small arena pit almost completely surrounded by a horseshoe of steeply rising wooden tiers divided by iron railings, each tier packed mostly by young medical students wearing black beaver top hats, nearly all of them smoking pipes or cheroots, and puffing out clouds of acrid tobacco smoke. The noise of talk and laughter was almost deafening in the confined space.

James stood at his uncle's side on the topmost tier staring about him, absorbing the scene. The small pit of the arena had a peculiarly fashioned table in its centre shaped like a long rectangular board with raised edges and hollowed-out troughs leading to holes at each corner. On the floor beneath each hole was a shallow wooden box half filled with sawdust, and at

2

regular intervals along the edges of the board fixed leather straps dangled towards the floor.

There were no windows in the room, instead the daylight came through large dirty fanlights set in the roof directly above the table, and more light from the flaring gas jets on the greasy dark walls. In the far wall facing the open end of the tiered horseshoe was a pair of closed double doors.

'Dr Nairn, how are you, sir?' A young florid-featured man pushed through the close packed bodies.

'I'm very well, Mr Milcheap. What is Dr Barnes doing today?'

'Amputation of the leg. Rumour has it he intends to beat his record.'

'Are you betting?' Nairn smiled.

'Only a couple of sovs.'

'For, or against?'

Arthur Milcheap's florid features became guarded, and he glanced from side to side as if fearing being overheard, then leaned forward to whisper hoarsely, 'Against. I believe that the old fellow has lost something of his speed lately.' He mimed as if he were drinking from a glass. 'Become overfond of the grog, I'm told, and can't cut so dextrous any more.'

Nairn nodded. 'I've heard the same.'

'Do you want to lay anything? I can get you odds of three to two against,' Milcheap offered.

'I'll lay five against.' Gold coins chinked as money changed hands.

'I'll be back in a jiffy.' Milcheap pushed away from them.

James looked questioningly at his uncle.

Nairn chuckled. 'Don't look so shocked, Nephew. It's an ancient custom to bet on the speed of an amputation. It adds to the excitement.'

James was uncertain about his own feelings on the matter and made no reply.

He began to find the air uncomfortably hot and nauseous, saturated by unwashed flesh, scented pomades, gas fumes, acrid tobacco smoke. A sheen of sweat broke out on his forehead.

'You appear to be rather heated, Nephew. Are you feeling perfectly well?' Nairn enquired quizzically.

'I'm perfectly well, thank you, sir,' James replied stiffly.

Milcheap returned and Nairn told him, 'My young companion here wishes to become my apprentice, Milcheap.' He winked slyly. 'Since this is his first operation I want him to have a good view. Perhaps you would be kind enough to ensure that he does so.'

The florid features grinned knowingly. 'But of course I will.' He took James's arm. 'Come with me.'

Pulling James behind him he began to push down towards the pit, shouting loudly, 'Make way for a raw 'un. Make way for a raw 'un!'

Men moved willingly and in brief seconds James and Milcheap were pressed up hard against the bottommost iron railing only scant distance from the operating table.

The double doors opened and a man appeared carrying a flat wooden case and a chair.

'That's Charlie Wood, he's acting as Barnes's assistant today,' Milcheap informed James.

The newcomer opened the case and took out a series of knives, scalpels, saws, clamps, tourniquet screws which he laid out on the chair. He then waxed some ligature threads which he pulled through his buttonhole.

A roughly dressed, tough-looking man came through the double doors.

'He looks like a boxer!' James exclaimed.

'He's one of the regular attendants.' Milcheap grinned. 'They need to be tough. Some of the patients can need a deal of restraining.'

Dr Barnes came next, in company with another man, both wearing frock coats that were thick with dried blood and bodily fluids.

The noise died away instantly and there was an expectant hush.

Barnes was tall and white haired, his voice thin and reedlike as he greeted his audience.

4

'Good afternoon, gentlemen.'

'Good afternoon, sir,' a deep chorus replied.

There sounded a clattering of boots as stretcher-bearing attendants entered through the double doors, and James experienced a rush of pity for the young man they carried.

He wore only a shirt and his eyes bulged with terror in his pallid emaciated features. He cried out in pain as the attendants lifted him on to the table.

James hissed in horror when he saw the greenish-black mass of rotten flesh that was the patient's lower right leg. The rancid stench enveloped him, and his stomach heaved involuntarily.

Milcheap grinned as he saw James's queasy expression. 'Now you know why we smoke in here. It helps to smother the stink.'

Under the directions of the assistant surgeons the attendants used the leather strapping to secure the patient to the table. While they were doing this Barnes told the audience, 'The patient is twenty-two years old and was employed as a common labourer. Like most of his class he is uncaring of any hygienic and healthful practices. Consequently he has spent his life in filth and ignorance, as a result of which, although his muscularity is well-developed, nevertheless his constitution has been greatly undermined, his vital forces diminished, and he is subject to scrofulus disorders, and the Itch.

'He has recently suffered compound fractures of the right tibia and fibula, luxation of the knee with lacerations spreading traumatic gangrene, thus making amputation imperative in order to save his life . . .'

While he spoke an attendant brought in a bucket of water, some sponges and roller bandages and placed them on the floor to one side of the table.

'. . . I shall amputate at the middle of the femur using anterior and posterior flaps formed by transfixion of the members, in the first entrance passing behind the vena saphena. By the formation of the flaps from the flexor and extensor muscles of the thigh a better covering can be made for the end of the bone.'

James could not take his eyes from the patient, now trussed

and helpless like some sacrificial victim, moaning loudly, terror-filled eyes rolling in his deathly grey face.

Barnes turned back to the table.

'Is all ready? Very well. Mr Woods, you will take the arteries. Mr Hampshire, the soft parts.'

He lifted his face to his rapt audience and smiled. 'Time me, gentlemen, if you please.'

Pocket watches were snatched from fobs, and from the upper tiers voices bellowed, 'Heads! Heads! Heads!' until the men on the lower tiers removed their top hats to clear the sight path of their colleagues.

Barnes lifted the long-bladed knife, his assistants took position, and a concerted hiss of breath sounded as the steel was thrust through living flesh.

James jerked in shock as the patient's anguished scream filled his ears. Beside him Milcheap was counting aloud: 'One second, two seconds, three seconds, four seconds . . .'

Other voices were shouting out the seconds and there was a tumult of noise.

The patient's crescendoing shrieks were like lances thrusting into James's head. Nausea shuddered through him as he watched brutal hands gripping raw bleeding flesh, bending it back from white glistening bone, while blood steamed and trickled down troughs and dripped on to the sawdust. He heard the savage rasping of the saw teeth and sudden blackness whelmed over him.

'Thirty-seven seconds! I told you that the old boy had lost his speed, didn't I . . .'

As the darkness slowly lightened James could hear Milcheap exulting in his own sagacity.

'. . . I've realised it for months. I knew he'd begun to fail when he took that woman's foot off. He was fumbling then, and that was months ago. It was plain to me, if not to you.'

James opened his eyes to find that he was lying on his back surrounded by towering figures who appeared to be ignoring him completely.

6

'I do believe your would-be apprentice has rejoined us, Dr Nairn,' another voice announced.

Dazedly James struggled to push himself into a sitting position.

A fresh wave of darkness threatened to roll over him.

Supporting hands gripped beneath his armpits, and the threatening wave ebbed and rolled back.

'Don't try to stand until you are completely recovered,' Nairn's voice instructed.

James was suffused with shame and embarrassment.

He clambered to his feet, holding the iron railing to steady himself until the pounding dizziness in his head should subside.

'I must apologise, sir, for my weakness.' He forced himself to meet his uncle's eyes.

To his surprise he could discern no scorn, no contempt in their dark depths.

'You have nothing to apologise for, Nephew.' Nairn's tone was kindly. 'You're not the first by a long chalk that has found their first operation too much to endure. Isn't that so, gentlemen?'

'Indeed it is, Dr Nairn.'

'By God, yes.'

'I keeled over the first time I was at an operation.'

'It's nothing to be ashamed of, young man.'

'You will harden to it with custom.'

James was genuinely moved by their sympathetic understanding.

'And now we must take our leave, gentlemen,' Nairn announced.

The two men walked back through the city in silence, the cold damp air helping to clear James's head and calm his nausea, but doing nothing to lift the depression which lay heavy upon him.

As soon as they arrived back in his uncle's hotel room James felt driven to apologise again.

'I'm sorry that I disgraced you and myself so, sir.'

'You have disgraced neither of us, Nephew,' his uncle assured him. 'But I am wondering if you still wish to become a surgeon.'

7

James could find no ready answer. What he had witnessed in the operating theatre had deeply shocked and disturbed him. Up to this point in his life he had led a somewhat sheltered existence upon his widower father's small and remote country estate in Leicestershire. Educated by tutors, kept on a close rein by his overly strict father, now at twenty years of age he had little first-hand experience of life's brutalities.

Septimus Nairn shrewdly surmised the young man's troubled thoughts.

'Don't say anything yet, Nephew. Let us sit down and take a glass of wine, and allow you time to marshal your thoughts.'

After several glasses of the dark sweet Madeira, James' depressed spirits began slowly to lift.

Both men remained silent for several minutes, but Septimus Nairn was covertly observing his nephew, who sat with downcast head. The young man was tall and strongly built with the dark hair, fresh complexion and blue eyes of his Celtic ancestry, and had inherited the pleasant features of his long-dead mother, Nairn's only sister.

Eventually Nairn broke the silence.

'What was it that disturbed you most about the operation, Nephew?'

'There were many things that disturbed me, sir,' James answered thoughtfully. 'But I think that the worst thing was the screaming of that poor man.'

'What was the next worst thing?' Nairn pressed on.

James hesitated, reluctant to appear condemnatory. But the displayed attitudes and behaviour of the men in the operating theatre had been completely at odds with his idealised conception of the surgeon, that it had been his life-long ambition to become.

'Answer truthfully, Nephew,' Nairn encouraged. 'I shall not take anything you say amiss.'

The young man drew a deep breath and then said bluntly, 'It was the callousness. The sheer brutal callousness. Those men there today were behaving as if they were at a prizefight. They seemed to take no heed of that poor devil's sufferings.'

8

Nairn nodded. 'There is some truth in what you say.'

He paused as if inviting further opinions, and James continued.

'The patient was treated like an animal. He was brought in and displayed as if it were some sort of an entertainment. How must he have felt hearing men talking and laughing, hearing Dr Barnes discussing him as if he were a specimen in a freak show. He must have been completely mortified.'

'I am of the opinion that the patient was so terrified at what confronted him that he was completely oblivious to anything but his own terror,' Nairn answered reasonably. 'But let me explain something to you, Nephew. What you perceive as callousness, is in fact not that trait at all, but instead is the strength and resolution of character which all surgeons must possess.

'The suffering of the patient is a heavy burden that the surgeon must bear without complaint. You must always remember that the primary duty of the surgeon towards his patient is to ignore the screams, the pleas, the struggles of that same patient.

'Consider today. If Barnes had shown any hesitation in carrying out that operation, if he had permitted the screams of the patient to disturb his concentration, to deflect him from his purpose, then that patient would now be facing the speedy onset of death. The gangrene would have killed him in just a few days, maybe even in a few hours.

'We surgeons are engaged in a war against a seemingly all-powerful enemy. That enemy is Death. We must be hard and unflinching in our battles against Death. Any display of softness, of weakness on our part means defeat. Every time we hold back Death, no matter for what length of time, we have gained a victory.'

He paused to allow his words to sink home, waiting until he perceived the effect that they were having on his listener, and then went on.

'The surgeon inflicts a justifiable suffering upon his patients, because he is doing it in good faith and with a pure heart. He is

9

endeavouring with all his strength and purpose to save his patients, not to destroy them . . . To save their lives, Nephew.' Now he stopped and said no more.

James sat for long minutes silently considering what he had been told. It was the calm conviction his uncle had displayed which impressed him the most strongly. His recent perception shifted as now he realised that as his uncle had stated, it was not callousness he had witnessed today. Instead it was strength and resolution. His enthusiasm fired afresh when he considered himself as a warrior fighting an implacable, merciless foe.

'I still want to be a surgeon,' he said quietly. 'And to become your apprentice.'

Nairn experienced a pleasurable relief. He was at heart a very lonely man. A lifelong bachelor, grim-featured, stocky and at times taciturn, he had made very few close friends in his life, although he had many acquaintances who both admired and respected him. But now he was going to have kin of his own to share his life, to relieve his loneliness. Even perhaps to become, although a surrogate, the son he had always wished for.

He sprang to his feet and crossing to James' chair patted the young man's shoulder.

'I shall make a fine surgeon of you, Nephew.'

'I hope that I shall be able to become a fine surgeon, sir. But I can't help but wonder if I will ever be able to find sufficient strength and resolution to be able to bear the screams of the patients with equanimity.'

'You will harden to it, Nephew. It may take time, but you will harden to it, as we all have had to do.' Nairn smiled warmly. 'Come, I shall hire a post-chaise and we'll go home to Worcestershire directly.'

10

TWO

Hamlet of Tardebigge, Worcestershire

'**M**aster James? Come now, Master James. It's time you was up.'

James opened his eyes to see the rosy round face of Alice Biddle, his uncle's housekeeper smiling down at him.

'Have you slept well?'

He pushed himself upright, stretched his arms wide and returned her smile.

'I have indeed Mrs Biddle, thank you.'

He felt wonderfully alert and eager to embark upon his new course of life.

'There's a jug of hot water on the dresser there for you. Now make haste, for your uncle can't abide lay-a-beds.'

She bustled from the room.

The events of the previous day flooded back into James's mind and he felt a sense of relief that after a night's sleep the memory of the operation had somewhat lessened in its power to disturb him.

It was all so new to me, that's why I was so weak, he reasoned, and dismissing the subject from his mind he washed and shaved.

Downstairs he found his uncle accompanied by a bulky-bodied, red-faced man with close-cropped grey hair and startlingly blue bulbous eyes

'James, allow me to present my assistant, Mr Sean Fitzgerald.'

'Honoured to meet you, Jamie.' Fitzgerald greeted him in a broad Irish brogue.

11

The breakfast fare was fresh bread, thick slices of salted bacon and fried eggs washed down with tart-tasting cider. James ate and drank with relish.

Silence reigned until the meal was finished. Both elder men lit up cheroots, puffing out great clouds of rank-smelling smoke with evident satisfaction. Then Nairn said, 'I've something that I want to discuss with you, James,' and took the young man into his book-lined study.

'Now, Nephew, I can have an indenture drawn up today which will legally bind you to me as an apprentice Apothecary-Surgeon for a period of three years. The customary premium is three hundred pounds.

'It is advisable after the completion of that apprenticeship for you to spend at least another year walking the wards of a hospital. That costs a further forty pounds in fees. Then there are your living expenses and the purchase of the necessary books and instruments. In total it probably will amount to nearly one thousand pounds.'

He paused on observing James's shocked reaction to this very large sum, and smiled grimly.

'It's a great deal of money, is it not?'

'It is indeed, sir,' James agreed ruefully.

'And you do not have it, do you?'

'Not that amount, sir. I've two hundred and seventy pounds that my mother bequeathed me.'

'And your father, is he prepared to finance you?'

'No, sir. My father is adamantly opposed to my becoming a surgeon. He does not consider it to be a suitable profession for a gentleman to follow. We have quarrelled because of it, and he has disowned me.'

'Your father has always been a stupid snob, Nephew. It is one among many reasons why he and I have never been friendly,' Nairn deliberately baited.

James flushed and retorted, 'With all respect, sir, even though he and I are now estranged, he is still my father, and I can't allow you to insult him. He sincerely believes that he knows what is best for me, even though I can't accept his views. If you are not prepared to speak politely of him then we should part company now, for I've no wish to quarrel with you.'

He waited with some apprehension for a furious reply. If his uncle rejected him, his lifetime cherished dream of a medical career for which he had already sacrificed his parent, home and material security, would be left in ruins. But still he was determined that he would leave rather than stand and tamely submit to hearing his father insulted. If it had been a stranger doing so, he would have knocked that stranger down, but he could not bring himself to raise his fist against his mother's brother, his own blood relative.

The strained silence stretched until James's tension became almost unbearable, then relief flooded as Nairn replied with evident satisfaction, 'Well said, Nephew. You've passed a test of your loyalty. If you hadn't reacted as you have I should have thought much the worse of you and not accepted you as my apprentice.'

He rubbed his hands together briskly. 'Now here is what I propose. You will sign the indenture, and I shall forgo the premium, supply the books and instruments and give you bed and board here. That arrangement will continue so long as you give me satisfaction in your studies and progress.

'You must use the money your mother left you to pay for your own pleasures, but you may have the use of my horses on occasion. Is this acceptable to you?'

James nodded happily. 'Indeed it is, sir. And I thank you with all my heart.'

Nairn waved away the thanks and demanded, 'What medical knowledge do you have?'

'I've read a great many texts, particularly on anatomy, sir.'

'Have you now. Then you will know all about the trochanters?'

'They are found on the head of the femur, sir. The greater and lesser trochanters are prominent processes of bone which afford leverage to the muscles which rotate the thigh on its axis . . .'

13

For the next two hours Nairn relentlessly grilled the younger man on his knowledge of human anatomy.

Sometimes James stumbled, at other times he was forced to confess ignorance, but he was able to answer the majority of the questions with some degree of fluency.

At length Nairn ceased his interrogation and congratulated his nephew. 'You have done well. But from this moment on you will make the study of anatomy one of your primary purposes in life.'

Nairn rose from his chair and selected several books from the shelves which he placed on the desk in front of James.

'You will also study these works. Liston on Surgery, *The Manual of Therapeutics*, the *Materia Medica*, Buchan, and whatever else I decide that you should. Is that understood?'

'Yes, sir.'

Nairn's grim smile briefly curved his lips.

'You will also acknowledge our familial connection by addressing me as Uncle, and not as Sir.'

James experienced a burgeoning affection for this hard-featured man before him.

'Very well, Uncle.' He grinned happily.

Three

The first three months following his arrival at Tardebigge was a period of hard and unremitting work for James. Practically every waking hour of every day was spent in studying medical textbooks. His uncle proved to be a harsh task-master who demanded every last degree of mental effort from him. Each week, one night would be set aside during which Nairn would subject James to a relentless inquisition on what he had learned, and castigate him mercilessly for any errors in his answers.

'You're a damned fool, Nephew! That mistake could cost some unfortunate soul their life. Get back to your books, and this time study harder.'

Yet James did not resent these strictures, or the constant driving of his uncle, or the circumscribed, almost monastic life he was leading. If this was part of the price he had to pay to achieve his life's ambition, then he was more than ready to pay it.

At breakfast on the Friday of the last week in April while Nairn and Fitzgerald were smoking their cheroots, Nairn announced, 'I think it time that you were introduced to the practice, Nephew. Today you will accompany Mr Fitzgerald on his rounds, if that is acceptable to you, Sean?'

'Of course it is,' the Irishman agreed affably. 'It's about time I got to know this young man better. Here we've been living in the same house for more than the quarter of a year and I've yet to do hardly more than pass the time of day with him, you keep him so hard to the grindstone.'

He spoke without exaggeration. Although living in the same admittedly very large house James had seen comparatively little of the man.

'Who d'you want me to attend on, Septimus?' Fitzgerald asked.

'Go and see Neasom first, and then Mrs Landser. If she makes complaint tell her that I'll call on her tomorrow.' Nairn turned to James. 'Pay careful heed to whatever Mr Fitzgerald shows you today, and obey him as you would myself.'

'I shall, sir,' James agreed dutifully, already excited by this unexpected break from his normal grinding routine of study.

'Let's be making the start then, Jamie.' The Irishman grinned. 'For we've some riding to do.'

He led James outside to the stable block at the rear of the large house, shouting as he crossed the yard, 'Tommy, saddle up the brown mare for young Jamie, if you please.'

Inside the stables Tom Biddle, the housekeeper's squat-bodied, weather-beaten husband, stared with friendly interest at the young man but said nothing.

'Good morning,' James greeted.

Biddle only grinned and tugged his grizzled forelock, then busied himself with saddling the shaggy-coated brown mare.

'Tommy is not noted for his sparkling conversation,' Fitzgerald grinned. 'So his missus does enough talking for the both of them. I hold to the opinion that that's the reason that Tommy here never speaks. It's so long since he's been able to get a word in with his missus that he's lost the power of speech.'

James laughed. 'Perhaps that might be a blessing in disguise, Mr Fitzgerald.'

'I'm glad to see that you've a sense of humour,' the Irishman told him, and held out his hand. 'I know that you and I are going to become good friends, so no more Mr Fitzgerald, if you please. I'm to be Sean to you from now on. So let's shake on it.'

James shook the big boney hand with warm gratification at being proffered this new friendship.

*   *   *

16

The air was fresh and clean and James drew it deep into his lungs and blessed his present good fortune which had brought him to this adventure on which he and Fitzgerald were riding side by side, the Irishman with a wickerwork pannier strapped behind his saddle.

As they rode Fitzgerald poured out information in a constant stream.

'. . . We're betwixt the Redditch needlemaking and the Bromsgrove nailing but most of our practice is with the farming folk. Having the canal running through Tardebigge means we get a few cases from the bargees, and it's handy for Birmingham or Worcester if you choose to travel by boat . . .'

'. . . I was intended for the priesthood back home in Limerick. But when I was young I'd too much liking for the drink and the ladies to be wanting to wear a black cassock. Of course I was too young and green to know then that there's many a one wearing the black cassock who gets as drunk as a lord every night and has their sweethearts as well . . .'

'. . . I'm what they call a country doctor, Jamie, because I never went to the university but served my apprenticeship as an apothecary-surgeon back in County Meath. These university fellows with their Latin and Greek look down on us country doctors, but we're superior to them, because we've learned our profession by first-hand experience, and not sitting on our arses snoring though the lectures.

'Just take your uncle now. He served his apprenticeship to old Dr Taylor in Redditch, and then had a year walking the wards in the London hospitals. Some of them university scuts might sneer at him for that, but he's the finest surgeon I've ever known of. He gets called on to operate on patients all over this county, and even across into Warwickshire as well because he's so skilful.

'He's a great bone-setter is your uncle. A bloody marvel at it. I've seen him reduce dislocations where a dozen other surgeons have tried and failed. And he's a dab hand at pulling the teeth as well. Once he gets a grip on a tooth it just surrenders and comes out as sweet as a daisy . . .'

17

'Your uncle is a great man, Jamie. I feel honoured to be his assistant. And he pays me extraordinary well. Sixty pounds a year salary with bed and board, the use of a horse, and a share of the profits. I doubt there's another assistant in this entire country who gets treated so generous . . .'

James listened contentedly, now and again interjecting a question into the constant flow.

Their first call was at an isolated farmhouse where barking dogs came running out to greet them, followed by a ruddy-cheeked large-bodied woman and two buxom, fresh-complexioned girls who stared at James and smiled invitingly as he returned their gaze.

Fitzgerald grinned salaciously and whispered, 'It looks like you might do very well among the women hereabouts, me boy. They like young gentlemen better than the farm clods who they have to wed.'

Then he reined in and greeted the woman. 'How is your goodman today, Mrs Neasom?'

'He's still burning with the fever, Mr Fitzgerald. Last night he was tossing and turning and groaning so bad that I never got a wink of sleep.' Her eyes were fearful. 'Then he come downstairs a couple of hours ago, took a couple of swallows of hot gin toddy and said he felt funny and giddy. Then he just fell back in the settle and went senseless. He's been laying there ever since.'

The Irishman dismounted and told her soothingly, 'Now don't you fret yourself, Mistress, I'll soon have him as right as a tick.'

He unstrapped the pannier. 'I've a new physic made up special for him by Dr Nairn himself. It's a sure cure for the type of fever that your goodman is suffering from.'

'This new medicine, Mr Fitzgerald,' the woman looked doubtful, 'is it costly?'

The Irishman stared sternly at her. 'Yes, Mrs Neasom, it is costly. But how can you put a value on your goodman's health?'

She looked shamefaced and her ruddy colour heightened.

'Lead on, if you please,' Fitzgerald ordered grandly.

The woman entered the house followed by Fitzgerald, James

18

and the two girls giggling and nudging each other as they brought up the rear.

In the big kitchen a fire roared in the cooking range and the air was stifling. A hugely fat man swathed in blankets was half-lying on a wooden settle before the fire, breath snoring, sweat streaming down his broad dark-red face.

Fitzgerald stared down at the fat man. 'How long has he been like this did you say, Mistress?'

'About two hours. He come downstairs, drank a couple of glasses of gin toddy then said he felt a bit queer, and went off like he is now.' Her ruddy face frowned worriedly. 'Is he going to die?'

'Not at all. Not at all.' Fitzgerald smiled confidently.

The two girls seemed unconcerned by their father's condition. They merely giggled and nudged each other whenever either of them managed to catch James's eye.

'I'll have to ask you to leave the room, Mistress, while I examine your goodman. And you also, ladies.'

The Irishman shepherded the woman and her giggling daughters out of the room, then bent over her husband and spoke sharply into his hairy ear.

'Mr Neasom, can you hear me?'

The only reaction was a twitching of the closed eyelids.

Fitzgerald felt for the pulse in the man's throat and beckoned James to him, taking his fingers and placing them where his own fingertips had rested.

'Do you feel how thin and thready the pulse is, James?'

The young man nodded.

'Do you see the colour of the face, and the heavy sweating?'

'I do.'

'It's apoplexy, without a doubt. And it doesn't surprise me. I always knew that he was likely to have an attack of it.'

'How could you know that he might?' James was deeply interested.

The Irishman's tobacco-browned teeth bared in a grim chuckle.

'Because he's a gross bugger, with gross appetites and passions, my boy. Just look at the fat on him. He eats like a pig,

19

drinks like a fish, does no work, and he's got the temper of a mad dog.'

'Will he die?'

'Probably. Or be paralysed down one side. Or end up speechless and helpless. Or maybe feeble-minded. Unless God takes pity on him, of course. Then he might well make a decent sort of fist of recovery.'

'What can we do for him now? Surely we can aid his recovery?'

Fitzgerald chuckled with genuine amusement. 'By Jasus, you've a lot to learn about our profession, young James. And the first thing to learn is that we can do nothing of any real use in a severe case of apoplexy. However, we have to earn our fee, so fetch that pannier across here.'

He moved to the door and shouted loudly for Mrs Neasom. When she appeared he told her gravely, 'Your husband has suffered a very severe attack of apoplexy, Mrs Neasom. I have to tell you that his condition is very grave. I shall have to call in Dr Nairn for further consultation.'

She frowned anxiously. 'We're poor people, Mr Fitzgerald. The farm hasn't been doing so well lately, what with Mr Neasom's sicknesses. How much more will it cost to have Dr Nairn come here again? I don't know as how we can afford to pay the both of you.'

'Now you're not to worry about the money, Mrs Neasom,' Fitzgerald soothed kindly. 'You can rest assured that Dr Nairn and myself will not charge you more than you can afford to pay. We're both Christian gentlemen who endeavour to show charity towards the poor and afflicted.'

'Thank you, Mr Fitzgerald,' she uttered with visible relief.

'You go off and have a bit of a rest now, Mrs Neasom. I know that this has come as a terrible shock to you.' The Irishman gently ushered her from the room. 'I'll call you the very moment I finish the treatment.'

He was grinning broadly as he came to join James by the side of the unconscious man.

'Jasus! She's a caution, that one, isn't she just. Compared to

20

her, your man Shylock was a generous fool with his money. I'll tell you now, Jamie, all these bloody farmers are forever pleading poverty, but I've yet to see a thin one.'

James couldn't help but smile at the older man's drolleries, and then felt discomfited by his own self-perceived callousness in the presence of a gravely ill patient.

Fitzgerald took a large brass bowl which was flattened on one side and etched on its inner surface with lines and numbers. He explained as he did so, 'See these marks and numbers, they're to let you know how many fluid ounces you have in the bowl. I'm going to draw off twelves ounces from his arm. That should ease the plethora and congestion around his heart. Then I'll draw eight ounces more from his jugular vein to ease the congestion of the vessels in his brain.'

The lancet he took from his pocket case was pitted with rust, and he cursed. 'Dammit to hell! I was going to give this a good oiling and rubbing but I clean forgot.'

He tested the cutting edge with his thumb.

'It's sharp enough though, so there's no harm done.'

His eyes roved around the room and he grinned. 'Ahh haa! There it is.'

'There's what?' James was puzzled.

'The gin toddy your woman was blethering about.'

He lifted the half full pewter jug from the hearthside and drank from it.

'Not bad.' He grinned, smacking his lips loudly. 'Bit too much sugar for my taste, but beggars can't be choosers, can we. Here, take a pull at it. It'll help steady your nerves.'

'My nerves are steady. I don't need a drink.' James considered that Fitzgerald was displaying a brutally cavalier attitude. But then he thought that perhaps he himself was reacting with undue sensitivity. 'I'll take just a mouthful.'

The toddy was strong and sweet, and burned its way pleasantly down his throat.

'Good man, yourself,' Fitzgerald applauded. 'Let's get to it.'

He stripped the blankets away from the night-shirted man, pushed the sleeve up and fixed a leather tourniquet around the biceps of the left arm causing the lower veins to bulge and stand out against the skin.

'Hold the basin under his elbow,' he instructed. 'Now watch and listen carefully.'

He pointed the lancet at the distended veins in the bend of the arm.

'These are the median basilic and the median cephalic veins, both large enough to give a good flow of blood. But the basilic overlays the brachial artery at this point, so it is advisable to open the cephalic, that way the risk of cutting into the artery is much reduced. When making the cut use an oblique angle like so . . .'

He grasped Neasom's arm and sliced into the vein. The dark red blood flowed, dripping noisily into the basin.

James marvelled at the confident stroke the Irishman had made. He experienced no sense of queasiness at the sight and smell of the blood, only a rapidly burgeoning eagerness to try such a procedure himself.

When the desired amount had flowed, Fitzgerald released the tourniquet and used lint and adhesive plaster to staunch the blood flow, then fashioned a sling for the arm.

'Now, Jamie, when opening the jugular it is necessary to take great care. Help me move him to a suitable position.'

When they had moved the heavy flaccid body as needed, Fitzgerald placed James in position with the flat edge of the basin pressed hard against the man's lower neck, and instructed, 'Watch and listen carefully. I shall talk you through this as I carry it out.

'The vein is opened where it lies upon the sterno-mastoid muscle. It's covered by a layer of platysma-myoides muscle which must be opened first to reveal the vein.' He grinned. 'Just hark at me. Aren't I the most marvellous anatomist you've ever heard? And it's your uncle who's taught me most of it. Now just watch this . . .'

The razor-sharp blade incised skin and flesh.

'I now compress the vein with my thumb and finger here above the clavicle and below the point where I shall enter the lancet. This compression makes the vein rise and also prevents the entrance of air which could lead to a fatal result. There now, that's it!'

Once more blood snaked into the basin before James' entranced gaze.

A pad of lint and strips of adhesive plaster staunched the blood flow, and Fitzgerald congratulated his young colleague.

'I do believe that you're going to be a fine surgeon, James. You've the strong stomach. I reckon you enjoy seeing the lancet at work, don't you?'

James considered for several moments before admitting, 'I'm not sure about the enjoyment of it, Sean. But I do know that it fascinates me to watch you use it, and I feel the urge to use it myself.'

Fitzgerald tapped the bowl with his stubby forefinger and quipped, 'Go and throw that away quick. Because I'm sure that if Mrs Neasom gets hold of it she'll use it to make a black pudding, mean tight bitch that she is. Then we'll get this fellow to his bed and be off.'

As they rode away from the farmhouse Mrs Neasom and her plump-breasted girls waved them goodbye.

'I reckon that woman might be in the market for a new husband if her goodman dies,' Fitzgerald offered thoughtfully. 'A man could do a lot worse than marry her. It's a fine farm and she's got some tasty meat on her bones. I wouldn't mind shagging her, and that's a fact.'

He glanced slyly at James.

'And yourself? Could you give her one? I'll bet you've done some shagging, haven't you now? Let's be hearing about it.'

James's only experience of sex had been a few clumsy kisses and fumblings with a couple of girls in his native parish. He had never had sexual intercourse, and although possessing a strong sexual drive was a romantic where women were concerned.

Unwilling to confess his virginity and risk being jeered at for his lack of experience, he merely shrugged and smiled.

Momentary pique showed in the bulbous eyes of his companion.

23

'Ah well, if you don't want to tell me, then keep it to yourself. I was only having the crack with you.'

They followed a path for several miles through the fresh-budding greenery of extensive apple and pear orchards, woods and fields until they reached the canal.

Fitzgerald led the way along the towpath and ahead James could see several close-set plumes of smoke rising to create a pall in the still air.

'That's where we're going. The salt works at Stoke village.' Fitzgerald winked salaciously. 'You'll see some sights there that'll make your eyes water.'

The salt works were a huddle of large low-roofed wooden sheds on both sides of the canal connected by a bridge. Each shed with its tall, smoke-belching chimney. The air was acrid with sulphurous smoke and James coughed as the initial intake of the fumes irritated his throat.

A swarm of dirty ragged noisy urchins came to greet them, and Fitzgerald chuckled.

'Look at this lot, near everyone of them born a bastard. Their mothers stay the whole week from Monday to Saturday living at the works here, and spending their free time drinking and whoring.'

The works office was a small red-brick building and upon their arrival a dandified man with shiny pomaded red hair and a sweep of mustachios came out from its door.

'That's George Landser, the proprietor of this establishment,' Fitzgerald informed.

'Good afternoon, Mr Fitzgerald,' the man said as they reached him. Landser displayed a fine set of white porcelain false teeth in a beaming smile.

Fitzgerald introduced him as Nairn's nephew, and Landser turned his smile upon him.

'I am honoured to make your acquaintance, Mr Kerr. Now, gentlemen, I suggest that we take some refreshment before you attend upon my wife. I know that you will have had a tiresome journey.'

In the shabby office, its sole furnishings a battered pigeon-

24

hole desk strewn with papers, and several leather upholstered chairs, Landser poured generous measures of gin into glass tumblers and toasted. 'To my wife's speedy recovery, gentlemen.'

'That recovery is assured now that she is under the care of Dr Nairn and myself,' Fitzgerald asserted positively, and drained his gin in a single gulp. 'Agghhh. That's superb! You have the connoisseur's taste in Hollands, Mr Landser.'

The porcelain teeth flashed with gratification.

'I purchased a couple of dozen bottles from a small select distillery which has just come to my notice. I must insist that you take another glass, Mr Fitzgerald.'

James sipped his own drink, feeling somewhat bemused by the lack of urgency in attending to the sick woman.

'And how is Robert doing?' Fitzgerald enquired, and informed James, 'Robert is Mr Landser's son. He's at Oxford University, isn't he, Mr Landser?'

'He is.' Landser beamed proudly. 'And he's doing very well. He numbers several young noblemen among his friends there.'

'That must cost you a pretty penny then, Mr Landser, to enable him to keep up with their pursuits,' Fitzgerald suggested, and Landser's smile faltered.

'A very pretty penny indeed,' he agreed ruefully. Then his smile beamed once more. 'But it's money well spent. His noble friends will prove of great service to him in the future, I've no doubt of that.'

Almost an hour later, with the bottle emptied the three men made their way to a detached house some distance behind the office.

'Liddy? Liddy, where are you, my dear?' Landser shouted as they entered the musty smelling hallway.

There was a sound of hurrying footsteps from the floor above and then a petite young girl appeared at the top of the stairs and remonstrated in a low voice, 'Don't bellow so, Pa. Mamma's head is paining her dreadfully.'

'Here's Mr Fitzgerald and Mr Kerr come to see your mother,

my dear. I'll await you in my office, gentlemen.' George Landser made his departure.

The girl stood waiting for Fitzgerald and James to ascend. 'This way, if you please, gentlemen.'

She opened the bedroom door and stood aside to let them precede her. As he passed James nodded pleasantly to her, and the sweet fresh scent of her shapely, slender body filled his nostrils.

She returned him a fleeting smile, and he noted how white and even her teeth were. He found her very attractive with her lively blue eyes, the smattering of freckles across her pert nose and her vivid red hair hanging in a long net snood down her back.

Close up he could see that she was slightly older than he had first thought, and he judged her to be perhaps a couple of years younger than himself.

The bedroom was close-curtained and gloomy, the air heavy with a stale, sickly sweetish odour.

Beatrice Landser's features were gaunt, her eyes feverish and prenaturally large, her shoulders and arms painfully wasted. She raised herself from the heaped pillows to croak petulantly, 'Where is Dr Nairn? Why hasn't he come? He is supposed to be treating me in person.'

Fitzgerald smiled and told her soothingly, 'There now, dear lady, do not distress yourself. Dr Nairn has been unavoidably prevented from coming today. He sends his most sincere apologies and promises that he will attend upon you tomorrow afternoon at the very latest.'

'I could be dead before then,' she retorted, and was shaken by a fit of weak, breathy coughing.

The Irishman moved towards the bed, but before he had taken two paces the sick woman threw out her hands as if to push him back.

'No! Only Dr Nairn shall examine me,' she gasped.

Fitzgerald accepted the rebuff equably. 'As you wish, dear lady. We will withdraw and trouble you no further.'

Lydia Landser followed them out on to the landing and closed the door behind her.

'I must apologise for Mamma,' she told Fitzgerald, 'but she has had a very bad night and day of it.'

'Please, I fully understand.' Fitzgerald graciously waved away her apology, then became brisk and businesslike. 'Has you mother been taking the Peruvian Bark and Chalybeate Wine that Dr Nairn prescribed?'

'She has,' the girl confirmed. 'The dose every four hours as the Doctor instructed.'

'And her stools and urine? No trace of blood or pus?'

James stared questioningly at the Irishman, shocked that he could speak of such indelicate matters to a young gentlewoman.

But Lydia Landser seemed perfectly at ease. 'No, none.'

'Good.' Fitzgerald nodded. 'Well, we shall detain you no longer, Miss Landser. Dr Nairn will call tomorrow and make the examination of your mother.'

James hoped for another smile from this striking girl, but she only turned and went back into the bedroom without looking at him, and he felt a momentary pang of chagrin that he had obviously made no impression upon her.

Outside again he asked, 'What is the matter with Mrs Landser?'

'She has the Wasting Consumption. There's nothing we can do for her,' Fitzgerald informed him casually. 'It's amazing that she's lasted this long. I should think it will be a blessing for her husband when she goes. Her treatment is costing him a small fortune.' He grinned. 'She's been a good earner for us, we'll be sorry to lose her.'

James was disturbed by the implications of what the Irishman had told him.

'But if you can do nothing for her why not tell her husband so, and let him save his money.'

Fitzgerald showed amazement. 'Jasus Christ, boy! What do you think that we're running here? A bloody charity? Doctoring is a business like any other. Good profitable patients like Mrs Landser don't come along every day of the week. A whole lot of the buggers die on us or get well before we can start to show any decent profit on them.' He abruptly stopped and stared hard into James's eyes, then grinned. 'I can see that you're an idealist. You think that doctors should be selfless saints who go around treating the sick for free. You've a lot to learn, my young friend.'

Back in the office George Landser poured out gin for the three of them, and asked Fitzgerald, 'Can you recommend a good nursing woman, Mr Fitzgerald? I fear that my Liddy is carrying too heavy a burden in caring for her mother.'

The Irishman frowned doubtfully. 'Well now, that's a little difficult right this minute, sir.'

'I'll pay her well.'

'I'll see what I can do.'

'Thank you very much.'

'Well, regretfully we must leave you, sir. But before we go could I show my young friend here where the salt is made?'

'But of course.' Landser came to the door with them. 'And you'll not forget about the nurse, will you?'

'I'll make enquiries immediately,' Fitzgerald assured him.

As James and Fitzgerald walked towards the nearest of the great sheds the Irishman muttered indignantly, 'And pigs will fly before I'll send another nursing woman here. We've recommended four already and none of them stay more than a couple of weeks, because Beatrice Landser is a nasty, evil-tempered bitch who treats the women as if they're shit. I feel sorry for young Liddy having to put up with the bitch, as well as run the house for her pa.'

'Surely they've a maidservant or two?' James queried.

'The servants never stay more than a couple of weeks either. Why should a woman put up with being treated like shit when she can earn wages a lot easier elsewhere. Especially in these works.'

His bulbous blue eyes sparked with anticipatory pleasure.

'You're going to love seeing where the salt is made, Jamie. Just wait and see if you don't.'

The interior floor of the shed was filled with a great shallow evaporation pan fashioned from wrought iron and filled with bubbling boiling brine. The damp ammoniac air was thick with steam, and the heat caused James to sweat heavily before he had been many seconds inside. On each side of the pan was a raised wooden walkway some five feet wide and lined with wooden boxes in which the salt crystals were cooled and drained.

'Now isn't that a sight to gladden your eyes.' Fitzgerald indicated two figures busy about the wooden boxes on the nearer walkway.

James peered through the steam-misted air and blinked unbelievingly. The figures were two young women clad only in thin wet translucent shifts which clung to their bodies like a second skin and did nothing to hide their breasts and private parts.

The women saw the men but made no attempt to shield their bodies, only exchanged words and smiles with each other and stared back boldly.

'I've not seen you two before,' Fitzgerald called.

'That's because they warn't here before, Mr Fitzgerald.' A third woman materialised through the thick steam behind the men. She was middle-aged and like the other women wore only a thin wetly translucent shift, and James felt a rush of embarrassment as he found himself staring at her large drooping breasts and distinct triangle of pubic hair.

'Hello, Milly.' Fitzgerald's tongue ran over his lips. 'They look to be likely girls. I must make a visit.'

'They are, and you must.' Milly laughed. 'But for now I'd like you to bugger off and let us get on with our work. If we don't produce then we don't get wages. So sod off, if you please, Mr Fitzgerald, and take this young bugger with you. If his eyes pops out any further he'll never get 'um back into his head. I'll bet he's never seen a woman's cunt afore, has he?'

Fitzgerald led the way outside, and James felt sharp relief to escape Milly's mockery, and feel the cool air upon his heated sweaty face.

As they rode away from the works James asked curiously, 'How do you come to know that woman? Is she a patient of yours?'

29

'Only in a manner of speaking.' Fitzgerald laughed. 'On occasion I've given her the treatment.' His eyes dwelt on James's puzzled face for a couple of seconds, before he went on. 'It's as I told you, the women come here on Monday morning and stay at the works until Saturday afternoon. They sleep in the sheds at the back there. I reckon the heat of the work makes them randy, because nearly everyone of them is more than ready to play the whore for a couple of shillings or a bottle of gin.

'There's more than a few respectable gentlemen of this parish who come sneaking in here at night, I can tell you. I do myself from time to time. Of course, absolute discretion is necessary.'

'And does Mr Landser know what's going on?'

The Irishman shrugged. 'I think he acts like the three wise monkeys. He's a good-hearted man so I shouldn't think he begrudges them having their fun and earning themselves some extra money.'

His bulbous eyes glanced slyly.

'Maybe you'd like to come over with me the next time I pay a visit?'

James had no wish to buy any woman's body. He would enjoy coming back here only if it were to further his own acquaintance with Lydia Landser. But not wanting to offend his companion he answered with a smile, 'The state of my finances prevents me from even thinking about it at present, Sean. But maybe when I earn some money I'll accompany you.'

'Well, you'd better not leave it too late, else those two new ones will have lost their bloom. It don't take very long for fresh meat to taint and go off, you know.'

'No! Don't open that window. You know how the cold air affects me. You're a bad wicked girl to torment me so,' Beatrice Landser snarled furiously.

Liddy's own fiery temper sparked momentarily. 'The air in here is foul, Mamma. And it's not cold outside.'

'The air outside is full of smoke,' her mother retorted. 'You know very well that it makes me cough.'

30

'The wind is presently blowing the smoke away from us. That's why I wanted to take advantage of it and let some fresh air in here,' Liddy argued.

'Just go away and leave me in peace,' the sick woman demanded. 'I know that you want to see me dead. You both do, you and your father. Robert is the only one who cares for me in this family. Only Robert loves me. He's not looking forward to my death as you and your father are. Thank God I birthed a loving son and not another unnatural wicked creature like you to torment me.'

Liddy sighed as she endured the familiar tirade, accepted defeat and left the window closed. She and her mother did not share any close or loving relationship. Beatrice Landser had always favoured her son, and had never displayed any parental affection for her daughter. In consequence over the years Liddy's natural child's love for her mother had died. Now she felt only some degree of pity for the woman's physical sufferings, which to her credit she did her utmost to soothe and alleviate.

She bent over her mother and the reek of fresh faeces invaded her nostrils.

'I must bathe you, Mamma, and change your nightdress and bedding. And afterwards I'll make you some beef tea?' she offered. 'You've eaten nothing today. You must make the effort to take something.'

Her mother's clawlike fingers lashed viciously across Liddy's cheek, and she cried out in shock and pain and lifted her arms to shield her head.

'I eat nothing because I'm feared that you will poison me. Just leave me alone, will you. Go from my sight.' Beatrice Landser's eyes glared with savage hatred.

Without another word Liddy went out from the fetid room and downstairs. She stood in the kitchen, fighting to control her anger. It was my own fault for dropping my guard, for becoming careless and unwatchful, she thought.

Since her mother had fallen ill, these physical attacks had been of frequent occurrence. Although bitterly resentful of them, Liddy tried to accept that these outbreaks of violence were caused by a mental imbalance brought about by her mother's illness, and that the older woman was not responsible for her own actions at certain moments.

Despite her brief eighteen years, Liddy was not some foolish, flighty, mentally innocent girl. Living in such close proximity to the rough, hard-bitten salt workers she had unavoidably heard much foul language, and witnessed crude behaviour, fights and drunkenness. She knew the sexual proclivities of many of the women, and that most of the babies they gave birth to were illegitimate. Also, since the onset of her mother's illness, she had come to know intimately the painfully harsh realities of constant verbal and physical abuse, and all the foulnesses of diseased, decaying flesh.

Calmer now, she glanced out of the kitchen window and saw Fitzgerald and his young companion riding out of the dusty yard. She had been aware of the admiration in James Kerr's eyes and in her turn had found him very attractive.

She sighed regretfully. For her, romance must remain only a daydream. She was trapped here, caring for her sick mother, keeping house for her father. But she did not resent her father's need of her. She loved him dearly and always excused his failings. She would say to herself, It's not his fault that he's a drunkard. Being married to Mamma would make a saint turn to the drink . . .

'Lydia? Lydia? I need you. Come up here, I need you. I'm suffering.'

Beatrice Landser's querulous shouts echoed from above and, sighing resignedly, Liddy went back upstairs.

32

Four

Aﬁter the medical men had left him George Landser prepared to receive another expected visitor. From a desk
drawer he took out ledgers and papers, comprised of bills of
sale, receipts, tables of costs, geologists reports, order forms,
business correspondence, and sorted them into their respective
sections. Then he left the office, locking the door behind him,
and made his way through the works complex to a wide expanse
of barren heathland on the opposite side of the canal. The
heathland was dotted with wooden railed enclosures several
yards square, and it was to the furthest of these enclosures that
George Landser now headed.

When he reached it he climbed over the fence and walked
slowly to the edge of the gaping well-hole in the centre. He
stood on the edge of the hole for some moments, then picked up
a stone and dropped it down into the black depths of the shaft.
Scant seconds later a faint splash sounded, and he grimaced
despairingly.

George Landser was a desperately worried man. Ten years
previously he had used all his available capital to buy the salt
works. Most of that capital had been his wife's money. Initially
all had gone well with the business and after a few years he had
decided to expand the works. He had negotiated large loans
from several sources to finance the sinking of new shafts into
the subterranean brine beds and the installation of more sheds,
furnaces, evaporation troughs and new steam pumps. The
interest on the loans would take a major part of his income,
but he was untroubled by this, confident that as soon as the new
brine beds were tapped into and with his vastly enlarged works,

33

his salt production would more than treble, and his profits increase accordingly. He would be earning enough to repay all the capital sums and clear his debts within a few years, and then would go on to make a fortune.

But all had not gone to plan. The new buildings and equipment had been constructed and installed, but were still empty and idle. The geologists who had mapped out the subterranean brine beds had failed to detect the existence of underground fresh-water streams criss-crossing the heathland. The well-diggers had sunk shaft after shaft, only to break into a stream each time. Consequently they had been forced to abandon those shafts because if they continued to dig downwards then the fresh water would flood into the brine bed, contaminating and rendering it worthless.

The cumulative cost of sinking all these fruitless shafts, coupled with the interest payments, had proved crippling. In an attempt to cut his financial outlay Landser had sacked the works manager and taken over the day-to-day running of the business himself, and wherever it was possible replaced the male work hands with cheaper female labour. But this had gained him only a temporary respite and he had been unable to meet some interest payments in full. This in turn had led to heated confrontations with the affected creditors and threats to have him commited to the debtors' prison.

Now, though he still presented a bold front to the outside world, George Landser despairingly feared that his own world faced imminent ruin.

As Edward Harcourt Esq., Justice of the Peace, banker, and Chairman of the Parish Board of Guardians, neared the salt works he reined in his horse to a walk so that he could make a leisurely examination of the complex. He counted the chimneys from which smoke rose, and noted that they were a small minority. He saw that there was only one barge moored at the works canal wharf and that the labourers loading the cargo of hessian-wrapped blocks of salt were female. You're in serious trouble, Landser, he concluded.

He kicked the horse into a trot and rode across the canal bridge and up to the small detached works office.

A shabbily dressed woman was standing outside the office door and as he neared her told him, 'If you wants the master, he aren't here.'

He made no acknowledgement but rode on to the house and dismounted. After tethering his mount he hammered on the door with his riding crop.

When Liddy appeared he smiled. 'Good afternoon, Miss Lydia. I've come to see your father.'

'Is he not in his office, Mr Harcourt? I know he's expecting you.'

'I wouldn't be knocking your door if he were in his office, my dear.'

Harcourt was a wealthy bachelor, and even though middle-aged he still had a good figure displayed to full advantage by the elegant clothes he favoured. His teeth were sound, his brown hair still thick and only sparsely streaked with grey. Many of the local matrons regarded him as the finest catch in the parish for their unmarried daughters, and gossip had it that he was constantly pursued to this end.

Liddy herself had known him for some time, and his manner towards her was consistently kindly, even avuncular, yet Liddy always felt a vague sense of unease in his presence. There was something in his eyes when he looked at her that made her think of the predatory wolves in the fairy tales she had read as a child.

'He's not in the house, Mr Harcourt, but I'm sure he can't be far away. Would you care to step in and wait for him?'

'No, thank you, my dear. I'll have a stroll about the works. Perhaps I shall find your father.'

He touched his hat brim and walked away.

Then he saw George Landser approaching from the direction of the heathland and changed course to meet him, but the shabby woman hurried in front of him.

Harcourt heard their talk as he came up to them.

'Our Dot's leg has gone bad ways, Master. Her foot's all swelled up and red hot.'

George Landser's reaction was one of genuine concern. 'You'd best go and ask Dr Nairn to come to her, Rosie. Tell him that I'll pay . . . And here' – he rummaged in his pockets and handed her some coins – 'buy some delicacies for her. It might cheer her up.'

'I will, Master. God bless you.'

The shabby woman hurried away, and Harcourt shook his head and remonstrated, 'That money will go on drink, no doubt of it. You're too soft with them, George. And to have Dr Nairn to her will end up costing you dearly.'

'Rosie has worked for me for ten years, Edward; she'll not spend the money on drink. And as for the doctor, young Dot's been badly scalded by boiling brine. I can't just abandon the poor girl. She was one of my workers after all, and a good one at that.'

'She can go into the workhouse. She'll get medical care there.'

Landser smiled wryly. 'I think the poor girl would rather starve to death than enter the "Bastille". She has too much self-respect to become a pauper inmate.'

'The labouring classes don't know what self-respect is. They're little better than brute beasts,' Harcourt scoffed contemptuously.

'Some of them are, but not all,' Landser qualified pleasantly. 'However, you haven't come here to talk about the labourers, so will you come to the office please? I've all the necessary information ready for you.'

As they walked side by side Harcourt remarked casually, 'I went to the house in search of you and saw Lydia. She's suddenly blossomed into a beautiful woman, hasn't she?'

'Well, I think so, of course. But then, I'm her father and greatly prejudiced in her favour.' There was fond pride in Landser's voice.

'How old is she now?'

'Eighteen years last March.'

'It's high time she was married then. Has she a suitor?'

'No.'

'But surely there must be some young bucks hovering around her? Bees always swarm around honey.'

Landser was becoming disturbed by the tone of these prying questions, and answered shortly, 'My Liddy has no suitors, and no wish to get married. She is perfectly content as she is.'

Harcourt's smile was a sneer. 'How fortunate for you. It saves you the expense of employing a housekeeper.'

Too much was at stake for George Landser to show any resentment of the insulting implications of this remark. So he forced himself to smile.

'Yes, I'm well aware of that fact, Edward.'

In the office Harcourt refused the offer of a drink and immediately sat down and began intently scrutinising the documents and ledgers.

Landser sat watching, trying to hide his nervous tension, knowing that the future of himself and his family depended on Harcourt's decision whether or not to advance him the loan he sought.

It didn't take long for Edward Harcourt to satisfy himself that certain whispered rumours he had heard among the business circles of Birmingham contained much more than a grain of truth. In these balance sheets and ledgers, George Landser had very skilfully disguised his true financial plight, but Edward Harcourt could recognise clever artistic accounting when he saw it.

He didn't tax Landser with his findings, however, but continued to pore over the documentation, deriving cruel enjoyment from the knowledge that every minute that passed intensified the other man's torment.

At long last he stretched and yawned, and leaned back in his chair.

'I've seen enough, George.'

Landser eagerly craned forwards. 'It's not a large loan I'm requiring, Edward. And I'm willing to pay a higher rate of interest than the norm. All I need is sufficient to resume shaft-sinking. I'm convinced that the spot I've selected for the next shaft will be trouble free. I've had a dowser here, and he assures me that there are no underground streams anywhere near the new site. I could be tapping into the fresh brine bed and producing its salt within weeks only.'

Harcourt frowned doubtfully. 'The new brine bed lies deep, and the cost of sinking the shaft will be accordingly high. I can't believe that this warlock you speak of can guarantee the absence of fresh-water streams. And if a stream is broken into, then a great deal of my money is lost for nothing.'

'The man isn't any sort of male witch,' Landser argued, and now he was betraying his desperation, unconsciously raising his hands in a pleading gesture. 'He is a widely known and trusted finder of underground waters. He came to me with the highest of recommendations from other gentlemen for whom he has discovered water sources. All I need is this one shaft, Edward, and then I shall be on the road to riches. I only need this single shaft.'

'Let me consider the matter a little further, George.'

Harcourt steepled his fingers before his chest and bent his head until his chin rested upon his fingertips. He closed his eyes, pursed his lips and appeared to be thinking deeply. Landser could only sit fidgeting, anxiously waiting for the decision.

The seconds lengthened into minutes, and for George Landser those minutes seemed like hours. Then finally, Edward Harcourt looked up and smiled.

'We have known each other for many years, George, and I like to think that we have become friends in that time. Because of this I'll advance you the money you need, and at the usual rate of interest only.'

Relief made Landser feel momentarily weak. Then he poured out profuse thanks. But those words of thanks would have been strangled in his throat had he known that Edward Harcourt had a secret agenda. An agenda that included not only the salt works, but Landser's beloved Liddy as well.

Five

'I 'm sorry I was not back in time to see you last night, Nephew. You were in bed and asleep when I returned and I didn't wish to wake you. However, Mr Fitzgerald has informed me that you behaved very well yesterday,' Septimus Nairn told James across the breakfast table, and with a sly gleam in his eyes teased, 'He said that you didn't flinch when he let blood from Neasom. Indeed, quite the opposite, you appeared to relish the sight. I have to confess that surprised me after what happened in Birmingham.'

James took the banter in good part. 'I wouldn't claim that I relished it, sir. But I confess that I was able to eat a hearty dinner upon our return here.'

The older man nodded, well satisfied with that answer. Then he became more serious.

'Mr Fitzgerald also informed me that you appeared somewhat doubtful concerning our practice.'

'I don't understand, sir?' James was puzzled.

'That you seem to believe that we should tell our patients when there is nothing that can be done to cure them?'

'Yes, I did say something along those lines,' James admitted candidly.

'A cardinal principle of medical practice is that you must always allow the patient to hope. Believe me, Nephew, I have witnessed instances of miraculous recovery, when I would have wagered my own life that the patient was going to die. So never, ever, tell the patient that they are doomed. Always tell them that they will recover. Because there is always the chance that they may do so.' He smiled sardonically. 'Despite the ministrations of we doctors.'

'Very well, sir,' James readily accepted.

Sean Fitzgerald came into the room with a bunch of keys jingling in his hand.

'That's a fine specimen that Cull delivered last night, Septimus.'

Nairn nodded. 'Yes, as a twisted curvature of the spine it is interesting enough.'

'I must have dropped off, because I never heard him arrive. What time did he come?'

'It was just before two o'clock this morning,' Nairn told him

Fitzgerald nodded sagely. 'It's always better to have the late delivery. Less prying eyes are abroad.'

'Just so,' Nairn agreed. 'Now I have to give Mrs Biddle some instructions, Sean, so will you show James the new specimen? I'll follow directly.'

Fitzgerald led James outside to the stable block but walked on past it to a large red-brick outbuilding which stood on its own behind a huge stinking pile of stable manure and rotting straw. Its door was chained and padlocked and Fitzgerald unlocked it and led the way inside with a proprietorial air.

'You're going to see something special here, James. It's a rare thing altogether, for your uncle only buys the rarest.'

James stared about him with intense interest. The windowless room was well lit by a huge fanlight and smelled of formaldehyde and carbolic acid. The floor was stone-flagged and sloped slightly towards a long drainage channel opposite the entrance door. Shelving stretched around the limewashed walls laden with books, medical instruments, mortars and pestles, oil lamps, earthernware pots, several wooden buckets and rows of great glass jars filled with a clear liquid in which floated strange objects. There was a large stone sink and hand-pump against one wall next to a deep cast-iron open-topped tank containing the formaldehyde. Dominating the centre of the room were two long, broad, shallow, lead salting troughs of the type used to salt and preserve meat. On the nearer trough a small mound was covered with a tarpaulin sheet.

Fitzgerald closed and bolted the door, then moved to the

trough and with a showmanlike flourish whipped off the tarpaulin.

'There now! What do you think to this?'

James stared in shock at the pale naked body of a young male child lying in a foetal position.

'It's a beauty, isn't it,' Fitzgerald observed with satisfaction. 'Fresh as a daisy. They don't often get such fine ones as this in the anatomy classes at the universities, or in the teaching hospitals, I'll tell you. Most of the students there are lucky if they get half a rotting body to dissect throughout their entire time.'

James initial shock ebbed rapidly away. The close view of a dead body was nothing new to him. Death was a domestic commonplace and even the youngest children were taken to show their last respects to corpses of kinfolk and acquaintances before the funeral and burial. He studied the small corpse. The child's features were peaceful as if he were merely sleeping, and the white flesh bore no trace of injury or malnutrition.

James noted the grotesquely twisted spine and experienced a rush of pity.

'The poor child. He must have endured a great deal of suffering with his back so deformed.'

Fitzgerald's rubicond face was impassive. 'I expect so, James. Still, he's beyond all care now, isn't he? And that spine of his will make a fine addition for our collection.'

'Collection?' James questioned.

Fitzgerald waved his arm at the great glass jars. 'We keep the most interesting specimens.'

James peered more closely at the jars containing the strange objects which, knowing now what they were, he found rather distasteful to look at.

The Irishman chuckled at his expression. 'Don't worry, Jamie. In a few weeks you'll be eager to get your hands on such as these.'

James looked again at the small corpse and intense curiosity suddenly overwhelmed him. Who was this child and where had he come from? What did he die of? How did this man – what was his name? Cull! – how did Cull get hold of the child? A disquieting suspicion roused.

'Is Cull a resurrection man, Sean? A body-snatcher? How else does he obtain such a small child as this one?'

Fitzgerald shook his head.

'Cull is a bit of a mystery man for me. Your uncle says that he's not a resurrection man, and that there's no foul play involved, so I don't press him on the subject. I'm not that interested to tell the truth!'

He took a cheroot from his pocket and struck a lucifer match to light it, puffing out clouds of rank-smelling smoke with evident satisfaction before going on. 'One thing to remember though, Jamie, is that we don't talk about our collection to others. It's not that we're doing anything wrong, but the people hereabouts are only country bumpkins and being ignorant and superstitious might get the wrong notions about our specimens. So it's best that you don't talk of this to anybody either.'

James could understand this reasoning, and the need for discretion. He accepted that the ignorant and uneducated natives of this parish could quite easily attribute evil motivations for this collection of anatomical specimens. In his native parish in Leicestershire the locals had believed in witchcraft and black magic, and had unmercifully persecuted an old woman whom they believed to be a witch.

He nodded with ready agreement. 'Very well, Sean.'

'Good man yourself.' The Irishman grinned broadly.

There was a knocking on the door and Fitzgerald unbolted it and let Nairn in.

'I'll leave you to it now then.' He left them together.

Nairn selected a scalpel from a case on one of the shelves, then went to the small corpse and gently straightened its legs.

'He's been dead more than forty-eight hours, Nephew, that's why the rigor mortis has gone. In my experience it can be generally stated that the process of rigor commences about six hours after death and begins to wear off after about thirty-six hours.'

James was feeling increasingly apprehensive about what was

to happen. He expected his uncle to direct him to cut open this dead child, and he was very uncertain that he would be able to bring himself to mutilate such pathetic human flesh. For several years he had practised dissection on dead frogs, birds, rabbits and other small creatures, even a dog once, but never on human remains.

Something else was beginning to trouble him also. Although not a particularly religious man, he nevertheless had been influenced by the Christian teachings of his childhood. Such a young child as this should surely have been given a Christian burial instead of being brought here as a curiosity? He could not help but feel that it would be a desecration to dismember this body.

As if he were party to these thoughts, his uncle displayed an almost uncanny percipience.

'The soul that was the living child has left this flesh,' he said softly. 'These poor remains are merely the vehicle that the soul utilised here on earth. Yet we shall treat them with respect. And afterwards they shall be given a Christian burial. Arrangements have already been made to transport them to another parish where a churchyard grave awaits them, and a priest whom I've long known will perform the final offices.'

He stroked the grotesquely twisted spine, and his face showed compassion.

'You must bear this fact uppermost in your mind, Nephew, that if we are to save children from the bodily sufferings this poor little fellow underwent in life, then we must discover what is the cause of such afflictions. And the only way we can make such discovery is to examine the human body. To dissect and study what that dissection lays open to our eyes.

'Now help me to position the subject so that we may begin our work.'

James shivered involuntarily as his hands touched the cold skin, and Nairn urged gently, 'Remember, he is no longer here. This is only the fleshly shell.'

A sharp nausea assailed James as the scalpel made the first long incision and the lifeless white skin was retracted back to

43

disclose the dark flesh. But gradually as he watched and listened to Nairn's explanations he became imperceptibly absorbed in the wonders his uncle's deft, skilful fingers were unfolding before his fascinated gaze. And when finally Nairn handed him the scalpel he was ready and eager to embark upon his own voyage of discovery within this miraculous creation that was the human body.

Six

L ydia Landser was humming happily as she cleaned her older brother Robert's room in preparation for his homecoming. Ever since her father had written to Robert telling him he must return home as soon as possible she had been eagerly waiting for his arrival. The summer had been an unhappy time for her. The new shafts had been disasters. All had gone very well at first, and her father had been as cheerful as a light-hearted schoolboy. Then, only scant feet from the brine bed the well-diggers had broken into yet another stream. A further shaft had been sunk, only to meet the same fate. The effect upon her father had been catastrophic. He now filled his waking hours with constant drinking and had become morose and depressed, seeming to have lost all his drive and energy, even his once perennial optimism. Liddy was praying that Robert's arrival would cheer her father up, if only a little.

Robert Landser returned home in a foul temper, trudging through the gates of the salt works in the early dusk. He saw the lamplight glowing through the windows of the office and surmised that his father was inside. He entered the small building without bothering to knock.

George Landser was sitting slumped at his desk, a bottle of gin in front of him. He blinked drunkenly and, recognising his son, shook his head gloomily.

'This is a sad day for me, Rob. A sad day indeed.'

'It's a sadder day for me, Pa,' Rob declared heatedly. 'You've ruined my life.'

'I've no money left, Rob. I can no longer afford to keep you at university,' George Landser informed him miserably.

The young man pointed at the bottle and sneered contemptuously. 'You can afford to drink though. You should have spent more time working and less time getting drunk, then perhaps you wouldn't have ruined my life.'

Stung by his son's open display of contempt, Landser counter-attacked furiously.

'Don't talk to me of work. You've never done a day's work in your life. All you're good for is spending my money and wasting your time with all those other fine college gentlemen who have never done a day's work either. All you're good for is to spend money that I've sweated to earn. You're like a leech on my pocket.'

Robert was untroubled by these strictures, and mocked, 'Then it's a case of like father like son, isn't it, Pa? Or have you forgotten that most of the money you once had came from Mamma? You did precious little sweating to earn her money, did you? And you call me a leech.'

This harsh truth struck home with telling force, abruptly draining all heat from George Landser's anger, leaving him feeling utterly spent. He visibly sagged in defeat, and lifted his hand in a weary gesture of dismissal.

'I've no wish to fight with you, Rob. I've troubles enough to face. Just leave me be.'

He looked suddenly much older, and Robert experienced pangs of guilt. But his resentment still seethed and he could not bring himself to apologise.

'I'm going to Liddy and Mamma,' he muttered, and left the office.

George Landser sighed heavily, refilling his glass with gin.

'Oh, Rob! It's so good to see you again!' Liddy cried out delightedly and rushed to embrace her older brother, so alike to her in features and colouring that they could have passed for twins.

46

He smiled as he hugged her. They had always been close-bonded, and although Robert Landser was by nature selfish, self-centred and spendthrift, he was genuinely fond of his sister, while she, knowing his flawed character, still adored him.

'Where's your baggage?' she wanted to know.

'I had to leave it at the Crown to be collected later.' He scowled. 'No one would hire me a gig on credit. As soon as I made myself known the impudent bastards demanded cash in advance for the hire. It was the same story at the Golden Cross. Apparently Pa owes money at both places.'

'Have you seen Pa?' she enquired hesitantly.

He nodded, frowning. 'He's drunk. I didn't waste much time with him.'

Liddy's dismay showed plainly on her expressive features. 'You've quarrelled, haven't you,' she guessed. 'Oh, that's awful! To quarrel now when such troubles are come upon us.'

'What's the truth of it, Liddy?' he demanded.

'The truth is that we're in sore straits. But Pa's not to blame for what has happened. It's just bad luck!' She went on to explain about the failure of the new shafts.

'But what about me? What am I supposed to do now?'

'I don't know,' she said sadly.

There sounded a sudden thumping from the ceiling above them.

'Mamma must have heard us. She'll be so happy to see you, Rob. You must go up to her straight away.'

The young man seemed reluctant to move. 'How is she? Is she any better yet?'

'No, she's not. Dr Nairn comes regularly, but no matter what he prescribes she shows no improvement.'

Although he was his mother's favourite upon whom she had always doted, Robert Landser did not reciprocate her depth of devotion. He had liked her well enough when she was in health, and had been able to accept her physical displays of affection with equanimity. Particularly when those kisses and hugs had been accompanied by presents. But since her illness he had resented her pain-induced querulous moods, and

47

during his visits home had viewed her deteriorating physical condition with initial distaste which had escalated to a positive repulsion.

The thumping impacts became louder and quicker in tempo.

'You must go up, Rob. She's becoming very agitated,' Liddy urged.

He sighed and grudgingly agreed. 'Very well. Can you prepare some food for me? I've not eaten since midday.'

'There's some cold mutton, and pickles, and fresh bread and butter. Will that do?'

He shrugged sulkily. 'It will have to if there's nothing else. But I've become used to better fare.'

Liddy could not resist a gentle teasing. 'Well, you'll just have to get used to our plain country fare again, Rob. We can't match the High Table of Oxford.'

'You cannot match anything of Oxford in this midden heap,' he gibed spitefully.

'I don't think that we'll choose to match the bad manners you appear to have learned there,' she retorted spiritedly. 'I know it's come as a terrible blow to you having to leave the college, Rob. But life hasn't been very pleasant for me either these last months.'

He was instantly contrite. 'I'm sorry, Liddy. I should not take my anger out on you.' He smiled and held out his hands. 'Am I forgiven?'

She smiled readily. 'Of course you are.'

'Robert! My dearest!' Beatrice Landser's eyes were wet with tears of joy. Her clawed hands clutched his shoulders and her lips greedily pressed on his mouth.

The foul stench of her breath and body sickened him, and he had to fight against the impulse to push her from him.

He stoically endured her embrace for some seconds then managed to release himself and to draw back so that her breath no longer gusted against his face.

'Is your health improving, Mamma?'

Her huge eyes hungrily devoured him. 'Now you are home

again I shall soon get better, my darling.' A gleam of cunning shone. 'It was your absence that made me fall ill in the first place. I'm sure of that. You must promise me that you will never leave me again. Never! You must promise that you will stay by my side and never leave me again.'

'Now, Mamma, that may not be possible.' Her manner was making him feel uneasy. There was something in her expression that he felt vaguely fearful of.

'They want me dead, you know,' she declared vehemently.

'Who wants you dead?' he exclaimed.

'Those two.' Her voice dropped to a rasping whisper, her eyes glittering feverishly. 'George Landser and his hell-bitch daughter. They want me dead. If you leave me alone with them again, then they will surely murder me.'

Robert drew a sharp intake of breath as his vague fears suddenly crystallised into absolute certainty. She was mad!

'Mamma, you're talking nonsense!' he reproved sharply. 'That is a wicked thing to say of Pa and Liddy. They both love you.'

'Love!' She screeched so loudly that he jerked in shock. 'No one loves me, except you, my darling. Only you, my sweet boy.' She pushed herself upright, her clawed hands reaching for him, pleading hoarsely, 'Come, kiss your mamma, darling. Kiss me. Kiss me. Kiss your mamma.'

He was racked with horror as her fingers gripped and her rancid breath came hot against his face.

'No!' He broke free and stumbled back from the bed, and she tried to follow but was too weak to raise herself further, and collapsed sideways to lie with her head over the side of the mattress, sobbing and moaning unintelligible words.

He turned and rushed from the room and down the stairs shouting, 'Liddy? Liddy, where are you?'

His sister came from the kitchen.

'What is it?'

He gabbled breathlessly, relating what had happened, and to his amazement she merely said, 'You'd best come back upstairs with me and help me to settle her comfortably.'

49

He shook his head, baffled at her apparent incomprehension. 'Do you not understand what I'm telling you? Mamma is acting as if she's insane! As if she's raving mad!'

She nodded and answered calmly, 'I do believe that you're right, Rob. That at times she is insane.'

'What?' He stared at his sister as if she were an alien being. 'How can you behave so coolly? Have you no feelings? How have you become so callous?'

Liddy's cheeks flushed and she told him hotly, 'For months now, Pa has been escaping from his troubles by drowning them in a bottle. You've been enjoying yourself in Oxford, while I've been struggling here.' Angry tears glistened in her eyes. 'I've endured Mamma's insane rages and suffered her blows and abuse. I've nursed her without anyone to help me. Don't you dare to tax me with having no feelings, to accuse me of being callous.'

For the second time since his return he experienced pangs of guilt.

'I'm sorry, Liddy. It's just that the shock of seeing Mamma like this has confused me. Why didn't you write and tell me of what was happening here?'

For a brief moment she was sorely tempted to tell him: because he was a selfish weakling, who would have reacted exactly as he was reacting now. But seeing the genuine distress in his eyes she softened towards him.

'I didn't write because I hoped that matters would improve. That Mamma would get better, and Pa might be able to salvage the business. Besides, there was nothing that you could have done to better the situation.'

He stared at her for long long moments, and then like a small child beseeched, 'What is going to become of us, Liddy?'

She forced a smile, and spoke with a confidence she was far from feeling.

'So long as we all stick together and do our best to help each other, then everything will be all right. Now sit at the table and I'll bring you some food, then I'll go and see to Mamma . . .'

Seven

From the early hours of this crisp September morning, people had been converging upon the great mansion of Hewell Grange to witness the Grand Review of the Queen's Own Worcestershire Yeomanry Cavalry.

Septimus Nairn's house stood on the roadside some two miles distance from the mansion, and James Kerr was sitting at his bedroom window watching the passing cavalcade of carriages, horsemen, and pedestrians. At times officers and troopers of the regiment came by and James found himself wishing that he too could be wearing the dashing uniform of the scarlet coatee, the black shako with its flowing white plume, steel scabbarded sabre and white crossbelt.

His uncle entered the room and came to stand at the window.

'Today we shall go to see the Review,' he announced. 'You deserve a holiday. You've worked hard and well. I'm more than satisfied with your progress. In fact I'm delighted by it. It is quite exceptional.'

James felt tremendously gratified by these rare words of praise. In the months since his arrival here he had devoted almost every waking hour to hard study and practice of his new profession. His high intelligence, retentive memory and intense eagerness to learn had enabled him to make very rapid progress. He had absorbed large amounts of theoretical knowledge, and had gained considerable practical experience also by frequently accompanying his uncle or Sean Fitzgerald on their rounds. He could now competently bandage and plaster, draw blood, lance abscesses, sew up cuts, apply blisters and clysters, use dry cups and scarification, fit trusses for hernias, and set and splint simple minor fractures. He was gaining experience of diagnosis and could identify the symptoms of a variety of diseases and prescribe the specifics for their treatment. He had also proven to be adept with the scalpel and was dissecting with a confident dexterity of touch that many much more experienced students would envy.

Twice every week his uncle subjected him to long and detailed examination and discussion on what he had learned, and so far James had acquitted himself well.

To his disappointment there had not been any opportunity to witness or help with any major operations or amputations or with massive traumatic injuries. But as Septimus Nairn pointed out, 'Operations are the last desperate resort for any patient and we're not the only doctors in this parish able to saw off an arm or leg. And as for any massive traumatic injuries, well, we just have to trust to luck to get our hands on them. They're not such a common occurrence in these parts after all.'

Now his uncle urged, 'Make ready then, and we'll be off to the Review.'

When James came downstairs Nairn was standing holding a hat box.

'I've got a small present for you, Nephew.'

He reached out and plucked James' tasselled cap from his head and tossed it into the corner of the room. He then opened the box and lifted from it a shiny new black beaver top hat.

'This is the correct hat for a medical man like yourself to wear. Here. Try it on.'

James flushed with pride and pleasure. He moved to stand in front of the mirror and placed the top hat on his head, tilting it to achieve the desired hint of devil-may-care rakishness.

There was pride in Septimus Nairn's eyes as he watched his nephew, and he nodded.

'Yes, it suits you very well.'

'Thank you, Uncle. This is a fine present.'

James examined himself from different angles. Although not vain by nature, he couldn't help but feel pleased at how the top hat imparted a new maturity to his features. He felt that it made him look like a man instead of a callow youth.

He went to stand with his uncle on the gravelled forecourt of the house, waiting for Tom Biddle to bring the horses from the stable block.

A voice hailed from an approaching open carriage.

'Good morning to you, Doctor. Are you attending the Review? Pull up, driver.' The carriage halted.

George Landser was sharing the carriage with his son and daughter. James experienced a sense of pleasure as he saw how fresh and pretty Lydia Landser was looking in her white gown and pale blue shawl, a flowered broad-brimmed sun-bonnet upon her bright hair, which she was wearing in demure ringlets.

'Can I offer you a lift to the ground, gentlemen?' Landser asked.

Nairn bowed. 'It's not necessary, thank you, Mr Landser. We're waiting for our horses. How are you, Lydia, Robert?'

James was introduced to the sullen-looking, dandified young man, whom he now saw bore a startling resemblance to his sister.

Robert Landser nodded perfunctorily and grudgingly muttered, 'Your servant, sir.'

James instantly surmised that he was never likely to become a friend.

But Lydia Landser smiled at him, and he bowed and lifted his hat. 'I'm happy to see you, Miss Landser.'

'And I you, Mr Kerr.'

'We'll get on then.' George Landser appeared to be very tense. 'Perhaps we shall meet together at the Review, gentlemen.'

'Indeed,' Nairn replied pleasantly, then as the carriage crunched away over the gravel grumbled jokingly, 'I see that he has money enough to hire a carriage and pair, but he has yet to settle the bill for my last call on his wife.'

'How long is she likely to live, Uncle?' James enquired interestedly.

'She could last for some considerable time to come. She has a powerful will to survive, Nephew. It is amazing how the power of the will can keep life in a body that is hopelessly decayed.'

Tom Biddle led their horses on to the forecourt and as they mounted another voice hailed.

'This is well met, Septimus. I was coming to call on you after the Review.'

A tall, slender man, dressed in the glittering uniform of a Yeomanry Captain, reined in beside them. He was strikingly handsome with olive skin, black curly hair and dashing side-whiskers, and James could not help feeling somewhat plain and dowdy beside this resplendently uniformed exotic.

Nairn introduced him as Carlos Wybergh and his smile was friendly as he shook James' hand and greeted him warmly.

'It's a pleasure to meet you, Mr Kerr. Your uncle told me previously that his nephew had come to live with him. But may I address you as James, and you must call me Carlos, for I hope that we shall become friends.'

Pleased and flattered, James readily concurred.

'Do you come to the Review, Septimus?' Wybergh asked.

'We do.'

'Excellent, then we shall keep each other company.'

Riding three abreast they joined the traffic passing along the road.

James quickly became conscious of how the elegant captain attracted admiring stares from the men, and coquettish looks and smiles from the women in the carriages they passed. But Carlos Wybergh appeared to be completely unaware of the attention he was attracting. He was telling Nairn gravely, 'My father is now quite determined upon a lithotomy. But he insists that no one but yourself shall perform it.'

'It is a severe ordeal to undergo, Carlos,' Nairn pointed out. 'And your father's strength has been greatly diminished during these last months. It would have been much preferable if he had agreed to the operation when I first suggested it. I confess I am somewhat reluctant to perform it now. I fear that the shock could well have a most deleterious effect upon his constitution.'

'What is certain is that he cannot continue to endure the

agonies that afflict him. His sufferings increase almost daily. You are his only hope. Please, you must agree to perform a lithotomy. Please, Septimus, you must . . .' Wybergh continued to press until Nairn conceded.

'Very well, Carlos. I'll carry out the operation this coming Saturday. Is your mother at home yet?'

'No. She is still in Madrid. But I've sent a letter asking her to return immediately.'

Now that these arrangements had been made, James was drawn into the conversation and Carlos Wybergh asked him many questions about his interests and pursuits.

'You must come and dine with me very soon, James,' Wybergh invited. 'And allow me to introduce you to my friends. They're good fellows who know how to enjoy life. You will have a high old time in our company, I can assure you.'

James was conceiving a rapidly burgeoning liking for this new acquaintance, who radiated a smiling charm, but was surprised by his uncle's lack of response when the invitation was issued.

They entered the park of Hewell Grange through ornately gilded gates and James exclaimed in pleasure when he saw the great mansion with its Grecian portico and pilasters, surrounded by thirty acres of gardens and lakes, and wide vistas of well-wooded parkland.

'It makes a fine sight.'

'It was the seat of the Earls of Plymouth. Our colonel, the Honourable Robert Clive and his wife Lady Harriet, Baroness Windsor, inherited it upon the late Earl's death,' Carlos Wybergh informed James. 'Herbert, the colonel's younger brother, is a close friend of mine. It's a shame that he's not here at present, I could have introduced you to him. He's a jolly fellow.'

James was greatly impressed by this claim of intimacy with the aristocracy, and he glanced at his uncle to see his reaction. But the grim features displayed only their customary dourness.

'There must be several thousands here.' James twisted his

head and looked around at the thronging well-dressed men and fashionable women who were strolling across the greensward, picnicking by the sides of carriages, clustering in animated laughing groups. Several flag-decorated marquees and smaller tents were dotted across the park, and on a grassy knoll the band of the Yeomanry were playing a selection of martial tunes.

'Regretfully I must leave you now and report for duty. But perhaps I shall be able to join you later in the day.' Carlos Wybergh saluted and rode away towards a large flat stretch of parkland where the bright-scarlet uniforms were congregating.

'What a nice man he is,' James remarked. 'I shall look forward to dining with him.'

Septimus Nairn frowned slightly. 'He's very pleasant mannered, I grant you, Nephew. But I don't believe that he would be a suitable friend for you at present.'

'Why not? He's a gentleman, isn't he?' James could not understand his uncle's attitude.

'And too rich for your empty pockets to keep company with, Nephew. His father is very wealthy, and far too indulgent. Carlos spends most of his time roistering with a group of rackety scapegraces. They are to be found at every prizefight, race meeting, badger-baiting, and cock fight for miles around. They drink and gamble incessantly and keep company with boxers, jockeys, actors, tavern keepers, rogues, and whores. I would not wish you to waste your days as they do.'

James could see the many attractions of such a hedonistic life. He had all youth's natural desire for gaiety and pleasure and excitement.

'Well, Uncle,' he smiled wryly, 'all work and no play makes Jack a dull boy. Isn't that so? And Carlos must have some seriousness of purpose, after all he is an officer of the Yeomanry.'

'Oh yes, he takes his yeomanry duties seriously,' Nairn acknowledged readily, but then irony crept into his voice as he went on, 'And like the rest of that gallant band he is always ready and willing to maintain law and order. To use force against poor and starving wretches like the Black Country miners when they are driven by their sufferings to protest against those who exploit them so mercilessly.'

'Why, you sound like one of those Radicals, Uncle,' James exclaimed.

'I speak only the truth,' Nairn asserted and then lifted his hand to forestall any reply. 'I would much prefer that we talk no more on this subject, Nephew. Naturally I accept that you are old enough to choose your own companions, and I cannot forbid you to make closer acquaintance with Carlos Wybergh. Nevertheless I will state my opinion, which is that he is an unsuitable person for you to become a close friend to. That having been said, I shall say no more on the subject. You must do as you choose.'

James made no answer. Conflicting emotions were warring within him. He had become very fond of this grim man beside him and had no wish to offend or upset him in any way. Yet at the same time he resented what he considered was Nairn's attempt to dictate his choice of friends.

A strained silence fell between them as they rode on towards the paddock where their horses could be left in the care of white-smocked estate labourers.

Strolling through the terraced gardens, admiring the fountains and statues, Liddy Landser was enjoying this rare holiday. By her side her brother walked in morose silence. George Landser had disappeared into a refreshment tent immediately upon arrival.

'I do wish you'd cheer up, Rob,' she gently chided. 'It's such a beautiful day. Can't you at least try to enjoy it?'

'What's to enjoy?' he retorted. 'We've had a ride in a hired carriage, and Pa's getting drunk as fast as he can, and I've not got a penny to spend.'

He fell silent as they encountered a family group of portly, opulently dressed father, plump bejewelled mother, and six children of varying ages being shepherded by two neatly caped and bonneted nursemaids.

'Can't you realise how difficult it is for me, Liddy?' he

57

demanded bitterly when the family were out of earshot. 'A few weeks ago I was a gentleman amongst gentlemen. And now through no fault of my own I'm reduced to a pauper. I dread meeting any of my old friends today. It will be your fault if I am humiliated here. I didn't want to come, but you nagged me into it.'

'Well, you don't look like a pauper.' Impatience with his self-pity spurred her to speak sharply. 'So unless you tell people about your empty pockets no one will know that they are so.'

A whining note entered Robert Landser's voice. 'I don't know why Pa was so insistent on coming here anyway. Wasting money on hiring a carriage and acting as if he's lord of all creation. And where is he now? Why, in the refreshment tent naturally. Swilling down drink and standing treat to anybody who'll give him the time of day, I'll bet. Yet when I ask him for a few shillings he pleads poverty and refuses me. Can you really wonder at me being so down?'

'Pa hasn't come here for pleasure, Rob.' Liddy sprang to her father's defence. 'He's come to try and talk with Edward Harcourt. You know well that that man has been avoiding him, and making excuses as to why he can't see him at the bank. And as for acting like a lord of creation, I think Pa is merely trying to show a brave face to the world. And I admire him for it. It's a pity that you can't try and show a little more bravery in the face of our troubles, instead of whining and complaining all the time.'

Her words stung Robert Landser and he felt ashamed. But unwilling to admit to this, he countered sneeringly, 'Edward Harcourt? What does Pa think that Edward Harcourt will do for him? Lend him more? That would be throwing good money after bad, don't you think? Edward Harcourt has never been noted for doing that.'

'Might I point out, George, that I do not make a practice of discussing affairs of business in such surroundings as these.' Edward Harcourt stared with scarcely veiled distaste at the man before him.

58

The refreshment tent was filled with noisy men drinking wines, spirits, and ales.

George Landser had desperation in his eyes. 'But all I'm asking for is sufficient funds to enable one more shaft to be sunk. I've been assured by the dowser that these further brine beds are completely separated from any subterranean streams of fresh water.'

Harcourt's mouth twisted mockingly. 'That same dowser who failed to discover the other fresh water stream, I assume.'

Landser tried a different approach. 'You know very well that until the contamination the works were highly profitable. And they will be so again as soon as we successfully sink a shaft. If you won't help me further then I shall be forced to declare bankruptcy, and we shall both be losers. You're not my only creditor. The others would come swarming to dispute the share-out of assets. Everyone will end up out of pocket.'

Landser's desperate threat to declare bankruptcy was the signal Edward Harcourt had been waiting for. He could now move on to the next phase of his secret agenda.

'Let's go outside, George. I can't hear myself think in here.'

Harcourt had no intention of allowing Landser to become bankrupt yet. It was as the man had stated, there were other creditors to demand their share of any assets that could be realised. Now Harcourt could force Landser to tell him who exactly the other creditors were and how much he owed them.

'Have you approached anyone else for more finance?' Harcourt asked as they walked away from the tent.

'The Morani brothers in Birmingham have said that they are prepared to advance me further loans,' Landser told him.

'They are usurers.' Harcourt dismissed them with a contemptuous snort. 'They will bleed you white with their interest charges.'

'They are doing so now,' Landser admitted ruefully and truthfully.

'Well, on reflection I'm inclined to help you, George. I know that you've fallen into this present predicament through no fault of your own. But I must have all the details of your current financial affairs. All debts and rates of interest.'

George Landser's relief was such that he felt momentarily light-headed.

'But of course, Edward. I can supply all such details at your convenience.'

Harcourt smiled. 'Come to the bank tomorrow morning. We'll see what's to be done.'

'Thank you. Thank you very much.' Exultation coursed through Landser.

'Pa?' Liddy called as she and Robert came walking towards the two men. 'Pa, I do believe the Review is about to begin.'

Liddy saw the happiness in her father's face, and her own spirits soared as she realised that he must have been successful in his quest.

Edward Harcourt stared appreciatively at Liddy's shapely figure. He bowed and said gallantly, 'You're looking very beautiful today, Miss Lydia.'

Liddy was not in the least flattered by his compliment. She disliked the way his eyes were lasciviously examining her rounded breasts. She looked levelly at him and replied coolly, 'My mirror tells me that I am not beautiful, sir.'

'Then your mirror lies.' Harcourt smiled easily, not at all disconcerted by this unfavourable reception of his compliment. He liked the women he targeted for pursuit to be spirited. It heightened the pleasure of the chase and eventual conquest.

'No, sir. It doesn't lie. On the contrary it always is truthful, even to the point of giving offence.'

Harcourt's smile did not waver. He was going to enjoy capturing this pert young miss, and then breaking her spirit.

'Is it like its mistress in that respect?' he asked, and again his eyes moved over her breasts.

Liddy's fiery temper sparked. 'I don't wish to continue this conversation, Mr Harcourt.'

'Then I shall wish you good day, young lady. I'll see you tomorrow morning, George. Come at nine o'clock.' He bowed slightly and sauntered away.

George Landser frowned uneasily at his daughter. 'You were very rude to Mr Harcourt, Liddy. Whatever possessed you to behave so badly?'

'Didn't you see the lecherous way he was ogling me, Pa?' she demanded angrily. 'It was him who was behaving badly.'

'He was merely admiring you.'

'I can do without that sort of admiration.'

A trumpet call sounded and Robert demanded petulantly, 'Are we going to watch the cavalry? Or do you intend standing here arguing with each other all day?'

George Landser smiled wryly at his daughter. 'Let's not quarrel, Liddy. The sun is shining, we're having a holiday, and Harcourt has agreed to help me, so we have ample cause to celebrate and enjoy ourselves.'

Liddy returned his smile. 'Very well, Pa.'

'Here, Rob.' George Landser pressed some coins into his son's hand. 'If you should meet any old friends then you now have money to treat them.'

The unexpected gift cheered the sullen young man up instantly, and the three were in good humour as they found a vantage point among the spectators on the rising ground overlooking the troops of trotting, jingling cavalry.

On the opposite rising ground across the wide flat area James Kerr and his uncle were also watching the cavalry. The colourful uniforms, the flashing sabres and stirring trumpet calls evoked a wistful desire in James. As a boy he had dreamed of becoming a soldier. A dashing Hussar or Light Dragoon.

Now he told his uncle of those youthful daydreams, and Nairn chuckled and confessed, 'I had the "Scarlet Fever" myself when I was young, Nephew. I think that most boys with any spirit suffer from it at some time in their lives. Unfortunately my parents couldn't afford to buy me a commission and allow me sufficient funds to live as a cavalry officer. But when you are qualified there's no reason at all why you should not join the army as a regimental surgeon. It would have to be a Line regiment of course. Only wealthy men

61

can afford a cavalry mess. But I'll help you all I can if you decide to enter the army in a few years' time.'

James felt a warm glow of affection for his relative. 'You've already helped me more than I could ever have hoped for, Uncle. I have to put childish daydreams behind me now.'

Nairn shook his head. 'Never stop daydreaming, Nephew. The man who does that is deliberately denying himself one of life's greatest pleasures.'

The unbidden image of Lydia Landser's bright hair, pretty face, and shapely body suddenly appeared in James' mind, and he smiled to himself.

I'll certainly not deny myself the pleasure of daydreaming about you, Liddy Landser, he thought.

'There you are, Septimus. I was hoping to find you here today. I'd like a private word with you.'

Nairn moved some distance away with the distinguished-looking man who had approached him, and engaged in a brief converation. Then the man walked off and Nairn rejoined James.

With an ironic smile he informed the younger man, 'That gentleman is one of the pillars of our local society, Nephew. Edward Harcourt Esq., Justice of the Peace, banker, and Chairman of the Board of Guardians. He is also a patient of mine who pays me very well.'

'A patient? But he looks the very picture of health!' James protested.

'He has the gonorrhoea. Not for the first time, I might add. He's an incorrigible lecher. He pays me very well for the treatment because he knows that he can rely on my absolute discretion.'

Once more the ironic smile quirked Nairn's mouth. 'Another cardinal principle of medical practice, Nephew: you must exercise an absolute discretion concerning your rich and power-ful patients' disorders. Poor patients, of course, can have their disorders shouted to the world.'

James frowned uneasily. 'But isn't that the practice of hypocrisy and double standards, Uncle?'

'It certainly is.' Nairn's smile was now sardonic. 'And that is the only way that we can survive in this hypocritical, double-dealing, wicked world . . . You must learn that lesson quickly, Nephew, if you are to succeed in your chosen profession.'

James' uneasy frown stayed in place, mirroring his uneasy thoughts.

Eight

At the breakfast table on Saturday morning, Septimus Nairn told James, 'You shall come and assist at the operation today, Nephew.'

James felt simultaneously excited and apprehensive. 'Do you think that I'm ready for this, Uncle?'

Nairn chuckled. 'I don't intend that you should cut for the stone. You will only be helping to secure the patient.'

'Oh.' James simultaneously experienced disappointment and relief. 'I thought that you intended to let me ligature the blood vessels perhaps.'

'There will not be any major vessels needing a ligature. I've had much practice at lithotomy. When I perform the operation there is only a minimum of bloodshed.'

There was no suggestion of boasting in Nairn's tone, only the plain recital of a proven fact.

'I've been reading about Civiale,' James said, 'and how he uses an instrument called a lithotrite to crush the stone inside the bladder.'

Nairn nodded judiciously. 'Civiale does indeed, and is reputed to be very skilful. I've used that same instrument myself and found it effective in certain cases. Unfortunately in many cases it will not serve. When the stone is too large and hardened the only way to remove it is to perform a lithotomy. Julius Wybergh has an extremely large stone. He should have let me attempt the lithotrite years ago when the stone was still small enough to be crushed.'

It was early afternoon when James and his uncle reached the large house some miles north of the town of Redditch.

As they rode up the long driveway between the rows of sentinel oaks Nairn glanced up at the black threatening clouds.

'There's a storm brewing fast. But at least we've had a dry journey here, even though we may get wet on our return.'

Dogs came barking and liveried footmen ran out to drive the animals away and take the newcomers' horses.

Carlos Wybergh came from the house and down the flight of balustraded entrance steps. Today he wore civilian clothes which were the epitome of elegance.

'Are my people here?' Nairn wanted to know.

'Yes, they've been here for several hours.' The olive features were anxious. 'My father is in terrible pain, Dr Nairn. I doubt if he's had a wink of sleep these last forty-eight hours.'

'Did you administer the laudanum doses I prescribed, and apply the hot bread poultices?'

'Yes, but I'm afraid it seemed to have little effect.'

'No matter,' Nairn said soothingly. 'I shall very soon relieve his sufferings.'

James unstrapped the medical chest from his horse and carried it into the house behind his uncle and Carlos Wybergh.

More male and female servants hovered in the large entrance hall and James was impressed by the family's wealth as evidenced by the number of servants and the luxurious wall hangings and furnishings around him.

At the foot of the broad staircase Nairn halted and told Wybergh, 'I would prefer you to remain downstairs, Carlos, and to keep all others in the household down here also.'

The young man frowned doubtfully. 'But is there nothing I can do to help? Perhaps my father would be helped to bear this easier if I were with him.'

'No,' Nairn said flatly. 'I must insist that you do as I request. Believe me, it is better so.'

'Very well,' Wybergh acquiesced reluctantly.

As they continued upstairs Nairn whispered to James, 'Another cardinal principle of surgical practice, Nephew. Never, ever allow relatives to be present at any operation. They are

65

always a hindrance because they complain about the patient's sufferings and often try to impede the operation.'

In the large bedroom a fire was burning in the tiled fireplace, rendering the air hot and stuffy.

Sean Fitzgerald was waiting in company with another man whom James remembered from his visit to the Birmingham Hospital, the florid-featured Arthur Milcheap.

The room was dominated by a huge four-poster bed hung with thick brocaded curtains.

Nairn moved to the bed and spoke to the naked man lying on its coverlet.

'Bear up, Mr Wybergh. Your agonies will shortly be relieved.'

James stared with concern at the patient. Julius Wybergh was so emaciated that he resembled a living skeleton. His eyes were deep sunk in his skull-like head, his complexion a peculiarly livid grey hue, the wispy strands of long white hair spreading from the half-bald scalp across the silken pillows adding to his grotesque appearance.

He lifted one bony arm, mumbling unintelligibly.

Nairn turned from him and became brisk and businesslike. 'Have his bowels been emptied, Mr Fitzgerald?'

'Yes, sir, I administered the first enema at nine o'clock, and the cold-water clyster at half past the hour. The second enema at half past ten, followed by the clyster of warm water. I've also administered a double draught of laudanum at eleven o'clock, and have shaved the perineum.'

'Good.' Nairn turned to Milcheap and with grim humour enquired, 'And you, Mr Milcheap – have you been laying any wagers on the speed of this operation?'

The florid features grinned broadly. 'Indeed no, sir. But when the other fellows heard that you had so kindly permitted me to come here, then there was a deal of speculation as to the size of the stone, and some wagers were struck as to that.'

Nairn chuckled amusedly. 'I trust that you inclined towards the larger size, you young rogue.'

'Indeed I did, sir.' Milcheap beamed. 'As I told a few select friends, if Dr Nairn is going to cut for it, then it is most certainly going to be extremely large.'

'The doctor only cuts for the very largest. The ones that others are too frightened to cut for,' Fitzgerald chimed in admiringly. 'That's why he's acknowledged to be the finest lithotomist in the Midlands.'

James could see that this fulsome praise was gratifying to his uncle, and told himself, Why shouldn't he be pleased to hear how good he is. It's only the plain truth after all.

By the French windows a large table had been set in place covered with a red blanket. Milcheap fetched a chair and from the medical chest took surgical instruments which he arranged upon the chair. A bucket of water and sponges were also set down by the table.

James regarded the instruments and couldn't help but wryly acknowledge that they resembled medieval implements of torture rather than modern instruments of mercy.

Nairn took off his travelling coat and in its place donned a black broadcloth frock coat plastered thick with dried blood, pus and human waste.

'There now, Jamie, that coat is the proof of dozens of successful operations. That's the emblem of a great surgeon,' Sean Fitzgerald murmured admiringly.

James stared with envy at his uncle's operating coat, a fierce longing pulsing through him for that day to come when he too would be able to wear such a splendid manifestation of honour and success.

'Bring the patient if you please, gentlemen,' Nairn instructed.

Fitzgerald and Milcheap lifted Wybergh from the bed and he moaned with pain as they carried him to the table and laid him on his back upon the red blanket.

'Nephew, you will hold the right thigh firmly. Mr Fitzgerald, take the left and Mr Milcheap secure his shoulders while I introduce the staff.' Nairn lifted a long thin steel rod which was curved at the end and grooved on its curved side. He greased the curved end with lard then took Wybergh's flaccid penis in his left hand and used his right hand to firmly insert the curved rod into the passage of the penis and push it deep inside the body.

Wybergh screamed thinly and heaved against the restraining hands.

James felt his own heart begin to thump rapidly, and suddenly the threatening storm broke with a deep growl of thunder and squalls of wind and rain lashing against the windows.

'Jasus, it's turned wild.' Fitzgerald grinned. 'I hope we don't get a thunderbolt through the window while we're in the middle of this.'

Nairn's eyes narrowed as he concentrated on his careful probing. Then he exclaimed with satisfaction, 'I have it. Make him secure, gentlemen.'

While James could only watch, the other two men trussed the patient with leather thongs, ignoring his protests and cries of pain and weak struggles. First they passed an extra-long broad leather belt across his chest and under the table, tightening it so that he could not raise his upper body. Then they expertly bound the palms of his hands to his feet, and passed straps around his wasted thighs and up around his shoulders until he was lying with knees thrust upwards, helpless to move.

The naked old man with his mottled, pimpled flesh bizarrely put James in mind of a chicken spitted and tied ready for roasting.

'Mr Milcheap, take the left thigh. You, Nephew, take the right. Spread them wide and hold very firm. Mr Fitzgerald, you will assist me.' Nairn was crisp and very sure.

'Play close attention, Nephew, Mr Milcheap. I have passed the staff through the uretha and into the bladder. It is now hooked against the symphysis. Mr Fitzgerald will hold it in that position.'

He nodded to the Irishman who carefully took the staff. Nairn then took up a knife with a long narrow blade. He frowned to see a smear of dirt upon the blade's surface, and spat upon it and wiped it upon his sleeve. He peered closely at it, wiped it again on his sleeve, then continued explaining.

'I shall enter the knife here into the perineum, an inch behind

68

the scrotum and cut down and outwards in a line roughly midway between the tuberosity of the ischium and the anus, and beyond that orifice towards the sacro-ischiatic ligament. I will introduce the forefinger of my left hand to guide the point of the knife into the groove of the staff and then turn the blade and follow the groove, cutting upwards through the uretha and opening the bladder.' He regarded the two younger men keenly. 'Be steady now, gentlemen.'

He sliced into the flesh.

Wybergh's shriek of agony pierced James's head like a lance, the thin white thigh jerking so violently that he all but lost his grip. Cold clammy sweat burst out on his forehead, and he felt it soaking his body. As the anguished shrieking went on and on his chest tightened unbearably, and he could not seem to draw sufficient breath into his straining lungs. He began to experience the peculiar sensation that somehow he had been transposed into a waking nightmare, as thunder roared, lightning flashed, and the howling wind hurled the rain against the windows with such force that it threatened to shatter the thin glass panes.

It was taking all his strength to hold the thin white thigh captive against his chest, and then his eyes met Milcheap's.

The florid features grinned at him. 'By God, this old bag o'bone has got some considerable strength left, ain't he? It's all I can do to hold the bugger still.'

'Be quite, damn you!' Nairn ordered sharply, and Wybergh's shrieking all but drowned out his words.

Then suddenly the frail body slumped and the skull-like head thumped backwards against the table.

James gaped in horror at the purpled features and slack hanging jaw.

'Has he died?' he beseeched his uncle. 'Has he died?'

Nairn shook his head curtly. 'No. He's only fainted. And that's a blessing. As a gentleman he should be ashamed to behave so badly. Caterwauling like a damned woman!'

He drew out the bloodied knife blade and Fitzgerald removed the staff then sponged the bloodflow away.

Nairn took up another knife, broader bladed and blunt pointed and reinserted blade and forefinger deep into the raw wound.

After some moments he grunted with satisfaction.

'I have it now. But I need to widen the aperture.'

He exchanged the knife for a conically rounded wooden stick which he thrust into the wound, pushing and turning to force the hole wider.

He discarded the stick and inserted long-handled, narrow-jawed forceps. His eyes narrowed in concentration, he deftly manouevred the forceps and then smiled as he slowly and carefully drew them out of the body.

He held the bloody jaws before his helpers' eyes so that they could all see the dull, whitish-grey, rough-surfaced bladder stone. It was larger than a hen's egg.

'By God, sir, that's a beauty!' Milcheap breathed in awe.

Nairn smiled with grim satisfaction. 'Does its size win you your wager, you rogue?'

Milcheap laughed. 'It certainly does, sir.'

'Take it for proof then.' Nairn dropped the stone into Milcheap's eager clutch. 'And for winning you your wager I shall expect a flagon of finest French brandy upon my table.'

'You shall find two flagons upon your table, sir,' Milcheap promised happily.

'Enough chatter now, there's work to be done here.' Nairn peered keenly at James's pale, sweaty face, but said nothing and turned his attention to the patient once more.

Julius Wybergh was still unconscious, rapid thready breaths rasping from his throat.

Nairn examined him briefly, and declared, 'He's all right and in no danger.'

Then he used a narrow metal scoop to complete the clearance of any further detritus from the bladder, bringing out several other small gravel-like stones, and only when he was satisfied that it was completely clear did he tell the others, 'The operation is successfully concluded, gentlemen.'

Fitzgerald and Milcheap applauded with muted cheers and

70

clapping hands. But James could only smile weakly. He felt dreadfully shaken and nauseous. Yet it was not the sight of blood or raw flesh that had affected him. It had been the shrieking of the patient.

'Now, gentlemen,' Nairn went on. 'I propose to insert an india-rubber drainage tube into the bladder. Because of the narrowness of my incisions there is little or no necessity for any stitching to close the wound. But I shall pack lint closely around the tube to absorb any flow of blood. The thighs will be bound close with a roller bandage and the patient's hands will also be secured until he regains full consciousness. Otherwise in his delirium he might well clutch at the tube and wrench it out.'

'How long should the drainage tube remain in situ, sir?' Milcheap enquired.

'Until the urine flows clear. Then it can be discarded, and if necessary stitches put in to close the incisions.'

Nairn inserted the tube and packed the lint, then told Fitzgerald, 'I shall leave you and Mr Milcheap to finish up here. I want you both to remain with the patient overnight and tomorrow and watch over him closely.'

'Shall I stay also, Uncle?' James volunteered.

Nairn shook his head. 'No, you'll return home with me. I've something that I must discuss with you.'

He washed his bloodied hands in the bucket and dried them on a strip of grimy towelling. Then took off the freshly blood-stained operating coat and laid it before the fire.

'I'll have to leave this to dry here,' he told Fitzgerald. 'Remember to bring it back with you.'

'Don't you fret. I'd sooner lose me life than lose that coat,' the Irishman assured him jovially.

Carlos Wybergh was waiting in the drawing room, and immediately they entered he rose from his chair and questioned anxiously, 'How is my father? Did everything go well?'

'Very well indeed,' Nairn reassured him.

'Can I go to him?'

'It's better that you should wait until he has fully regained his senses. The laudanum has rendered him somewhat dazed. My people will fetch you directly he is ready to see you.'

'And the operation went well?' Wybergh needed further reassurance and Nairn supplied it with practised smoothness.

'Extremely well. The extraction was difficult, but I achieved it without inflicting any undue suffering upon your father, and indeed with the very minimum of trauma to the tissues.'

'You have my deepest thanks, Septimus.' Wybergh's handsome face shone with fervent gratitude. And then he apologised profusely. 'But forgive me please, gentlemen. I'm being unpardonably remiss in not offering you some refreshment. What shall it be? Only name it and you shall have it directly.'

Nairn's eyes rested briefly upon James's still clammy sweated, pale face.

'For myself I'll take a glass of Madeira. And for my nephew a glass of brandy wouldn't go amiss, I think.'

The liquor stung James's throat, but he welcomed its comforting heat spreading through his body, and his tremorous nerves calmed and steadied as he drained the generous measure.

'And now we must leave you, Carlos.' Nairn made his goodbye. 'My people will remain here with your father throughout the night to ensure his comfort. And I shall call upon you tomorrow afternoon to make sure that all is going well with him.'

Wybergh accompanied them outside the house, thanking them both continuously for what they had done.

The storm had passed over as quickly as it had gathered, and now the rain had ceased. James drew deep breaths of the clean-washed air, relishing the way it cleared his head.

As they rode side by side along the narrow muddy lanes both men were immersed in their own thoughts. It was Nairn who finally broke their silence.

'Tell me truthfully now, what was it that disturbed you so greatly during the operation? I feared at one point that you were near to fainting again.'

'It was the man's screaming, Uncle,' James answered, and after a moment's hesitation went on to admit, 'In all honesty I don't know if I shall ever be able to harden myself sufficiently against the patients' agonies. I fear I'm too weak. That I lack the necessary strength and resolution, despite the fact that I truly want above all else to become a surgeon.'

He turned in his saddle to look fully into his uncle's face, and asked miserably, 'How can I harden myself against the shrieking? I am not disturbed by the sight and smell and feel of the blood and flesh. But the shrieking pierces me like a lance. It threatens to shatter my nerves and turn me into a coward.'

'I suppose some might suggest that you deafen yourself by plugging your ears with wax, Nephew.' Nairn frowned bleakly, then read the distress in the younger man's eyes, and went on more sympathetically, 'I can only reiterate what I have already told you, and that is that in time you will harden to the shricking.'

'Is there nothing that we can do to ease the pain of an operation, Uncle? Could we not give the patient raw opium or laudanum?'

'The dosage of either that would be necessary to deaden all pain is lethal. I know that from personal experience. All that can be done is to get the patient drunk or give him enough laudanum to make him drowsy, but it is much preferable that the patient should take no alcohol or drug before an operation, because those substances dangerously diminish the vital forces and increase the possibilities of death intervening.

'Believe me, Nephew, the pain inflicted by the knife has a most salutary effect on the patient's vital forces. It rouses him to full vigour and this gives them a much improved chance of surviving the operation. Always remember that God gave us pain for that purpose.'

His confident assertion did little to ease James's troubled thoughts.

Nine

During the days following the operation on Julius Wybergh, James accompanied his uncle on several occasions to the Wybergh house to examine the patient and change his surgical dressings.

On their first visit, Julius Wybergh, although suffering considerable pain from his operative wound, was quite cheerful and appeared to be recovering. But on the subsequent visits the old man was feverish, and complained of feeling extremely unwell and in increasing pain.

The wound itself was swollen and much inflamed, showing no sign of healing and was discharging a foul-smelling, yellowish brown pus which seemed to James to be increasing in quantity as time passed. After ten days abscesses erupted upon the wound, and when they came to him on the twelfth day they found that Julius Wybergh's physical condition had worsened dramatically.

Nairn made no comment on this fact as he changed the dressings and assured Wybergh, 'It is all healing splendidly, sir. You will soon be up and about again, and as frisky as a young colt.'

The old man's face resembled a livid living skull, the skin appearing to be stretched to breaking point over the bone, his eyes deep sunk and heavily bloodshot. He could only nod and mutter weakly, 'I hope so. Indeed I hope so.'

As they waited for Carlos Wybergh to join them in the drawing room, James was greatly troubled by this rapid deterioration in the old man's condition.

'Is Mr Wybergh's wound healing as quickly as it should, Uncle?' he asked tentatively.

'No, it's taking more time than I had anticipated,' his uncle replied casually.

'Can it be the abscesses which are impeding the wound from healing?' James suggested.

'Good Lord, no!' Nairn stated emphatically. 'Every healing wound discharges a laudable pus from suppuration. As the pus is discharged by the flesh it carries off all the foul and injurious vapours from the body and thus allows the wound to heal. It is our body's defence against the invasion of atmospheric contagions. Believe me, Nephew, it is the absence of laudable pus which causes the surgeon concern. Its presence proves that the body is reacting as Nature designed it to do.

'Have you noted the change in this pus? Initially it was thick and creamy, now it's more watery and has a brownish hue. That indicates that there is some atmospheric contagion in the wound.'

James persisted, 'But those abscesses that have erupted, surely that means that the contagion is taking a firmer hold?'

Nairn regarded the young man quizzically. 'Is the student now teaching his master?'

'Oh no, Uncle, of course not,' James protested in embarrassment. 'It's just that I . . .'

'Enough!' Nairn frowned, then nodded judiciously. 'It is pleasing to me that you display some doubt at times, Nephew. It shows that you have an active and enquiring mind. But you really must think before you ask your questions. If you had reflected for a moment you would undoubtedly have realised that the eruption of these abscesses is merely the manifestation that the body is increasing the strength of its efforts against the atmospheric contagions. It is, in military parlance, launching its most devasting attacks upon its opponents.'

The absolute conviction with which Nairn spoke served to dispel all James's doubts and increased his already intense admiration for his uncle's vast store of professional knowledge and expertise.

'Thank you for explaining it so clearly to me, Uncle,' he said sincerely.

When Carlos Wybergh joined them he was obviously worried. 'Is my father progressing as he should, Septimus?'

Nairn smiled reassuringly. 'He is progressing as well as can be expected, Carlos. Lithotomy is a severe ordeal for even the strongest to endure, and your father is aged and in ill health. But I am hopeful that he will make a full recovery in due course.'

During the ride back to Tardebigge, Nairn remained deep in thought for some time then told James, 'On reflection I have to say that it's almost certain that Julius Wybergh will die within the next few days.'

James couldn't believe that he had heard correctly. 'But you told Carlos that his father would certainly make a full recovery.'

Nairn shook his head. 'No, I did not tell Carlos that his father would certainly make a full recovery. I told him that I was hopeful that he would. There's a deal of difference between certainty and hope. But I confess that my hope was a matter of whistling in the dark.'

'What will he die of?' James asked puzzledly.

'Pyaemia. His blood is poisoned.'

'But you told me that his body is expelling the poisons through the laudable pus.'

'Indeed it is,' Nairn agreed. 'And is making a valiant effort of it. But unfortunately because of his age and ill health Wybergh's vital forces are so depleted that his body lacks the strength and vigour to expel the poisons in sufficient quantity.'

James could still not comprehend fully. 'But where did the poisons originate from?'

'They are a malignant miasma which undoubtedly invaded the house at some time in the last few days. The miasma then enveloped Julius Wybergh and forced entrance into his body.'

'Couldn't its entry into the house have been prevented?'

'Possibly. If it had been visible and the people in the house had recognised it for what it was, they might have been able to close all apertures until the wind had carried it on its way. But these malignant miasmas are rarely visible. They are the deadliest of enemies for we doctors to encounter and can create havoc when they come in the form of the cholera and other plagues.'

'Are they sentient?' James had a disturbing vision of intelligent, invisible miasmas actively hunting for human beings to attack.

Nairn chuckled with amusement. 'There's no need to frighten yourself with such notions, Nephew. No miasma is sentient, thank God! Otherwise the human race would have ceased to exist long ago.'

'That's a relief to hear,' James admitted.

They continued on in silence for some time, and then Nairn informed James, 'I'm going to send the boy's remains for burial. You can help me prepare him to go when we arrive home.'

Back in the outhouse at Tardebigge James helped his uncle to fish the dismembered sections of the corpse from out of the tank of formaldehyde and place them on the lead trough. The formaldchyde had impregnated and discoloured the flayed tissues and none of the dissected sections bore any semblance to the child that once had been.

James regarded them dispassionately. For him now they were merely anatomical specimens: they were the necessary study material that he must use in learning his profession. For a brief moment he marvelled at how quickly he had become accustomed to this particular aspect of his work.

His uncle picked up a dissected forearm and examined it closely.

'You did a particularly fine piece of work with this, Nephew,' he congratulated, and James was pleased by this unexpected commendation.

77

'What do we pack them in for the journey?' he asked and Nairn pointed to a small coffin-like wooden box.

James went to fetch it to the trough and reached for a section of the corpse which he dropped casually into the box.

'What are you doing?' Nairn demanded sharply.

'I'm packing them up.'

'Take it out, and put the box down also,' his uncle snapped curtly and James obeyed, starting at Nairn's grim frown in amazement.

'Have you forgotten my words to you when this child was first brought here?' Nairn demanded sternly. 'Let me remind you. I told you that his remains would be treated with respect. And when they had served their purpose they would be sent for Christian burial.'

'What would you have me do?' James questioned uncertainly.

'I would have you do as I told you. Treat these remains with respect. We shall restore him to some semblance of humanity, and he'll be wrapped in a winding sheet before being placed in his coffin. Then we shall say a prayer for his soul's salvation and he will lie here through this night with lighted candles at his head and feet while we keep the vigil.' He smiled bleakly. 'You are puzzled as to why I insist upon all this, are you not?'

'Yes, I am,' James told him frankly. 'With all respect, Uncle, it seems totally unnecessary. These are just anatomical specimens now, and anyway they are going to receive a Christian burial. Why do we have to pray and keep the vigil?'

'To remind ourselves that this flesh and bone once sheltered an immortal soul.' Nairn's dark eyes held a fanatical gleam. 'The surgeon must never treat the human body with contempt. We are not slaughtermen or butchers dismembering brute beasts. We are healers, and this flesh and bone lying here was fashioned in God's image. Always remember that, Nephew.'

James considered these words and a sense of shame burgeoned in his mind.

'I'm sorry,' he apologised quietly. 'And I will try to always keep that fact in the forefront of my mind.'

'I believe you, Nephew,' his uncle said gently. 'Now make ready the needle and thread, and we'll restore him as best we can to human likeness.'

Ten

'For as much as it hath pleased Almighty God to take unto himself the soul of our dear brother here departed . . .'

Reverend the Lord Aston's brandy-hoarse voice carried across the tombstones to the ears of the smock-clad labourers come to gawp from a distance at the spectacle of a rich man's funeral equipage. The ornate stately hearse, black-plumed horses, banner-carrying mutes, gentrified mourners and huge laurel wreaths.

One by one the chief mourners stepped foward and cast their handfuls of dirt down upon the coffin of Julius Wybergh.

'. . . We therefore commit his body to the ground; earth to earth, ashes to ashes, dust to dust . . .'

It was an indication of the Wyberghs' wealth and social standing that Lord Aston was presiding in person at this interment instead of delegating it to one of his curates. A bulky-bodied, dyspeptic man who still wore the traditional clerical wig on his bald pate, he was a worldly cleric, who even as he intoned was covertly eyeing the widow's slender waist and fine breasts.

Others among the mourners were also eyeing the widow and speculating upon her future. There would undoubtedly be many men eager to comfort her in her bereavement; and some of those men were present here, Edward Harcourt prominent among them. Lifelong bachelor though he was, a wealthy widow was a tempting incentive towards matrimony.

Behind the black veil the dark eyes of the newly widowed Mercedes Wybergh examined the sombre-clad crowd around the open grave. The women were veiled like herself, the men uniform in black mourning cloaks and top hats swathed with bands of black crêpe. One young man's face caught and held her attention. He was standing next to Septimus Nairn, and she surmised that he was Nairn's nephew, James Kerr, of whom Carlos had told her. She thought him very handsome, and visualised his smooth-skinned, muscled body hidden beneath the voluminous cloak.

'. . . in sure and certain hope of the Resurrection to eternal life through our Lord Jesus Christ, who shall change our vile body . . .'

Standing by his mother's side Carlos Wybergh was both saddened and relieved. He was saddened to lose his indulgent father, yet at the same time relieved that the old man was now beyond all bodily sufferings. Although he was reluctant to acknowledge it there was also a certain pleasurable sense of release. Now he was free to lead his life exactly as he chose without any paternal dictate or imposed restriction.

'. . . that it may be like unto His glorious body, according to the mighty working, whereby He is able to subdue all things to Himself.'

After further prayers the graveside service ended and the mourners moved aside to allow Mercedes Wybergh, leaning on the arm of her son, to precede them out of the churchyard to where the long line of carriages waited.

James and Nairn had both been invited to attend the select gathering at the Wybergh house after the funeral, and James was not looking forward to the occasion. He could not help but experience an uncomfortable sense of guilt. Julius Wybergh had died following the operation at which he had assisted, and he could not dismiss the nagging instinct that if the operation had not been performed, then Julius Wybergh might still be alive.

A tall lantern-jawed man, dressed all in black but without a mourning cloak or swathe of crêpe on his top hat, was standing to one side of the churchyard gate when the mourners filed through it. As Nairn and James neared him, he lifted his hand

81

in a discreet signal and walked some little distance away, then stopped and turned.

'It's Enoch Cull,' Nairn told James, and frowned in annoyance. 'He's chosen an unseemly time to come in search of me. I prefer not to be seen in company with him.' He sighed exasperatedly. 'Ah well. Let's keep it brief.'

When they came up to the man, Nairn voiced his annoyance. 'This is not a happy meeting, Cull. You know well that I prefer our acquaintance to be kept from others as much as possible.'

Cull showed no reaction to the rebuke. He was the tallest of the trio, raw-boned and physically powerful. James found him vaguely sinister and menacing with his peculiarly grey-hued face and cold, close-set eyes.

'Would you also prefer then for me to take my goods elsewhere, Dr Nairn?' he questioned flatly.

'I didn't say that,' Nairn retorted. 'But coming here was not well done. A gentleman's funeral is not an occasion upon which to carry out business transactions.'

The other man stayed silent for a couple of moments, betraying no emotion, then merely stated, 'I deal in perishable goods, Doctor, and so am forced to transact my business at the earliest opportunity, as well you know. However, if you wish I will leave you immediately.'

Nairn shook his head. 'You may as well stay.'

Cull stared at James and lifted his thick eyebrows in silent query.

'You may speak freely,' Nairn assured him. 'This gentleman is my relative, Mr James Kerr, and is in my confidence. What do you have?'

'Male. Very fresh. Aged about thirty. Well muscled. Got hit by a charge of shot. Several wounds on the body.'

'What price?' Nairn questioned.

'Fifteen pounds.'

'That's very high!'

'It cost me high to procure it.'

'Very well,' Nairn accepted after a moment's consideration. 'Make the delivery after midnight.'

Cull nodded, walked away and was quickly lost to view around the corner of the churchyard wall.

To James's surprise his uncle's mood changed immediately and he smiled.

'This is very timely, Nephew. I was hoping that an opportunity would arise to show you the effects of gunshot upon the tissues and bones. They can present most unexpected results.'

'How do you think the man came to be gunshot?' James asked curiously.

'He was probably a poacher,' Nairn theorised. 'There are quite a few shooting affrays between gamekeepers and the poacher gangs. If a poacher is wounded or killed then his accomplices always try to carry him away with them.'

'I can understand them taking risks to save each other from capture. I suppose that is what they call honour among thieves,' James remarked. 'But why take the risk of carrying away a dead man?'

'It's a matter of self-preservation, because if he was recognised it could lead to their own identities being revealed. And that could mean transportation or even the gallows for the poor devils.'

Remembering the depredations of poachers on his father's small estate James stated forthrightly, 'Poachers are thieves, taking by force what belongs to others. They must be punished.'

Nairn frowned. 'It's a cruel thing to send some poor devil to Van Diemens Land or hang him for the sake of a few rabbits or birds. The Game Laws are far too savage.'

'But without such laws there would be anarchy. No gentleman's property would be safe,' James riposted.

Nairn chuckled with grim amusement. 'By God, Nephew, there are times when you sound like a pompous prig of fifty years instead of a young sprig of twenty-one.'

The accusation struck home and James flushed with embarrassment.

His uncle regarded him keenly. 'The old saw is true, you know, Nephew. All work and no play makes Jack a dull boy. I

83

fear that I'm in part responsible. I've driven you hard and given no thought to your pleasures. You've spent too much of your time lately in the company of we dull old fogies; you need to spend some time in the company of lively young sparks.'

'I'm content enough with the life I'm leading,' James said truthfully.

'Nevertheless, I intend that you shall have some enjoyment. I shall send you to stay with Arthur Milcheap for a few days. He undoubtedly knows how to make merry.'

He lifted his hand to forestall any objection.

'You shall go to stay with Milcheap, Nephew, and that's an end to it. So, you may look forward to a holiday after I've shown you the effects of gunshot on the bones and tissues. And now we'd better make haste to the Wyberghs.'

At the Wybergh mansion they were ushered into the large drawing room where Mercedes Wybergh and her son were receiving their guests. The widow had lifted her veil and James was astonished when he saw her face. She was strikingly attractive, with dark, almond-shaped eyes, olive skin and high cheekbones. But it was not her good looks that surprised him as much as the fact that she looked so young. He could not believe that she could be the mother of a man who was two years older than himself.

Septimus Nairn correctly interpreted the expression in his nephew's eyes and whispered into his ear, 'Mrs Wybergh was hardly more than a child when she gave birth to Carlos.'

The room thronged with guests and servants moved among the gathering offering glasses of wine and slices of cake.

Nairn led James to where the widow was seated on a throne-like brocaded armchair. He bowed and told her, 'May I offer on behalf of my nephew and myself our sincerest condolences on your tragic loss, ma'am. It is a matter of the utmost regret to us both that we were unable to save him.'

'I know that you did all that could be done, Dr Nairn, and you have my profound gratitude for all your efforts.' Her voice was soft and accented with the musical timbre of her native

84

Andalusia. Her lucent dark eyes moved to James. 'You also have my gratitude, Mr Kerr.'

Close up James could see some lines on her broad brow and dark shadows beneath her eyes, yet for him these flaws did not diminish her physical attraction. Instead they suggested a womanly maturity which he found was affecting him powerfully. He felt a sense of shame that he was feeling a sexual desire for her at such a time as this. Her eyes held his for long moments and he experienced the sudden apprehension that she was aware of what he was feeling towards her. He was relieved when his uncle intervened.

'I beg that you will forgive us for leaving without further delay, ma'am. But you will understand that we have urgent cases to attend on.'

She bowed her head gracefully. 'Of course, Dr Nairn. I hope that you will dine with myself and Carlos when we are somewhat reconciled to our sad loss.' The lucent eyes gazed at James again, and a fleeting smile curved her full moist lips. 'And you must come with the Doctor, Mr Kerr.'

James bowed. 'I'd be honoured, ma'am.'

She held out her hand to each in turn, and James's heartbeat quickened as he felt a discernible lingering pressure from her slender fingers.

As they left the room James could not resist the impulse to turn his head for one final glimpse of her, and his breath caught in his throat when he found her gaze fixed on him. He was shamefully conscious that his cheeks were reddening, and hastened to get outside.

Edward Harcourt had also noticed the way Mercedes Wybergh had looked at the young man. So, that's the way of it, he thought, and chuckled inwardly. She's already feeling the pangs of the widow's hunger. I shall definitely present her with my own menu, and it might well be wise to do it sooner rather than later.

Outside Septimus Nairn looked keenly at his nephew's flushed cheeks but waited until they were mounted and trotting down the long driveway before remarking with outward casualness, 'Mrs Wybergh is a handsome woman, is she not?'

'She's more than handsome,' James answered unguardedly. 'She's beautiful.'

Nairn smiled dryly. 'And she's old enough to be your mother.'

James flush deepened, and he silently cursed his own physical reaction.

Nairn's smile broadened. 'They do say that there's many a good tune can be played on an old fiddle, do they not?'

Uncomfortably aware of his uncle's shrewd gaze James kept his own eyes to his front and made no answer.

Nairn chuckled amusedly. 'Yes, the holiday with Arthur Milcheap will do you a power of good, Nephew. That scallywag will know where to take you to expend some of your vital forces. Otherwise you might well explode at an inopportune moment.'

'I don't know what you mean, Uncle,' James was driven to reply stiffly.

'Oh, I think you do,' his uncle teased. 'I think you know very well what I mean.'

They continued on in silence, and James was able to ponder on the startling effect that Mercedes Wybergh had had on his emotions.

No woman has ever had such an effect on me, he marvelled.

She really is old enough to be my mother, he accepted with dismay.

'What the hell has happened to me?' he demanded angrily, unconsciously voicing this demand aloud.

He was shocked to hear his uncle state calmly, 'That question is very easily answered, Nephew. You have spent many months sublimating all your natural desires in the pursuit of knowledge. Immersed and enveloped in death and suffering and decay, without a respite.'

In James's mind embarrassment warred with the intense desire to unburden himself to this older, far far wiser man and to seek his guidance and advice. At last he asked tentatively, 'Can I speak frankly, Uncle?'

86

'Of course,' Nairn assented warmly. 'I am in the place of your parent, Nephew. But I am also your friend and you can confide whatever you wish to in me. I promise you, I shall not be shocked or offended by anything you might tell me.'

James spent many moments nerving himself to confess, 'I'm still a virgin.'

'That's nothing to be ashamed of,' Nairn assured him.

It was as if a crushing weight had been lifted from James's shoulders. All sense of embarrassment disappeared, and the words came in a rush.

'I felt a sexual desire for Mrs Wybergh, Uncle. I couldn't help it. It just overwhelmed me.'

'As it overwhelmed most of the men there, I don't doubt.' Nairn chuckled. 'I confess I felt a stirring of that nature myself.'

He paused, then smiling kindly went on, 'You have youth's hot blood, Nephew, and your natural bodily hungers cannot be denied for ever. My advice to you is that while you are staying with Milcheap, you find a willing woman and satisfy your hungers. Only take care that she is clean and free from disease. Milcheap will undoubtedly know such a one.'

'But she will be a prostitute!' James protested. 'It will be a sordid thing to do. A matter of buying someone's flesh to use. It seems so cold-blooded, somehow.'

'It's not so cold-blooded as seducing some poor ignorant servant girl, getting her pregnant and then abandoning her, as all too many of our young bloods of the gentry do,' Nairn asserted firmly. 'A whore who is good at her trade will have you feeling hot-blooded enough when the moment comes. It's amazing what flames a few drinks and a willing woman can fire in a man.

'St Paul said that it was better to marry, than to burn. Personally I'm of the opinion that he could equally well have advised that it was better to go with a whore, than to burn. Anyway, that is my advice, and whether or not you take it is entirely your decision.'

He leaned across and patted James's shoulder fondly.

'You're a good, decent lad, and I'm proud that you're my kin. You must do as you think fit.'

James grinned ruefully. 'Well, for the time being I shall just have to go on burning. I'll decide upon it when I'm staying with Arthur Milcheap.'

Eleven

January 1842

'You've broiled this beefsteak excellently well, Liddy,' Robert Landser congratulated as he ate his meal with tremendous gusto. 'I declare I've never eaten better at Oxford.' He tapped the glass of ruby-red claret with his fork. 'And this wine is very palatable I must say.'

Sitting by the fireside Liddy basked in her brother's praise. Since her father had obtained the new loan from Edward Harcourt she had paid the outstanding household bills and been enabled to improve the family's diet.

'Edward Harcourt certainly came up trumps for us, didn't he?' Robert declared. 'The fellow may be a bit overfond of himself, but I think that his heart is in the right place. All credit to him, he's proven to be a good friend to this family.'

'Yes, I suppose he has in a way.' Liddy harboured some considerable reservations as to how good a friend of the family Edward Harcourt might really be. Since the day of the Yeomanry review Harcourt had frequently visited the salt works, and although he treated her with friendly politeness there was always an expression in his eyes when he spoke with her that made Liddy feel both angry and uneasy.

Her brother now looked keenly at her, conscious of the lack of any warmth in her reply. 'You don't like Harcourt very much, do you, Liddy?'

'I neither like or dislike him.'

'But he's always very polite and kind to you, isn't he?'

'Oh yes, he's polite enough.' She pondered briefly. 'But

whenever he looks at me I always feel as if I'm somehow being hunted.'

'Being hunted!' Robert laughed 'That's a bit strong, isn't it? I'm sure the man only looks at you in the same way as any other man looks at a pretty girl. It's only a natural reaction.'

Liddy pursed her shapely lips, mentally examining her own feelings. She was well aware that many men found her attractive and stared at her with desire. But they did not make her feel uneasy and somehow threatened, as Harcourt did.

She shook her head. 'No, most men look at pretty girls with an honest admiration, or a natural healthy lust, but Edward Harcourt looks at me with the eyes of a predator.'

'Exactly as I say,' Robert declared emphatically. 'We men are hunters by instinct. And when we see a pretty girl we naturally look at her as a hunter looks at any desirable creature whom he would like to give chase to. That's all it is, Liddy, the thrill of the chase.'

George Landser had come into the room while his son was speaking and had heard the last few words.

'Thrill of the chase?' He smiled. 'Are you planning to go fox-hunting, Robert?'

Petulance sparked in the younger man's eyes. 'And pray do tell me, Pa, how I am to go fox-hunting when I don't own a horse?'

'You could follow the hunt on foot. There are many who do so,' George Landser suggested good-humouredly. 'I did myself during my younger days.'

'Oh yes, indeed there are many who follow the hunt on foot, but no gentlemen are to be found among them,' Robert gibed acidly. 'I don't doubt that it was the same during your younger days.'

George Landser's smile abruptly vanished.

'Come and sit down, Pa. I've your meal hot in the oven,' Liddy intervened quickly, hoping to deflect the looming clash between the two men.

Her father seated himself, and then said quietly, 'You know well that at this time we can't afford horseflesh, Robert. But I pay you money enough to enable you to hire a horse for a day's hunting.'

'A hired nag!' Robert sneered with exaggerated incredulity. 'A hired nag! No real gentleman would allow himself to be seen on a hired nag.'

'And no real gentleman would continually badger his own father for that which he cannot provide,' George Landser accused peevishly.

Liddy came from the kitchen with the plate of food and put it before her father. 'Now stop arguing the pair of you,' she commanded sharply. 'And eat your dinner, Pa, before it gets cold.'

The two men ignored her.

'But you have money enough now to buy me a horse,' Robert challenged. 'Edward Harcourt gave you money.'

George Landser scowled at his son. 'You know full well that Harcourt's money is a loan and it carries a high rate of interest, I can assure you. It must be used to sink the new shaft and pay out the wages and meet the bills. It cannot be wasted on inessentials. When matters improve, then you may have a horse. But you must be patient until then.'

'For how long?' The younger man's features resembled a spiteful child. 'Matters seem to be taking a devil of a long time to show any improvement.'

'They might improve the quicker if you were to help more!' George Landser retorted angrily.

'I do help,' his son declared indignantly. 'Don't I do the clerking? And a damned tedious, dull job it is working at those cursed ledgers day in and day out.'

'And a damned long-winded, bad job you make of those ledgers,' his father rejoined. 'I have to double-check every entry that you make. And you make precious few of them, don't you, and those that you do look as if they were entered by a babe-in-arms they're so scrawled and blotched!'

Robert took the napkin from his knees and hurled it on to the table. 'Let me remind you that I have been educated as a gentleman and not a damned counting-house clerk!'

He jumped to his feet and stormed out of the room.

George Landser sighed wearily. 'I've spoiled that boy. I've been too soft with him and given in to all his wants too easily.'

Liddy smiled at her father and told him fondly, 'There's nothing wrong with being an indulgent parent, Pa. It's far better than being a harsh one. Come now, eat your dinner.'

He returned her smile. 'What would I do without you, Liddy? Having you for a daughter makes up for all the other disappointments of my life.'

He had scarcely begun to eat when the outer doorbell jangled furiously.

'I shall go, and if it's someone for you I shall tell them to return after you've had your dinner.' Liddy hurried to answer the strident summons.

Edward Harcourt stood facing her. He bowed slightly.

'I'm seeking your father, Miss Lydia. Is he within?' His eyes lingered on her breasts, and her instant resentment caused her to answer shortly.

'Yes, he is. But he's just sat down to his dinner.'

'Has he now.' The suggestion of a smile touched his lips, and again his eyes lingered on her breasts. 'Well, I don't wish to take him from his meal. I shall entertain myself until he's done.'

He touched his finger to the brim of his top hat, and turned away to walk towards the office building.

'Who was it at the door?' George Landser asked as she re-entered the dining room.

'It was Edward Harcourt. He said that he'd entertain himself until you had done eating.' She was still seething with resentment at how Harcourt had stared so lasciviously at her breasts.

'I'll have to go to him.' Her father laid down his knife and fork.

'No, Pa!' she protested hotly. 'Finish your dinner. Let him wait.'

'I can't afford to let him wait, Liddy, my dear. I can't afford to do that.'

Liddy's anger fired and she mentally called down curses on

Harcourt's head for having turned her father into someone resembling a servile lackey.

'Why, Pa?' she demanded. 'Why must you act so lickspittle towards that man?'

He shook his head, and for a brief moment his shoulders sagged and he looked like a much older man. 'Because without his loans we'd all be in the workhouse, my dear.'

A thumping sounded on the ceiling above their heads. Liddy sighed, and made her reluctant way upstairs in answer to her mother's summons.

As he waited in the office for George Landser to come to him Harcourt mentally reviewed the progress of his secret agenda and was content. There were now only the finishing touches to be added, and within short weeks all would be achieved. He quickly scanned through the recent pages of the ledgers on the desk and found what he had hoped for. The sinking of the new shaft had met an obstacle in the form of a very heavy seepage which was causing delay and a great deal of extra work for the contractors. He grinned with satisfaction, confident that this new shaft was also destined for failure.

Now his thoughts turned to Lydia Landser. During the last months his lust to possess her had escalated into an obsession. So much so that when he made his regular forays into Birmingham or Worcester he found himself mentally superimposing the image of her face upon the faces of the whores he bought, and imagining that it was upon her fresh young body he was slaking his voracious sexual hungers instead of their much-used flesh.

One of the reasons that Harcourt wanted to bring George Landser under his complete dominance was his recognition of the deep bonds of affection that bound father and daughter. He reasoned that if he controlled the father, then it would be easier for him to bring the girl under his dominance also. That she might be forced to come unwillingly and fearfully to his bed did not trouble him. Possession of her body and subjection of her will was what he wanted, not her love or willing compliance.

Yet, impatient as he was to have her, perversely he could also

93

savour the waiting, knowing that a rare dish tasted all the sweeter if the appetite was made keener by long anticipation.

'Ahh, here you are, George. I hope I haven't taken you from your meal.'

'No, Edward. It was a small family matter which delayed me.'

'The seepage in the new shaft, how bad is it?'

George Landser had been dreading this question. He drew a long breath before admitting reluctantly, 'It seems to be more extensive than we originally thought it to be. The contractors have not been able to staunch the flow completely as yet.'

He waited apprehensively for an angry reaction, but to his surprise Harcourt suggested, 'Perhaps we should try elsewhere, rather than persist any longer with it. What do you think?'

'Well, it would mean more expense,' Landser answered hesitantly. 'But I think that it might be advantageous to sink another shaft further to the west of the present one. After all, this seepage is entering from the eastern side of the shaft; if we go to the west we might well find that it's completely dry.'

'Very well, that's what we'll do. I'll arrange the transfer of the money as soon as I return to the bank. Usual interest rate, of course.' Harcourt smiled warmly. 'In for a penny, in for a pound, my friend. I'm determined that we succeed in this endeavour, George, and I'll not let any extra expense deflect me from my purpose.'

George Landser inwardly blessed the happy moment that had brought him such a generous creditor.

Twelve

Bromsgrove
February 1842

A chill wind was blowing when, in late afternoon, George Landser came trudging down the turnpike road and into the long High Street. His feet were sore and his arms aching from the weight of the parcel of heavy ledgers he was carrying, and he stared longingly at the alehouses he passed. But he dared not go into any of their inviting doors because he was en route to a meeting with Edward Harcourt.

Harcourt had sent an urgent summons for him to bring his account ledgers immediately, and now Landser was dreading what that summons might mean. He was still desperately struggling to survive and if Harcourt intended to call in his loans then that struggle would be lost.

The clerk showed him into Harcourt's office.

Harcourt frowned from his thronelike leather chair.

'I expected you earlier, George. Sit down.'

Harcourt gestured imperiously towards the straight-backed chair standing before his desk, which had several rolls of vellum bound with red ribbons strewn across its broad leather top.

When Landser was seated, Harcourt smiled bleakly. 'You may well be wondering why I asked you to call at such short notice. I hope it didn't unduly discommode you?'

'Oh no. I'm always happy to come at whatever hour is most convenient to you, Edward.' Landser's porcelain teeth glistened in an obsequious grimace.

'I hope that you came on foot. I've a great objection to my

money being wasted on hiring gigs now that you've no vehicle or horseflesh of your own.' Harcourt enjoyed inflicting humiliation on his victims.

George Landser instantly sensed that something very unpleasant might be coming, and fear stirred, but he forced himself to assure pleasantly, 'Oh yes, Edward, I walked here, and I shall walk back.'

'As befits your present situation in life.' Harcourt's smile was feral. He pulled open a desk drawer and took out a bottle of brandy and a single glass, which he filled and sipped from appreciatively. 'This is French, George, from the Cognac region. The very best.'

Landser desperately needed a drink himself by now. He realised that the other man was playing some sort of cruel game, and dread enveloped him.

Harcourt's manicured fingernails tapped the rolls of vellum. 'Do you recognise these?'

'No.'

'You should do, George. They're your debts.'

'My debts?'

'Your debts. I've bought them from your other major creditors. Now I'm your sole creditor, apart from what you owe to the local tradespeople and shopkeepers. But of course those are only trifling sums, unlike the debts you now owe to me. Which are very considerable sums. Very considerable indeed.'

Landser squirmed uncomfortably upon the hard wooden chair.

Harcourt's feral smile metamorposed into a snarl. 'And how long will it take to increase the present abysmal levels of your production sufficiently for you to be able to meet all the interest payments in full?'

Landser spread his arms in miserable appeal. 'It's impossible to do that until the new shaft is finished, Edward. You must appreciate that fact well enough. But the shaft is progressing uncommonly well, and is bone dry.'

Harcourt clicked his fingers, signalling for Landser to place the ledgers on the desk before him.

96

The broad pages rustled as Harcourt quickly scanned through them, then he read one entry which caused him to look up frowning.

'I see that from last September 1841, you've been employing your son at a salary of eighty pounds per annum. What exactly are his duties?'

'He does some clerking and makes himself generally useful. He earns his wages.' Landser was defensive.

'Does he indeed? I pay my head clerk forty-five pounds per annum, and my other clerks thirty-five pounds. In my opinion your son is grossly overpaid. You'd better get rid of him immediately.'

Stung into anger, Landser flushed and retorted, 'I can employ whomsoever I wish at my works, Edward, and pay whatever salaries I choose to pay.'

The banker shook his head.

'Oh no, George. From now on you will do as I say.'

His fingers moved over the rolled sheets of vellum as if he were caressing them.

'If I laid these before one of my fellow magistrates, I could have you committed to the debtors' prison before the week is out. And if you were in prison then your family would be rendered homeless and destitute.'

Fear shivered through Landser.

When Harcourt saw the effect his threat had on his victim, the feral smile reappeared.

'Don't be alarmed, George. I've no desire to harm you or your family.'

George Landser's tense body sagged in relief. But that relief was short-lived, as Harcourt went on, 'That is why I propose to employ you to manage the salt works for me.'

'What?'

Harcourt ignored the shocked exclamation.

'I shall pay you a salary of sixty pounds per annum and you may remain in the house rent free. I consider that to be a most generous offer.'

George Landser was utterly bewildered and wondered if he were going mad. He lifted his hand in protest.

97

'What are you saying, Edward? It doesn't make any sense!'
'Oh, but it does make sense, George.' Harcourt beamed happily. 'You see, because I now own all your major debts I can call for the instant repayment of the capital sums. I've had my lawyer closely examine all the loan agreements that you signed. I fear that you obviously didn't read the small print as carefully as you should have. To cut a long story short, the situation is that you have two options. You can either sign the works over to me, or I can have you made bankrupt and committed to prison for debt and come to an agreement with the receivers to purchase the works for a nominal sum . . . The first option will ensure that you will have a salaried position and a house to live in. The second option will place you in prison and make your family homeless and destitute.'

He stopped talking, and gazed intently at the bewildered man before him.

George Landser was having great difficulty in absorbing what he had heard. He was totally confused but slowly amid the jumble of his thoughts one fact was becoming paramount. Edward Harcourt was going to steal the salt works from him. No matter that legally Harcourt would commit no crime, it was still morally an act of theft. A murderous rage flared within him, and for a brief instant he was on the verge of hurling himself at the banker, but even in the grip of that murderous impulse he was racked with the sickening realisation that he was completely in Harcourt's power. He had hostages to fortune in the shape of his children and his sick wife. If he killed Harcourt, then he would be laying a further burden of suffering upon them.

Harcourt himself was tense. He had seen the murderous spasm of rage upon Landser's face and readied himself for a physical attack. But as the moments passed he realised that the threat of violence was receding rapidly, and thought contemptuously, You're a coward, Landser. I'd have killed any man who did to me what I've done to you.

Aloud he said consolingly, 'I know that this is very hard for you to accept, George. But believe me when I tell you that I'm acting in your own best interests. You were facing inevitable ruination. In signing the works over to me you will escape ruin and the material security of your family is assured. Do you see that?'

Seething with anger and resentment though he was, George Landser knew that for the sake of his family he would have to suffer whatever humiliation Harcourt chose to inflict upon him. He nodded and replied dejectedly, 'Yes, it is clear.'

'Then you'll sign the works over to me?'

'What other choice have I?' Landser spat out bitterly.

'Good. I'm happy that we've arrived at an amicable understanding.' Harcourt relaxed now that he knew he was in complete control of the situation. Rising from his seat he came around the desk to pat the other man's shoulder and tell him in a friendly fashion, 'I shall instruct my lawyer to prepare the necessary documents for the transferral of ownership. I also intend to help your son to find other employment. That's if you wish me to, of course. I have some business connections in London that can perhaps find a position for him.'

Landser nodded.

'Now we'll drink a toast to our joint future. I've plans for the salt works, George, that will greatly benefit both of us.'

Harcourt filled two glasses with brandy, but George Landser stood up and snarled, 'I've no wish to drink any toast. I'll bid you good day.'

Harcourt shrugged unconcernedly. 'As you like, George.'

George Landser stepped into the street seething with anger against Harcourt. But that anger was quickly overwhelmed by a black depression. He muttered, 'I need a drink.'

He stepped into the first tavern doorway he came to and called for gin.

Thirteen

J ames Kerr's head was throbbing painfully, his mouth was
sour and dry, his stomach nauseous. In the bed beside him
the woman lay on her back, snoring loudly. James levered
himself upright and looked down at her painted face.

In the daylight the thick layering of rouge and powder could
no longer disguise the raddled complexion, and the seductive
young beauty of the previous night had metamorphosed into an
ugly ageing drab.

My God! he thought, I must have been drunk out of my
mind. He felt a twinge of self-disgust as he remembered how
greedily he had sated his hunger for her body. Then he admitted
ruefully, But it was marvellous at the time.

An involuntary sense of satisfaction suddenly overlaid all
else: I'm not a virgin any more.

He looked more kindly at the woman, recalling how patiently
she had guided him in the mechanics of lovemaking, shown him
how to lengthen his pleasure, aroused him again and again.

He smiled wryly: And now I can't even think what your name
is.

He felt a warmth towards her and took care not to wake her
as he left the bed and began to dress.

His consideration was wasted, however, when a thunderous
hammering shook the door and Arthur Milcheap shouted,
'Can I come in, Jamie?' and entered without waiting for a
reply.

The woman stirred, her eyes opened, and she cursed savagely, 'You noisy bastard!'

Milcheap's florid features wore a beaming grin. 'Come on, Jamie. It's past noon and we've got to meet the fellows. And you'd best hurry up and get out of here, Dorry, because my cleaner is coming shortly and if she finds you here then my good name will be lost.'

'You've never had a good name to fuckin' well lose,' the woman accused good-naturedly.

'Did you look after my friend properly?' Milcheap questioned.

'You'd best ask him that,' she retorted. 'He wasn't complaining anyway. He couldn't get enough of it. I earned me bleedin' money last night, I'll tell you. He's wore me out, so he has.'

James flushed with embarrassment, and the other two both laughed raucously.

She got up and dressed quickly then left, patting James's cheek fondly as she said goodbye. 'I enjoyed meself with you last night, my handsome. You're a regular stallion, you am. I might even let you have it at cut price next time.'

Despite his embarrassment James could not help but feel a glow of gratification at this endorsement of his sexual prowess. He made a hurried toilet and then the two young men set out to cross the city.

James had now been in Birmingham for a week. He had been to the theatre, and the music-hall and the dancing-rooms, and every night had centred around drinking and carousing with Milcheap and his raffish friends, Conky and Tim.

'Where are we supposed to be meeting the fellows?' he asked now.

'They should be at the hospital mortuary. Conky wants to assist with an autopsy on a woman who died of puerperal fever, and Tim is bound to be there with him.' Milcheap grinned quizzically at James. 'Your uncle tells me that you're a star at dissection, so you might be able to give Conky a couple of pointers. He's useless with the scalpel.'

James shook his head. 'I doubt that I could show you fellows anything. You're all far in advance of me.'

'Don't you believe it.' Milcheap laughed heartily. 'We're all such dunces that I pity the poor patients who put their trust in us.'

The mortuary was a large gloomy room with several troughlike stone tables on which the corpses were laid for dissection. It stank of carbolic and formaldehyde and rotting flesh. When James and Milcheap entered there was an uproar of shouts and laughter going on, and a crowd of students were clustered around two fresh-faced youths who were fighting a mock duel, using amputated legs as their weapons.

Conky and Tim, young dandies with luxuriant side-whiskers, together with an older man with patrician features and bald head, were bending over the body of a woman on one of the tables.

'That's Professor Wilcox,' Milcheap informed James. 'He's in charge of the lying-in section. A damn fine obstetrician. Good morning, sir,' he greeted the older man. 'May we watch?'

Wilcox, intent on what he was doing with his scalpel, nodded without looking up.

James quickly became absorbed by what the skilful wielding of the scalpel was revealing.

'You will take note, gentlemen, that the symptoms in all cases of puerperal fever are the same, namely: suppuration and inflammation of the uterus, the lymph glands, the veins, the pleura, the peritoneum, the pericardium, the meninges. In many cases the liver, spleen and kidneys are also affected.'

As James watched and listened he kept on remembering the symptoms that Julius Wyberg had displayed.

The patrician features lifted to James. 'Let me pose a question to you, young man. Why does puerperal fever attack so many of the women of the lower orders who come to have their babies in the hospitals, while ladies who come to the childbed in their own homes are less likely to suffer from it?'

102

'I don't know, sir,' James admitted readily.

'It is simply answered, young man. Puerperal fever is epidemic. It is caused by atmospheric, cosmic, tellurian influences, which invade the body through the open wounds of those women who are in labour or have just given birth. We have not found it possible to prevent the entry of these malignant influences into the lying-in wards of our public hospitals. While in the houses of the better classes some defences can be put in place.'

James had a sharp mental image of Julius Wybergh's suppurating wound in his mind when he queried, 'Excuse me, sir, but is not post-operation fever or wound fever the same as puerperal fever?'

Wilcox frowned sternly. 'Certainly not. Whatever put such a nonsensical notion into your head?'

James quickly related the story of Julius Wybergh's death. '. . . and his wound was inflamed and suppurating like this woman's organs, sir. My uncle said that the cause of death was pyaemia, and that that had been caused by malignant atmospheric influences. Given the similarity between the inflammation and suppuration in these two cases, I would think that wound fever and puerperal fever are one and the same thing.'

The patrician features reddened slightly. 'And I would think that you are trying to run before you have even learned to walk, young man.

'I know Dr Nairn and I have not the slightest doubt that his diagnosis was absolutely correct. But the tellurian miasma which infected Mr Wybergh's wound is not of the type of malignant influence which causes puerperal fever.'

'But why then are the symptoms and end results the same, sir?' James persisted.

The patrician features displayed anger. 'The symptoms and end results are not the same. And in future, young man, it would be to your own advantage not to question the answers of those of us who are in the position of mentors to our profession.'

He dropped the scalpel into the open cavity of the corpse and wiped his hands on a dirty piece of rag.

'I have to conduct an examination of a patient, gentlemen. You may continue dissecting if you wish.'

He directed an icy glare at James, and stalked away.

'My word, you've definitely ruffled the old bird's feathers, Jamie,' Milcheap chortled. 'It's a good job for you that you're not walking the wards here. He'd have you slung out on your ear if you were.'

Conky fished the scalpel out of the cavity, stroked the dead woman's thigh and told her, 'Much as I'd like to stay and explore your charms further, my dear, I'm afraid that my thirst prevents it. However, I promise that I'll attend upon you tomorrow afternoon.'

'And I promise that I shall ensure he does so, my sweet.' Tim playfully tweaked her prominent nipples. 'So don't you dare go flirting with anyone else in the meantime.'

James bit back the words of remonstrance that rose to his lips. He knew very well that many students did not hold his uncle's beliefs that the dead should always be treated with respect, and that for many other students displaying such callous bravado was a means of helping themselves to cope with that constant intimate proximity to death which their profession demanded from them. So, while he himself subscribed to his uncle's strictures, he felt that he could not try to force their acceptance on others.

'Right then, what shall we do to amuse ourselves?' Conky questioned.

'First we shall eat,' Milcheap announced and put his arms around James's shoulders. 'And then, since it's Jamie's last night of holiday, I think we should introduce him to another pleasure that I doubt he's experienced before. I propose an ether revel, gentlemen.'

Conky and Tim applauded enthusiastically.

'Have you ever been to an ether revel, Jamie?' Tim wanted to know.

James shook his head. 'No. Never. In fact I've never even heard the term before. What is it?'

'You'll find out in due course, my boy,' Milcheap chuckled, and in high spirits the four of them left the mortuary.

The apothecary's shop was at the end of a dingy alley and in its bowed windows the gaslight glimmered on the huge richly coloured glass jars.

The apothecary himself was a stunted, pasty-faced man enveloped in a voluminous white apron. He bowed to the four young men, rubbing his hands together and smiling ingratiatingly.

'Good evening, gentlemen. What's your pleasure tonight?'

'Some flasks of ether to begin with, Mr Jenkins, and later perhaps some nitrous oxide,' Milcheap told him.

'Nitrous oxide. That's the laughing gas, isn't it?' James sought for clarification.

'It is indeed, my friend.' Milcheap beamed. 'And it makes for cracking entertainment.'

The room behind the shop was furnished with several chairs and a table. As the four men seated themselves around the table, James was feeling a sense of eager expectation tinged with a shimmering of apprehension, very much as he had felt when he had decided to sleep with a prostitute.

And look how much I enjoyed that, he reminded himself. This will also be great fun, I'm sure.

Jenkins brought in four small glass flasks, stoppered with corks and half filled with a cloudy liquid.

'Here you are, gentlemen, the ether. I'll go and prepare the nitrous oxide directly.'

'Let's go to it,' Milcheap urged and each man uncorked his flask.

'Take a good long sniff, Jamie.' Conky grinned and followed his own advice.

The pungently sweet vapour filled James's nostrils and he could taste it in his mouth.

For a time no one spoke, all sat breathing in the fumes. James quickly began to feel light-headed as if he were becoming drunk.

105

'Dammee, this is good stuff, I'll be damned if it ain't,' Milcheap exclaimed, and James suddenly found his florid features inexpressibly droll. He laughed uproariously, and his laughter triggered the others who also began to laugh.

James soon lost all track of time, he was so delightfully intoxicated.

At one point he found himself cradling a large rubber ball from which a petcock protruded.

'Turn the tap and breathe in,' Milcheap told him, and he obeyed, filling his lungs with nitrous oxide.

He seemed to be inhabiting a dream world where he found himself doing things without conscious volition or chronological progression. He was singing, he was shouting, he was dancing, he was lying on the floor, he was standing on the table, he was embracing his friends, he was reciting poetry, he was laughing uproariously, he was drifting through a seemingly endless warm velvety darkness . . .

'Jamie? Come on, Jamie. Wake up now. Wake up.'

Milcheap's voice at first came from far away, then nearer and nearer as the darkness lightened.

'Jamie? Can you hear me?'

James opened his eyes to the greyness of early dawn. He found that he was lying in a corner of the room. He pushed himself up on to his hands and knees and a wave of dizziness struck him.

The other three were sitting at the table eating bread and cheese and drinking from a jug of beer.

'You see, I told you that he would regain his sanity, didn't I.' Milcheap chuckled. 'Come and have some breakfast, Jamie.'

James gingerly stood upright, evaluating how he felt. Slightly queasy, light-headed, and apprehensive as to what he might have done.

He became aware of a dull throbbing pain in his lower left leg and he bent and pulled up his trouser. His shin was cut and badly bruised, covered with dried blood.

'You must have done that when you kicked the table over for the second time,' Milcheap bantered.

James stared bemusedly as recollection came flooding back. He had indeed twice knocked the table over when he had been dancing.

He joined them at their meal but took little part in the general talk and chaffing. He found that he could remember much of what he had done, but one thing he could not remember was injuring his shin.

And yet it must have hurt like the very devil. It's damn sore now. But I couldn't have felt it, could I, he told himself wonderingly. Why didn't I feel it? Why didn't it hurt me?

As he rode back to Tardebigge later that day with his shin wound throbbing painfully, the question of why he had not felt that injury when it was inflicted continually revolved in his mind. He suddenly experienced a flash of inspiration: it was the laughing gas, the nitrous oxide. It had the effect of banishing the pain.

Even as he thought his, another part of his mind was decrying the idea: no, it can't be. If nitrous oxide banished pain then my uncle would know of it already. Nitrous oxide is not a newly discovered gaseous element, after all. It's been known for years. No, it can't be possible that it banishes pain.

But argue against it though he might, still he could not dispel the notion that the nitrous oxide vapour had acted as an anaesthetic.

I must tell Uncle Sep what happened, he thought. Perhaps we can conduct some experiments.

The thought filled him with excitement, and eager to get home he heeled his horse into a canter.

Septimus Nairn exploded with anger when James related the events of the previous evening.

'You young fool! You could have killed yourself. Nitrous oxide acts as a cerebral poison. Don't ever meddle with it again. And when I next see Arthur Milcheap I shall take him to task for his criminal stupidity. You are all lucky to be alive.'

107

James was quite shaken by the furious reaction of this normally calm and undemonstrative man.

'But none of us have suffered any ill effects. And the fellows say that gas parties are all the rage here and in America,' he attempted to placate his uncle, but without success.

'I don't give a damn what cretins do to amuse themselves.' Nairn's grim features were purplish with rage. 'They can all kill themselves if they wish and the world will be well rid of them. But you will never inhale any such vapours again while you remain under my tutelage and roof. Is that understood?'

James bowed before the storm. 'Yes, Uncle.'

Nairn calmed a little, but stabbing his finger at James's face threatened grimly, 'I love you like a son. But I will kick you from me as I would a cur dog if at any time in the future I come to know that you have disobeyed me in this matter.'

'I will obey you,' James promised. 'But can I ask you one question?'

'You may.'

'Would you object to me carrying out some experiments with the vapours using animals for subject?'

Nairn considered for a few moments, then answered negatively: 'I can't allow you to be diverted into such channels at this stage in your studies. When you are a fully-fledged doctor, then will be the time for you to begin any experimentation you wish for. But for now you must concentrate all your energies into achieving the successful completion of your apprenticeship.'

James's deep disappointment showed clearly in his expression, and loving the young man as he did, Nairn told him for consolation, 'My intentions are for you to take responsibility for your own cases as soon as possible, Nephew. Your progress has been remarkably swift and I believe that you are ready to be more severely tested in your abilities. You shall carry out the very next amputation that is presented to us. I give you my word on it.'

James's disappointment was drowned by the wave of elation that swept over him at hearing this.

'Thank you, Uncle. Thank you very much.'

108

'No need for thanks,' Nairn said gruffly. 'Now I suggest you get back to work. You still have much to learn.'

When James sat down and opened his textbooks, a visual image of Liddy Landser rose in his mind, and he smiled.

'I bet you'd be very impressed if you knew that I'm now judged ready to carry out an amputation, Liddy,' he said aloud. 'Perhaps you could come and see me do it.'

Then the memories of blood and screaming forced themselves into his consciousness, and his mood abruptly sombred.

'No, it wouldn't be right for you to witness it. Suffering is such an ugly thing to see . . .'

Fourteen

Stoke Village
April 1842

N ight had fallen when the shawled figure of a woman
slipped into the salt works and ran to merge with the
deeper shadow against the wall of an evaporation shed. Hidden
there she watched and waited.

George Landser did not see her as he walked past on his
return from the town. He went inside the office, slamming the
door closed behind him, and after a few seconds the watching
woman saw the glow of lamplight shining through the windows.

Still she waited, restraining her own impatience, wanting to
be sure that no one else was coming to see the man she was to
confront.

At last she moved, hurrying to the small building, and
sneaked a look through the window.

Landser was slumped in a chair, elbows on knees, hands
covering his face. A bottle and glasses stood on the desk at his
side.

She slipped through the door. 'Hello, Mr Landser.'

George Landser said in shocked alarm, 'What the devil? Who
are you? What the hell do you mean by bursting in here like
this?'

Meggie Kennedy slipped the shawl back from her be-
draggled, greasy hair and moved fully into the lamplight.

'Meggie?' He gaped in surprise, eyes wide and staring,
drunkenly bemused.

'Meggie? Is it you?' He shook his head as if he could not believe what he saw. 'What's happened to you, Meggie?'

The woman was painfully thin, her face badly disfigured with the scars of smallpox and her lips ulcerated, her clothing threadbare and badly worn.

'I took the smallpox up in Newcastle and nearly died of it.' Her eyes stared greedily at the gin bottle. 'Can you give me a drink? I've not had a drop for weeks.'

Landser was recovering from his initial shock, and now he poured out half a tumbler of the neat spirit and handed it to her.

She took it in both hands, sucking noisily at the drink, coughing as it stung her throat.

'Why have you come back here?' he asked, and there was a hint of anxiety in his bleared eyes.

Malice showed in Meggie Kennedy's expression and she jeered, 'What's up, Mr Landser? Are you feared that I brought your daughter along with me to meet her father for the first time?'

'My daughter?' he exclaimed incredulously.

'Yes, your daughter. Five years old she is now, and as bright as a button.'

Landser shook his head in bewilderment. 'You're telling me that I've a daughter of five years?'

Meggie Kennedy nodded. 'That's what I'm telling you.'

'You're trying to tell me that I've had a daughter with you?' Landser's drink-fuddled mind was making it difficult for him to ingest this totally unexpected information.

The ravaged face grinned mirthlessly, disclosing broken decayed teeth.

'That's right. That's exactly what I'm telling you.'

He shook his head in protest. 'But I wasn't the only man you were having connections with. There were lots of others buying your favours. Why should not one of them be her father?'

She shrugged. 'Truth to tell, I wasn't sure meself who the father might be, not until she was birthed. But when I saw her I knew she was your kid because she's the spittin' image of you, red hair and all. Anybody would only need to see you together to know whose daughter she is.' She hesitated as if uncertain of how to continue. 'There's summat else to tell you as well. She was birthed not properly made.'

'What do you mean, not properly made?'

'She's crippled.'

'Oh my God!' A spasm of distress crossed his features, and then he questioned, 'Why have you waited until now to tell me of this?'

Abruptly her manner changed, and the aggression disappeared from her voice.

'Because I didn't want to bring trouble on you. You was always good to me. You're about the only man that ever used me kindly.'

'When you told me that you wanted to leave the life you were living and begged me to help you make a fresh start in another part of the country, I gave you enough money to set yourself up respectably, didn't I? Why didn't you tell me then that you were pregnant?' Landser challenged.

'Because the bloke I went off with said he was going to marry me. I told him that the babby was his, because I wasn't sure who the father was then, was I. But he never did wed me. And when the money had all been spent, he did a runner. That was in Liverpool. I took up with a pedlar then, and went to Newcastle with him.' Bitterness twisted her mouth. 'But when I fell pregnant again, he run off and left me. That babby was born dead, thank God! And afterwards I went back on the game. Of course I took sick, but it didn't show for ages, the mercury cleared it. But then the bloody smallpox got me, and brought me down altogether. Men won't pay to go with a woman who looks like I do now.'

Landser's mind was clearing rapidly. Instinctively he knew that she was telling the truth, but he was still reluctant to fully accept it.

'You haven't produced any proof that the girl is mine.'

Gutter devil momentarily flashed in her eyes. 'Then let's see what the magistrates think, shall we? When I lay bastardy charges against you, they'll only have to see the two of you side by side to take my word as Gospel.'

112

He stayed silent, and then her shoulders sagged and she muttered dispiritedly, 'It won't matter what their eyes tell them, will it? You're a gentleman and I'm a common whore. If I say black is black, and you say black is white, it's you they'll believe.' Tears fell from her eyes. 'But I'm not lying to you, Mr Landser. Katie is your kid. You'd only need look at her to know it. And I'd never have come to you unless I was so desperate. There's nowhere else I can go, and nobody else I can turn to.'

He experienced sudden guilt that he had fathered a child into such a sordid life, and his innate kindness of heart won out as he regarded this broken creature before him, whom he could remember as a laughing, lively, saucy girl. He sighed ruefully.

'Don't weep so, Meggie. I believe what you tell me. Where's the child now?'

'In the Bromsgrove Workhouse.'

'Oh no,' he exclaimed in dismay.

'I had to take her in there. What else could I do? When I took the smallpox, me and Katie was put in the Newcastle Workhouse. But I'd got no settlement there, so as soon as I'd got over the worst of it me and Katie was turfed out and told to get to our own parish. I'd got no money and nobody who'd help me.' She gestured towards her badly disfigured face. 'Looking like this no blokes wanted me, did they? So me and Katie had to come on the tramp back to Bromsgrove, because I've got settlement here.'

'When did you get back?'

'Over a month since. They've split us up, you know. Took Katie from me and put her in the kids' ward. I hardly get to even peek at her. I've took the risk to sneak out to come here because I'm so desperate. If I'm caught I could get committed to the Bridewell for sneaking out without permission. You've got to help us, Mr Landser,' she pleaded brokenly. 'It's worse than prison in that bloody workhouse.'

He was genuinely troubled. 'I'll willingly help you, Meggie, but at present there's little I can do.'

'I'm not looking for charity, Mr Landser. Just give me work here and help me find a place to live so I can make some sort of a life for me and Katie.'

113

'I can't give you any work here, I'm not the master any longer.'

Disbelief showed clearly in her ravaged features, and Landser sighed wearily.

'What I say is nothing but the truth, Meggie. A man I thought was giving me help turned out to be a false friend. I can give you a few shillings now, and that I will do, and gladly. But that's about all I can do for you at present. Unless a miracle occurs.'

He rummaged through his pockets and produced a few coins, then hunted through the drawers of the desk and found a few more.

He laid them before her. 'Here, that's all the ready money I have. I'll get more for you. But you must promise me that you'll tell no one who Kate's father is. I can't have a bastard laid at my door, not with all the other troubles I'm facing. My family must never know about the child.'

When she made no immediate reply he urged, 'I mean what I say, Meggie. My wife's lying at death's door and if my children were to know that I'd fathered a bastard child then they'd turn against me, and that would destroy me. You would gain nothing from that. Neither would Katie. You must keep this secret, Meggie. And if you do then you have my word that I shall do whatever I can to help you and the child. Trust me in this, Meggie.'

She nodded. 'You were always honest with me, Mr Landser. I'll do as you ask and keep my mouth shut.'

'Thank you.' Relief brought a fleeting mirthless smile to his lips. 'And I give you my word that I shall do the very best I can for you both. But you must give me time.'

She swept up the coins and stowed them beneath her bodice.

'I could use another drink, Mr Landser. It's damp and chill outside.'

'Here, take it with you.'

He pushed the bottle into her hands, then opened the door and peered out into the murk.

'Go quickly now, and take care that nobody sees you. I'll be in touch.'

Closing the door behind her he slumped back against it. A terrible shame and guilt whelmed over him and he started to weep.

'That poor child!' he moaned aloud. 'God forgive me.'

Fifteen

I t began to rain heavily as Meggie Kennedy trudged along the turnpike road towards Bromsgrove, but frequent swigs from the gin bottle armoured her against discomfort and she went on without seeking shelter.

She clutched the coins George Landser had given her and told herself, I can trust him. He'll keep his word to help me and Katie. I reckon our troubles are almost over.

The foul weather had emptied the long street that comprised the main section of the town, but light shone from the windows of the many taverns and beerhouses, and the sounds of drunken merriment echoed along the rain-swept roadway.

Meggie was sorely tempted to join that merrymaking, but she knew that she dare not risk being caught in a tavern while she was an inmate of the workhouse.

I'll make up for what I'm missing just as soon as George Landser fixes me up with a place to live and more money, she promised herself, and walked on past those tempting doorways.

The Union Workhouse stood some distance from the town. A large wide-fronted, three-storeyed building surrounded by high spiked walls and iron gates it looked like a prison, well-deserving of its facetious nickname, 'The Bastille'.

The porter's lodge adjoined the double-gated main entrance, now locked and barred. Meggie Kennedy went to the small lodge window that fronted the roadway. Lantern light showed through a gap in its curtains and she squinted through the gap into the room beyond.

A thick-set man with a shock of greasy sandy hair and dirty-red, heavily pustuled face was sitting hunched over the small fire in the rusty grate.

Once satisfied that he was alone, Meggie tapped on the window.

He lumbered to draw back the curtain and stare out, and nodded to her. Then let the curtain fall and disappeared from view.

Meggie hurried around the high walls towards the rear of the complex.

He was waiting at a small gate in the rear wall. When he saw her approaching he closed the gate behind him and stepped forward to meet her. He lifted his hand and rubbed his finger and thumb together suggestively.

She gave him some coins. 'There's a tanner for you. Like we agreed.'

She made to pass him but he grabbed her arm.

'How much did you get?'

'That's none o' your business.' She dragged herself free.

'Well, a tanner aren't enough.' He shook his head. 'I could get chucked out o' my job for letting you out of here.'

'Then you'd best let me get back to me bed, hadn't you, before somebody finds out that I'm not there,' she retorted sharply.

He grinned, displaying blackened fangs of teeth.

'It don't matter to me if anybody does find out. All I got to say is that you must have snuck out without me seeing you.'

'And all I got to say is that you let me out of this very gate.'

'Oh yeah, you can do that, Meggie Kennedy. But who does you think that the Master 'ull believe. You or me?' He jerked his head in dismissal. 'Go on, fuck off! You're not coming through this gate. And you can tell anybody whatever you wants to tell 'um. I couldn't give a fuck! But you better remember that if the Master thinks you've run off, then your kid 'ull be made a ward of the parish and you'll lose her.'

The woman knew that he held the upper hand and that she could not risk losing her beloved child. She sighed in defeat.

'Look, Mr White, I knew you years ago, didn't I? When I

117

used to live here in the town. I was always all right to you, wasn't I?'

'No, you warn't. You was a stuck-up bitch and turned your nose up at me. You was only willing to sell your cunt to the bloody gentry, warn't you?'

She forced herself to speak in an inviting tone. 'Well, I'm not stuck up no more, Mr White. You can have me now if you want to.'

Daniel White snorted with exaggerated disgust. 'Have you now? Looking like you does? I'd sooner stick me prick into a heap of shit.'

His cruel rejection stirred her gutter devil, but simultaneously brought the realisation of her complete powerlessness.

'Please, Mr White, let me come back in,' she begged. 'I can get some more money for you next week.'

'It's tonight I wants more, not next bloody week.'

'I've got some drink,' she offered. 'Nearly half a bottle o'gin.'

He held out his hand. 'Give it over.'

She shook her head. 'Not until I'm back inside and in me room.'

He nodded and she wordlessly followed him through the gate.

At the door of her room she handed over the gin bottle, suppressing the almost overpowering impulse to smash it into his face.

Her bedmate was lying awake and as Meggie clambered into the bed questioned eagerly, 'Did you get any drink?'

'Half a bottle o' gin,' Meggie muttered bitterly. 'But that bastard of a porter has just took it from me.'

'He's a fuckin' pig, that Daniel White is,' the other swore viciously. 'I hopes his balls rots and falls off. He's a fuckin' pig!'

Sixteen

The hour had just passed eleven o'clock when Daniel White was again disturbed by a tapping on the lodge window. Cursing, he took a quick swig from the gin bottle then went to open the wicket gate.

The caller was a tall man, features half hidden by a scarf, top hat pulled low to shadow his eyes, and wearing a long travelling cloak.

'I've business with the matron. She's expecting me.'

'What name is it, sir?' White asked.

The man handed him a coin. 'No need for my name. Mrs Melen and I are old friends. I know where to go.'

He brushed past the porter and went towards the front door of the building.

White remained by the gate and watched as the door opened and the cloaked figure disappeared through it.

White grinned mockingly. ' "No need for me name", says he . . . No, Mr Enoch Cull. No need at all, because I knows it very well already.'

'What do you have for me, Mrs Melen?'

'A rare one, Mr Cull.'

'How old is it?'

'Three months less three days. I took special note of its birthday.'

'It'll be near to death then.'

'Not at all, Mr Cull. It's very healthy. I have to dose it twice a day to keep it quiet. It makes such a racket it gives me a headache.'

119

'The last one I bought from you didn't last two months.'

'That's not my fault, Mr Cull, I sold it to you in good faith. Monsters always need close watching, especially when they're newborn. That's why I kept this one back until it had gained some strength. God willing it'll last for years now.'

'How much are you asking, Mrs Melen?'

'Twenty pounds.'

'That's a high price.'

'This is a rare one, Mr Cull. Just look at the size of that head. I've never seen a bigger one than this.'

She took the lantern from the table and held it above the wooden box so that its light threw into sharp relief the unconscious baby's grotesquely swollen forehead and deep sunken eye sockets.

'You'll make your fortune with this one, Mr Cull.'

'I take leave to doubt that, Mrs Melen. It could well die before I earn a penny from it. But I'm prepared to risk ten pounds and take it off your hands.'

'I couldn't let it go for less than eighteen pounds, Mr Cull.'

'Fifteen pounds, Mrs Melen. That's my final offer.'

'Sixteen pounds and ten shillings, and that's my final offer, Mr Cull.'

Coins chinked as the money changed hands.

Amelia Melen fitted the lid on the box and roped it down firmly.

'The monster's been well dosed so it won't make any noise at all. It's just another box of oddments you've bought from me, isn't it.'

The man smiled bleakly. 'Oddments indeed, Mrs Melen. Very odd oddments.'

'And now, Mr Cull, I've got a surprise for you.'

'A surprise?'

'Oh yes. Something really special. A monster you've never seen the like of before. A monster that's as pretty as a picture.'

The man was greatly intrigued. 'Bit of a contradiction that, isn't it, Mrs Melen? A pretty monster?'

'I'll go directly and fetch it in here, Mr Cull. You can judge for yourself whether I speak truly or not.'

The small barefooted girl stared nervously up at the unsmiling, black-clad man towering above her like a threatening giant.

'What's your name, girl?'

'Katie Kennedy, sir.'

'How old are you?'

'Nearly six years I think, sir.'

'Let's have a good look at you.' His hands gripped her shoulders and she cried out in fright.

'Be still, the gentleman's not going to hurt you,' Amelia Melen scolded.

The child whimpered fearfully as Cull stripped the thin cotton nightshift from her body leaving her naked, and when he released her she crouched low to the floor bending almost double in an effort to hide her exposed genitals.

The man's fingers reached down to fondle the smooth, armless white shoulders and the child shuddered and cried out once more.

'Hold your rattle,' Amelia Melen shouted irately. 'The gentleman's not going to harm you.'

Cull patted the girl's cheek reassuringly and spoke gently to her.

'Stand up straight, Katie. Come now, and then you shall be dressed again.'

He pulled her upright and she whimpered as he turned her round and round, closely examining her body.

'She needs a deal of looking after, lacking arms as she does,' he stated.

'Oh no,' the woman denied. You haven't seen what she can do, Mr Cull. She can use her toes better than most people can use their fingers. Just watch this.'

The woman turned to the child and ordered sharply, 'Put your shift on.'

Whimpering and sniffing the child sat on the floor and using

121

her teeth, toes and feet pulled the shift over her head and shoulders.

'That's a good girl.' Amelia Melen took a small lump of sugar from a cupboard and pushed it between the child's lips.

Still whimpering and sniffing Katie noisely sucked the lump, her tear-filled eyes gazing down at the floorboards.

'You say that she's intelligent, Mrs Melen?'

'That I do. She can scribe letters. Just look at this.'

The woman fetched a piece of chalk from the cupboard and laid it on the floor in front of the seated child.

'Show the gentleman how you can scribe, Katie.'

Katie lifted the piece of chalk between the toes of her right foot and laboriously scrawled 'A B C' in large letters across the floorboards.

'There now, didn't I tell you. She's as bright as a button, she is.'

Cull's lantern-jawed features were thoughtful, his hard eyes fixed on the small figure between them.

'What price would she be, supposing I was willing to take her?'

Amelia Melen shook her head.

'She's not for sale at present, Mr Cull.'

'No matter then,' Cull accepted. 'I'll bid you good night, Mrs Melen.'

He lifted the wooden box which held the hydrocephalic child. 'I hope to recoup my outlay before this one dies on me.'

The woman chuckled comfortably. 'It'll live for years, Mr Cull, I've not the slightest doubt of that. Good night to you now, and have a safe journey.'

Pausing at the door he nodded towards Katie Kennedy. 'I might be willing to take her if the price suited.'

'I'll bear that in mind, Mr Cull. You may be sure of it.'

Henry Melen laid aside the book he was reading. The lamplight glinted on his spectacles as he removed them and his face was rosy from the glow of the fire in the black iron cooking range. He smiled at his wife.

'How did it go with Cull, my dear?'

'He paid the sixteen pounds, ten shillings. I told you he would, didn't I?'

'By God, but you're the sharp one for business,' he congratulated admiringly. 'If you'd been born a man you'd be a merchant prince by now.'

She drew a chair near to the fire and seated herself facing her husband.

'And he's hot to take Katie Kennedy as well. He tried on his usual trick, acting like he didn't care either way, but he didn't gammon me. I could tell he was hot to have her. I'll keep him waiting though until he's ready to pay my price.'

Henry Melen frowned doubtfully. 'We could never get away with selling her.'

'We could if her mother agrees to let her be adopted by some kind soul who'll give her a good home and have her educated.'

'Her mother will never agree to that. She loves that kid, no doubt of it.'

'Meggie Kennedy is a whore who lives only for the drink. I've seen hundreds like her. After a few months in here she'll be ready to agree to anything for the price of a bottle or two.'

Henry Melen was still not convinced. 'Listen, my dear, she must love that child dearly to have kept her. Most whores would have chucked the baby into the nearest cesspit when they'd seen she had no arms.'

'You let me worry about Meggie Kennedy,' his wife told him firmly.

Steam plumed from the spout of the kettle upon the hearth trivet. The man lifted the kettle and poured hot water into two glass tumblers already half filled with gin and sugar, then handed one of the tumblers to his wife.

They sat contentedly sipping the fragrant mixture, the silence of the room broken only by the loud ticking of the grandfather clock and the hissing of flaring coals in the fire.

The sounds of hobnailed boots echoed along the stone-flagged passage and halted outside the door. Henry Melen frowned and called, 'Is that you, White?'

123

'Yes, Master,' a hoarse voice replied.

'What is it now, damn you?'

'Just wanted to tell you that I let the gentleman out of the gate, and I've locked up for the night, Master.'

'All right. Get to your bed and let me have some peace,' Melen ordered irritably.

'Yes, Master. Good night, Master.'

The sounds of hobnailed boots diminished and died away.

'I can't help but dislike that man.' Melen frowned. 'He's not to be trusted. He'd cause trouble for us if he could, I'm sure of it.'

'You needn't worry your head about Daniel White,' Amelia Melen replied confidently. 'He knows that if he ever tries to cause trouble for us, then I'll open my mouth and tell what I know about him. I could get him hung.'

'What do you know about him that I don't?' Melen asked curiously.

She smiled archly. 'You must allow me to have some secrets of my own, my love.'

He took the empty glass from his wife's hand and mixed fresh drinks for them both.

After tasting his own, he asked, 'If it ever became possible to sell her, what price would you be thinking of asking for the Kennedy girl?'

'A hundred pounds.'

'What?' He stared in shocked disbelief.

'She's worth that, and more besides,' Amelia Melen stated positively. 'I can remember when I was a girl seeing that freak Jane Murrel down at Redditch Fair. The tent was packed out every show. They must have made a fortune from her.'

'I can't see Enoch Cull ever paying such a sum as that.' Henry Melen shook his head.

'If he won't, then I'll find some other who will,' his wife retorted.

They were silent for a while until Henry Melen said regretfully, 'It's a pity Kendrick died so suddenly. Now we'll have to try and come to some arrangement with the new doctor, won't we?'

'Whoever it is we'll have to tread carefully.' Amelia Melen frowned thoughtfully. 'He'll not likely be as easy to handle as that other drunken sot was. He'll maybe not sign a stillborn certificate for the price of a flagon of brandy. We'll have to tread carefully until I discover his weakness.'

Henry Melen smiled fondly at his wife and with absolute confidence told her, 'And you will find his weakness, my dear. Of that there's no doubt. No doubt at all.'

Daniel White went back to the lodge and sat down to finish drinking the gin. He was filled with a sense of wellbeing. This night had been a profitable one. Sixpence and gin from Meggie Kennedy. A shilling from Enoch Cull.

He caressed his genitals and grinned. The night was not over yet, and the best was still to come.

The midnight hour had passed when he drank the last dregs of the gin, and he belched regretfully at the empty bottle, then took up the shaded lantern and left the lodge to cross to the main building. He moved stealthily through its long dark passages until he reached the door that he sought. Setting the lantern down on to the flagstones he gently lifted the wooden latch and eased the door open. He slipped through the gap, closing the door behind him, and stood with his back to it waiting for his eyes to get accustomed to the gloom.

The air was chill and dank, thick with the stenches of unwashed flesh and foul breath, murmurous with moans and mutters, snores and snuffles.

White peered into the darkness and gradually the lighter shades of high narrow windows became visible and the shapes of low beds lining each side of the long room. He moved with infinite caution, his fingers touching the ends of the beds, mentally counting them off until he came to the one he sought.

Hannah Kearns lay rigid with terror, fists clenched, fingernails digging deep into the flesh of her palms. She whimpered as the dark bulk of the man loomed above her and his hand crushed hard upon her mouth.

'Come quiet now, Hannah,' he whispered menacingly into her ear.

Smothering her sobs she made no resistance as he pulled her from the bed. His excitement escalating almost uncontrollably, he dragged her after him down the corridor, across the wet mud of the yard, and into a wooden lean-to built against the outer wall. Its floor was covered with heaps of dirty smelly rags.

'Take this off.' He tugged at her shift, and now her sobs burst out.

'Shurrup, you little bitch.' His fist thudded deep into the softness of her belly, exploding the breath from her and she doubled over and fell to her knees, struggling desperately to draw in air.

'Now you listen,' he hissed savagely. 'You do what I want then I'll not harm you.'

He dragged the shift up and over her head and threw it aside, then dropped his trousers, pushed her on to her back and used his knees to bludgeon apart her thighs.

A high-pitched wail of agony tore from her as he rammed himself brutally into her virgin flesh.

'Shurrup, you bitch!' he threatened and, grunting, pounded down upon her until he emitted a shuddering groan of pleasure as his semen jetted.

He lay collapsed upon her slender body until his harsh panting eased then rose to his feet and stood staring down at her tear-wet face.

'You keep your mouth shut about this,' he snarled menacingly. 'Because if you don't then I'll fuckin' well kill you, you little bitch. Can you hear me? I'll fuckin' well kill you. And you won't be the first that I've served so.'

Fresh terror shivered through her.

'I won't say nothing. I won't. I won't,' she whimpered over and over again. 'I won't say nothing. I won't.'

Abruptly his voice changed, became coaxing. 'That's a good girl. I'll be a real friend to you if you're a good girl. Look how good I am to Maria. I'll get you extra grub as well, you'll see.

126

And after a bit you'll like being fucked. Maria likes it when I fucks her, don't she? And you will, you'll see.'

He examined his genitals in the lantern light, saw the smears of fresh blood and shone the lantern upon the girl's thighs. Dark trickles were writhing down the white skin. He ordered her, 'Wash yourself. There's water in the bucket there. And shove some rag up you to stop the bleeding.'

He wetted a piece of rag and wiped his own thighs and genitals and when the girl had done the same he told her to replace her shift and to follow him.

They went back across the muddy yard and re-entered the main building. At the door of her room he bent to whisper in her ear, 'Remember what I've told you. You speak one word and you're fuckin' dead.'

Her dark eyes were huge in her thin white face, and she shook her head whimpering, 'I won't. I won't.'

Again his tone changed dramatically, 'That's a good girl. I'll get you some extra grub tomorrow.'

He opened the door just wide enough for her to slip through and closed it behind her, then stood with his ear pressed against the warped panels listening hard for any voice greeting her return.

All was quiet and, satisfied, he crept away.

Hannah shivered violently as the shock of her ordeal took hold. Sick and faint she sank to the floor and lay on her side curled into a foetal position.

She cried out as hands suddenly came on her.

'Shhh! It's me. Shhh! Don't wake the others.'

Hannah recognised the voice of her bedmate, Maria Peat.

'Come on back to bed. Come on,' the other girl coaxed. 'It's over now. He won't come back again tonight.'

She half-pulled, half-carried Hannah back to their shared bed, and lay beneath the coverings cuddling her friend's trembling body close.

'It won't be so bad the next time,' she whispered. 'It don't hardly hurt me at all most times now. He's not so rough when you acts willing. Was he very rough to you?'

127

'I wish I was dead,' Hannah sobbed helplessly. 'I wish I was dead . . .'

'Shhh! You'll wake the others else,' Maria whispered. 'Go to sleep now. Go to sleep. It won't be half so bad the next time. And just think of all the grub he'll get us. Our bellies 'ull be full all the time.'

Seventeen

'**W**hat is God?'
The sonorous question reverberated over the rows of brown-clad paupers and in the pulpit above them the Reverend Henry Abevand's black eyes glowed with exultation.

'God is Love!'

Abevand's black eyes closed and his hands lifted upwards towards the heavens.

'For God so loved we miserable sinners that He gave His only begotten Son to save our souls from the Pit of Hell.'

The black eyes snapped open and swept across his congregation as if in challenge.

'What is our duty towards God? Our duty towards God is to believe in him, to fear him, and to love him with all our hearts, with all our minds, with all our . . .'

Aveband's sonorous voice rolled on and on and on, and Amelia Melen's boredom deepened. From her vantage point in the slightly elevated rear pew she was able to see the backs of most of the heads and shoulders and her gaze moved idly over them.

Here in God's House the paupers were segregated as strictly as they were in the workhouse. Males on one side, females on the other, with the broad centre aisle between them. Each division was subdivided and kept separated. Children under seven years of age. Boys between seven and fifteen. Girls between seven and fifteen. Able-bodied men and older youths. Women and older girls. Men infirm through age or other cause. Women infirm through age or other cause.

129

Amelia Melen's attention was suddenly caught by movement in the girls under-fifteen years' group. One girl was bending forwards, sobbing noisily, and her companions on each side of her were disputing over her bent head.

Annoyance stung Amelia Melen. She knew only too well that censorious eyes watched closely for any hint of misbehaviour during these once-monthly enforced congregations of workhouse paupers in the parish church. Any such occurrence was eagerly noted, gossiped about and reported to her employers, the Board of Guardians. Such adverse reports led in turn to a sharp reprimand for herself and her husband as the Matron and Master of the Union Workhouse.

The bloody Board should try bringing three hundred odd paupers to church and keeping them all in order, she thought disgruntedly now, they'd see for themselves how hard a task it is.

High-pitched angry shouting suddenly burst out from the group she was watching.

'. . . to keep our bodies in temperance, soberness and chastity. Not to covet nor desire . . .' Reverend Aveband's voice abruptly stilled and he stared down in shock at the violent struggle erupting between two of the girls.

'Jesus Christ!' Amelia Melen left her pew and hurried down the aisle as uproar ensued with the paupers rising up to see what was happening, some standing on the seating, others cheering, cat-calling, urging the combatants on.

Fast as she had moved, her husband, Henry Melen, had moved faster.

He dragged the struggling girls bodily from the pew and into the aisle and cuffed them heavily and repeatedly until they broke apart and cowered back, shielding their heads and faces with their arms.

He beckoned the workhouse nurse and thrust the girls towards her.

'Get these two back, Mrs Kings, and lock them up until I return.'

Then he stalked up and down the aisle and his fierce scowl

was threat enough to ensure a quick return to order and silence. Once satisfied he turned towards the pulpit.

'I apologise most humbly for what has happened, Reverend. I beg that you will continue.'

Aveband frowned and picked up from where he had left off.

'. . . not to covet or desire other men's goods, but to learn and labour truly to get our own livings, and to do our duty in that state of life unto which it shall please God to call us . . .'

Amelia Melen returned to her seat aware of the malicious eyes of parishioners watching from the gallery, and thought angrily, This will be carried back to the Board before I even get out of here. By Christ! I'll make those two little bastards smart for this.'

Her temper smouldered all through the remainder of the service; and the customary barrage of jeers and hooting of the urchins and hooligans of the town as she and her husband led the long crocodile file of paupers back along the main road towards the workhouse did nothing to soothe her lust to punish.

'You're an imp of the devil, Emma Taylor, but I'll thrash the wickedness out of you.' Amelia Melen swished the long thin cane threateningly through the air.

'It warn't me who started it, Missus. It was Maria Peat. I never did nothing to her. She started on me,' the girl wailed frantically.

'Hold your tongue!' Amelia Melen snapped and ordered.

'Make her ready, Mrs Kings.'

The raw-boned, masculine-featured workhouse nurse forced the undersized twelve-year-old on to the floor and despite her struggles pinned her face downwards.

Amelia Melen lifted the girl's long skirt exposing the small rounded buttocks and kicking legs. Her long thin cane swished through the air and the girl screamed as it bit into her flesh.

In the dormitory on the upper floor Maria Peat was also lying

131

face downwards on a bed, her long skirt pulled up to expose the angry red weals that criss-crossed her buttocks.

Hannah Kearns was bathing the wounds with cold water, her thin white face showing her distress.

Around the bed other girls clustered wide-eyed and excited.

'Why was you and Emma Taylor fighting, Maria?' one of the girls questioned.

Maria's puglike features were defiant. 'Because the cow kept on tormenting Hannah. And I'll tell the rest of you now, that if any of you torments my mate, then I'll give you what I give Emma Taylor.'

'What was she tormenting you about, Hannah?' the same girl wanted to know.

Maria Peat answered for her friend. 'About Daniel White. The cow was saying that Hannah liked him making free with her.'

'I reckon you ought to tell on the dirty bastard. You ought to tell the Missus about him,' another girl declared.

'Don't talk fuckin' stupid.' Maria Peat rounded on her, and her youthful features were momentarily haggard. 'Do you know what 'ud happen if we went to the Missus about that bastard? We'd be put in the bleedin' madhouse, just like Abby Coxwell was when she told on him. None of them 'ud believe her. They all said that she was lying about who give her that babby. And then they sent her to the bleedin' madhouse. I knows that's true because I was here when it happened.'

'But if you both went to the Missus and told her, then they'd have to believe you, 'udden't they?' the girl persisted.

'No, they 'udden't,' Maria declared with bitter certainty. 'Because they never does believe anything we say. And he says that if we speaks out he'll kill us. He says he's killed other girls who'se kicked up about it. And I reckon he has killed 'um, as well. He's such an evil bastard, so he is.'

Hannah Kearns burst into tears and Maria Peat sighed wearily.

'It aren't no use you crying, Hannah. You've just got to put up with it until we'em old enough to get out of this fuckin' rotten hole.'

One of the older pauper women came into the dormitory shouting angrily, 'Cummon, you lot. The Master says we've all got to work the rest of the day because of you kicking up a ruckus in the bloody church. It's all your bloody fault, this is.'

The chorus of complaint and protest was cut short when the woman threatened, 'Does you want me to fetch the Master to you? Because if you don't shurrup and come right now, I will do . . .'

Henry Melen, Master of the Bromsgrove Union Workhouse, always took care with his appearance before making the rounds of the establishment over which he ruled. Now he carefully brushed his fine black broadcloth frockcoat, arranged his cravat and adjusted the angle of his tall brown beaver hat. He examined his appearance in the full-length mirror and smiled with satisfaction.

Then a heavy knocking shook the panels of the door and he scowled and shouted, 'What is it?'

The door opened and the dirty-red, pustuled face of Daniel White appeared.

'I'm ever so sorry to bother you, Master. I'm ever so sorry,' the porter apologised subserviently, 'but one of the casuals is playing up, Master. He aren't done his task, and he's told me that he aren't going to do it neither.'

'Oh, won't he.' Melen nodded brusquely. 'We'll see about that.'

He took up a thick, steel-balled walking stick and a large ringed bunch of keys and commenced a slow majestic progress through the vast building, his iron-shod boots striking loudly upon flagstones still wet from a fresh scrubbing. Daniel White followed close behind Melen's tall strong figure, his bloodshot eyes gleaming with spiteful, pleasurable anticipation.

The stone-breaking yard was at the rear of the workhouse complex. Here male inmates and the wandering tramps who

133

had come to seek food and temporary shelter at the workhouse smashed waste rock into small gravel for road and path laying.

One wall of the yard consisted of a row of long narrow cells each with an iron grille built flat into the back wall above a kennel which accessed on to the lane outside. The pieces of rock were shovelled into these cells and lump hammers were used to crush the rock into gravel small enough to fall through the iron grilles into the kennels.

This part of the work, the most tedious and gruelling, was normally reserved for the 'casuals', the wandering tramps. They were locked in the casual ward overnight and early next morning to pay for their food and lodging were then locked into the yard cells until they had crushed sufficient gravel to gain their release to freedom.

'He's in that 'un.' White indicated a cell door towards the end of the row. 'What about this lot? Should I send 'um away?'

A group of ragged filthy tramps and male inmates clad in the pauper uniform of dark brown coats and trousers were stood watching intently, their breath pluming visibly in the sharp cold air.

Melen shook his head. 'Leave them be.'

Flanked by White he walked to the locked door and struck it with the steel ball of his stick.

'This is the Master. Why haven't you done your task?'

'Fuck off!'

The watchers sniggered at the raucous shout.

Melen showed no emotion. 'Do you realise that if you refuse to complete your task I can have you committed to prison?'

'Fuck you and the task! I'd sooner be in fuckin' prison than in here. We don't have to do no work on the Sabbath in prison.'

The watchers laughed openly.

'I'm giving you one last chance,' Melen tried again. 'Complete your task and nothing more will be said.'

'Fuck off! I aren't working on the Sabbath Day. God never did fuck all on the Sabbath and he said that nobody else has to do any fucking work neither.'

Melen unlocked the door and pushed it open.

134

The tramp stood defiantly facing him.

Melen coolly stepped forward and pistoned the steel ball of his stick into the tramp's face, striking again and again as the man stumbled, reeled and dropped to lie bleeding and half-senseless.

Melen stepped out for the cell and ordered White curtly, 'Keep him locked in here. He doesn't get out until he completes his task, and he gets no food or water.'

He walked towards the watching group and halted a couple of yards from them.

'You all saw that man attack me, didn't you?'

When they hesitated he scowled and raised his tone sharply.

'You all saw him attack me, didn't you? I hope none of you are going to lie. To claim that you didn't see him attack me.'

There was hasty agreement. 'Yes, Master . . . Yes, we saw him, Master.'

Melen nodded, then told the tramps harshly, 'Get on your way, and spread the word among your mates that anybody who comes to my workhouse does what he's told to do, or else.'

He left the stone yard and resumed his tour of inspection.

In one of the larger rooms men and boys were picking oakum: sitting on benches unravelling lengths of old rope down into single strands.

The hum of conversation stilled instantly as Melen entered the room, and the pauper overseer came to stand obsequiously before him.

'Yes, Master.'

'Any problems, Lammas? Is anyone complaining about having to do this extra work?'

'Oh no, Master. They knows what happened in church was a bad thing to happen. But if you please, Master, this present load of rope is very hard to work. It's all old ship cordage. It's making our hands very sore.'

Melen held out his own hand and the overseer gave him a piece of the rope. It was black with tar and iron-hard.

'Who are the worst affected?' he asked.

'Walter Smith and the Warman boy, Master.'

135

'I'll take a look at them.'

An elderly man and a rachitic youth came to show Melen their raw, bleeding fingers.

Melen pondered for a few seconds, then nodded. 'Very well. Take all this cordage to the stone yard, use the sledge hammers to give it a battering. That should soften it up sufficiently to be worked.'

'What about us, Master?' Walter Smith questioned.

'What about you?' Melen demanded.

The elderly man held his bloody fingers up in front of Melen's eyes.

'With all respect, Master, me and the lad can't go on picking oakum with hands like this, can we? We can hardly bear to touch the rope. It's agony, so it is.'

Melen stared hard into the gaunt, ravaged features, seeking for any hint of challenge to his authority. But Smith's expression was docile and respectful.

Melen nodded acceptance.

'No, you can't. You both report to the gardens. Tell Slater that he's to give you gloves and find work for you there for the next week.'

'Thank you, Master. Thank you kindly.'

Melen checked the time on his pocket watch, swung on his heels and walked ponderously from the room.

His wife came to him and handed him a note.

'This just came from that collier from Dudley. Sam Benson. He needs another boy.'

'What's happened to the one he's got?'

'Run away.'

'Small wonder, the way the bastard mistreats them.' Melen scowled. 'Well, I'm not inclined to supply him with another one.'

'Yes, you will,' Amelia Melen insisted. 'We need the money.'

'It's like taking blood money,' her husband objected. 'He's already worked two boys to death, and how do we know if this last one ran off? He could be dead as well for all we know. Benson could have hidden him down the coal pit.'

136

'Don't talk so stupid,' Amelia Melen hissed venomously.

'And what will the Board say? Benson's had three apprentices bound to him in the past five years.'

'The Board will say nothing. They appreciate that coalmining is a dangerous trade. There's men and boys being killed every day down the pits. But just to be on the safe side, Benson can apply with another name and town, and get somebody else to claim the boy.'

'Well, I'm not happy about this,' Melen argued stubbornly.

'You don't have to be happy about it. We're in sore need of the money, thanks to you and your bloody gambling. Now go and see Benson, and stop acting like a bloody Methody preacher.'

Melen sullenly gave way, and leaving the workhouse made his way to a mean alehouse in the High Street.

'Your usual is it, Mr Melen?' the landlord greeted affably.

Melen nodded, and raised his eyebrows in silent query.

The landlord gestured towards the small enclosed snug bar, and Melen stooped to pass through its low door.

The man waiting for him was a squat, shaggy-haired Black Country collier, his skin and clothes thick with coal dust.

'You took your time,' he grumbled.

'It's a pity you don't take more time in working your boys to death,' Melen said, scowling.

'It's not my fault that they'm wobbly-boned, you should feed 'um better grub in that fuckin' Bastille of yours. They might be strong enough for doing a bit of hard graft then.'

He clinked some sovereigns under Melen's nose. 'Same price as before, I take it.'

'All right.' Melen pocketed the coins.

The landlord brought in a pewter mug of mulled ale, and Melen waited for him to leave before telling the collier, 'You'll have to give a different name and town this time, and get one of your mates to come and claim him. I can't risk any of the Board remembering your face.'

'All right. We'll say that I'm Tom Nokes from Bilston, and the lad 'ull be working in the Half Moon pit there. When can I have him?'

'Two weeks next Wednesday.'

'Fuckin' 'ell!' Benson complained bitterly.

'It can't be done quicker. You've took sufficient boys from here to know that there's formalities to be completed. It's not like buying a bloody calf at market, is it?' Melen snapped curtly. He lifted his pewter pot, drained it with noisy gulps, and walked out of the room without bothering to voice any word of farewell.

Eighteen

T he Board of Guardians of the Bromsgrove Union had been summoned to attend at the workhouse board room at ten o'clock on Tuesday morning of the first week in July. Although the Board's number totalled eighteen it was very rarely that all attended, and this morning was no exception. By fourteen minutes past ten o'clock only four guardians had arrived.

Edward Harcourt stood at the window staring down at the road beyond the workhouse walls. When the clock chimed the quarter hour he turned and smiled pleasantly at those present.

'Well, gentlemen, it doesn't appear that any of the others are going to grace us with their attendance. However, we constitute a quorum, do we not, so let's get to the business in hand and have done with it.'

The other three guardians took their seats at the long polished table, and Edward Harcourt said to the elderly clerk to the guardians, 'I think that we can dispense with the minutes of the last meeting, Mr Pethwick, and proceed immediately with the election of the new medical officer.'

Pethwick sniffed disapprovingly, and Harcourt frowned.

'Is there any difficulty, Mr Pethwick?'

'Should not this appointment be discussed, and then voted on by the full Board in sitting, sir?'

'God Almighty, spare me!' Harcourt sighed impatiently. 'If any of my fellow Board members had wished to cast their vote for one or other of the medical gentlemen, they would un-doubtedly have attended this meeting, Mr Pethwick. Since they are not here then it would follow that they are happy for we

139

present to act on their behalf. So will you be so good as to record these proceedings in the minutes.'

The elderly man glowered but offered no further argument.

'Now, gentlemen, following the sudden and untimely death of Dr Kendrick, it is necessary that a replacement should immediately be appointed as Medical Officer of Health to the Board. Are we all agreed that Dr Septimus Nairn should be elected to the vacancy?'

The question was rhetorical because Harcourt continued without waiting for reply.

'. . . The ayes have it. Enter in the minutes that the appointment of Dr Nairn is confirmed by the Board, if you please, Mr Pethwick, and that his retainer is to be fifty pounds per annum with additional fees for midwifery, vaccinations and emergency attendances.

'That's settled then. Good! And I now move the motion that the meeting be closed,' Harcourt smiled genially, 'and that we should adjourn to the Crown Inn for some refreshment.'

'I second that motion wholeheartedly, sir,' one of the guardians said, chuckling. 'My throat's as dry as tinder.'

'Excuse me, Mr Chairman sir,' Pethwick snapped pettishly. 'There is still the matter of the reprimand to the Workhouse Master to be dealt with. I believe that Mr and Mrs Melen are even now waiting to attend upon the Board.'

'What reprimand?' Harcourt demanded.

'Concerning the regrettable incident that took place in the parish church during last month's service for the paupers, sir. Two of the female inmates began fighting with each other and creating a general uproar. When I spoke to Reverend the Lord Aston yesterday evening he was most insistent that the Master be reprimanded. His curate, Reverend Aveband, was most distressed by the unseemly behaviour and my Lord Aston feels that the Master and Matron are not enforcing the necessary strictness of discipline upon the paupers.'

There was a hint of a smug smirk quirking Pethwick's lipless mouth.

Harcourt's ruddy features reddened with quick anger. The

140

Melens' appointments had been made on his own personal recommendation and he took any criticism against them as an aspersion against himself.

'My Lord Aston has perhaps forgotten that Melen is an ex-military man and as such I do not believe that he needs any instruction with regard to the enforcement of discipline. Neither does Mrs Melen. I trust that you will convey to my Lord Aston my opinions on this matter.'

'You may be assured of it, sir,' the elderly man replied pettishly.

The youngest man present, Carlos Wybergh, smiled secretly. He found constant entertainment in the bitter rivalries and squabblings that were endemic between the members of the Board of Guardians. He had only stood for election to the Board because of his father's insistence that he carry out some sort of public service. Since his father controlled the familial purse-strings and he had no independent income of his own, he had been forced to accede to his wishes. Now that his father was dead he was intending to resign from the Board and devote all his time to his own amusements.

Harcourt scowled. 'Bring them in then, Mr Pethwick, and let's be done with this nonsense.'

Carlos Wybergh thought that the Melens made a striking couple: Henry Melen, tall and strong-bodied with the erect stance of a soldier, and hard-etched, weather-beaten features; his wife, a smaller, handsome woman, full breasted and shapely bodied, appearing some years younger than her middle-aged husband. They were both dressed in black, relieved only by Henry Melen's high white collar and the white lace fringing Amelia Melen's bonnet and framing her rosy face.

Carlos Wybergh found himself experiencing envy of her husband for possessing such a sexually desirable bedmate.

Henry Melen removed his top hat as he entered the room and the couple stood unsmilingly side by side.

'Mr Melen, my Lord Aston insists that you be reprimanded for the unhappy occurrence that took place during Sunday's church service.' Harcourt's tone was regretful. 'Needless to say,

141

I do not concur with my Lord Aston's opinion. I trust that the culprits have been punished?'

'Indeed they have, sir, and I have made report of it in the Discipline Register which my Lord Aston may read at any time he wishes to do so,' Henry Melen answered firmly.

'Very well.' Harcourt nodded and told Pethwick, 'Enter in the minutes the fact that I have complied with my Lord Aston's wish, and have informed the Workhouse Master and Matron of his reprimand.' He smiled at the Melens. 'That is all, you may go.'

'Thank you, sir.' Melen replaced his hat.

Amelia Melen dropped a slight curtsy and the couple left the room.

Pethwick sniffed loudly, and Harcourt baited him by instructing, 'Be kind enough to enter in the minutes my exact words to Mr and Mrs Melen, if you please, Mr Pethwick.'

Then he winked broadly at Carlos Wybergh and invited, 'Shall we adjourn to the Crown Inn, sir?'

'Indeed we shall, sir,' the young man readily accepted.

In the Tuesday evening dusk Septimus Nairn and James Kerr sat on their horses gazing up at the massive red brick and sandstone façade of the workhouse.

'There now, Nephew, look how fine our "Bastille" is. An ornament to the parish, is it not? It makes me proud to be its new medical officer.'

Nairn's tone was ironic.

James regarded his uncle uncertainly, unable to judge whether the older man was serious or not.

'Surely the appointment is a compliment to you, Uncle? Sean told me that other doctors hereabouts will all be disappointed that they haven't been offered the position. Sean says that it can be a useful source of extra income.'

Nairn shrugged dismissively. 'I fear that Kendrick made a poor living from it. Because of his drunkenness he had no private patients and existed solely on his salary from the Board and what extra fees he received for treating the outdoor

142

paupers. With Old Pethwick's son as the relieving officer I should think that those were few and far between.'

He saw James's incomprehension and explained: 'The paupers who are on outdoor relief have to get a ticket from Sidney Pethwick to receive any treatment from us, and we are then paid by the Board for that treatment; and believe me, Nephew, the Board begrudges every penny it spends on the treatment of sick paupers.'

He shrugged again. 'No, I don't expect to gain any great profit from this position. Indeed, many of my better-class patients will look askance at me for having accepted it. They don't like to think that the hands that touch them may have also touched pauper flesh.'

'Then why did you accept the position?'

'Because it will provide you with invaluable experience. I intend that you shall have constant practice in treating the paupers. It will be like having your own hospital ward to walk.

'Sean and I will overlook you until you have gained sufficient confidence to diagnose and treat them yourself, which shouldn't take too long.'

Nairn kneed his horse closer to the great closed gates and tugged on the bell-pull.

Daniel White pulled the gates open.

'Howdo, Dr Nairn, sir.' The man's black fangs bared in an obsequious grin.

'This gentleman is my assistant, Mr James Kerr,' Nairn told the porter. 'He is to be given access to the house at all times. Now I want to see the Master.'

'Gentlemen, I've been expecting you. Allow me to bid you welcome.'

Henry Melen came to the gate, smiling affably, hand outstretched towards the visitors.

As soon as the introductions had been made he invited them into his private quarters and produced a bottle of brandy and a plate of sweet biscuits.

'Ah, here is my lady wife. Do come and meet our new medical officer, and his assistant, my dear.'

143

Amelia Melen came through the door slightly breathless, face flushed as if she had just left off from hard physical exertions. She smiled delightedly and warmly greeted her visitors.

'I must apologise for disturbing you, ma'am.' Nairn bowed.

'You are more than welcome to call at any hour of any day, sir,' she assured him. 'And I'm very pleased that you've wasted no time in making yourself known to us. We've been most eager to meet you.'

James was surprised by the couple. Because of their low-ranking social standing he had expected to meet grim features, awkwardly stiff manners, stilted words, and instead here was this genteelly mannered, handsome couple smilingly at ease with their visitors even though these visitors were of a much higher social position.

But then when he compared his own work-a-day clothing with the opulent broadcloth of Henry Melen and the silk gown of Amelia Melen, he wryly admitted to himself that on first sight they could be taken to be of higher social ranking than himself.

Nairn was feeling weary and the congenial company, the warm comfort of the snug room, the frequently replenished glass of brandy quickly worked on his senses, making him disinclined to take the trouble of inspecting the sick ward and the rest of the workhouse. So when their visit ended three hours and a bottle and a half of brandy later all they had seen of its interior was the entrance hall and the sitting room of the Master, and had not set eyes on a single inmate.

As they trotted away from the workhouse, Nairn asked, 'What did you think to them?'

'I was pleasantly surprised.' James was feeling a half-drunken contentment. 'They were very mannerly.'

'They were certainly that,' Nairn agreed. 'It will be to our advantage to maintain a good relationship with them, because then they will be more ready to call us in for emergency attendances.' He smiled at his nephew. 'Perhaps we might show a small profit from this appointment after all.'

*   *   *

144

The Melens stood in the gateway waving farewell to their visitors until they had passed from sight.

'Well, my dear, what do you think of our new medical man?' Henry Melen wanted to know.

'I don't think he will cause us any problems so long as we help him to line his own pockets.' Amelia Melen smiled. 'Judging from what he was saying I think that as time passes it will be his nephew who will mostly come here. He'll be easy to handle. He's as green as grass.'

Henry Melen was somewhat doubtful. 'He seemed intelligent, my dear. The type who might sometimes be inclined to ask awkward questions.'

'No, he won't.' There was absolute certainty in her voice. 'He'll be easy for us to handle.'

'If you're sure.'

'I am,' she stated flatly.

Nineteen

T he day was hot and windless and the sulphurous smoke hung thickly in the air of the salt works, forcing Liddy to keep the doors and windows closed so that her mother would not be racked by fits of coughing.

As she prepared the meat and vegetables for the evening meal Liddy was bodily oppressed by the stiflingly close atmosphere inside the house, and mentally depressed by familial problems. Following a heated dispute with her father, her brother had left home and gone to London where he was now employed as a clerk in a business belonging to an acquaintance of Edward Harcourt, and was hating every moment of it. She had received a letter from Robert three days ago which had done nothing to cheer her, because it consisted of nothing but reproaches, recriminations and complaints.

Her mother, grief-stricken by Robert's departure, had withdrawn into her own inner world and appeared barely conscious of anything other than her own bitter sorrows.

At least she doesn't physically attack me any longer, Liddy told herself, drawing some bleak comfort from that fact.

George Landser himself was broken in spirit. Drinking himself into stuporous unconsciousness night after night, and continually weeping and maundering wildly that he was harbouring a terrible secret which would cause herself and Robert to turn against him should they ever discover it.

Poor Pa, Liddy thought, his troubles have only got worse since Harcourt took the works from him.

Yet although she disliked Edward Harcourt, Liddy could not really hold him responsible for her father's business disasters or his surrender to his alcohol addiction.

The family malaise appeared to have spread to the salt workers, whose previous rough good humour as they went about their daily tasks was now superseded by resentful sullenness.

They can't be blamed for it after the way that Harcourt forced Pa to cut their wages, Liddy accepted dispiritedly.

She finished peeling the last potato and then collected the pile of vegetable waste in her apron and went outside to throw it onto the rubbish heap. She heard a commotion of shouts and screams coming from the direction of the works and hurried round to the front of the house to see what was happening.

A rapidly increasing crowd of the workhands were clustered around the door of the nearest evaporation shed and as she ran towards them they moved on to the dirt of the yard and she saw that they were carrying a limp body.

'Who is it? What's happened?' she demanded.

'It's Susie Beech, Miss Liddy. She fell into the pan!'

'Oh no!' Liddy gasped in horror as she saw the young, heavily pregnant woman they bore in their arms.

The scant shift she wore had offered no protection against the boiling brine which had scalded and blistered her entire body, in some parts leaving her skin hanging in strips from raw red flesh.

'Does she still live?' Liddy questioned.

'No. God's been kind to her for once and took her out of this stinking life,' a half-naked, sweat-dripping woman spat out savagely. 'She should never have been working at her stage. She was ready to drop the babby.'

'Then why was she working?' Liddy wondered aloud.

'Because it was that or the bloody Bastille,' the same woman replied. 'We'em only paid starvation wages now, you knows that well enough, missy. If we was paid a proper wage the poor cow could have left off work until she'd dropped the babby.

147

Your dad ought to be ashamed of himself, paying us the pittance he does.'

'My father pays what he is told to pay.' Liddy sprang to her father's defence.

At that moment the door of the office opened and George Landser appeared, swaying and blinking owlishly.

'Oh, does he now,' the woman jeered. 'Well, he's pays himself money enough to be pissed morning, noon and night, don't he? Just look at the bugger now.'

There was a chorus of dissatisfied growling in her support.

'Cummon, let's take Susie and get out of here,' another woman shouted, and now the sound of displeasure was loud and sustained and the crowd surged on towards the gates.

As they neared the office George Landser stumbled out to confront them.

'What's going on?' He blinked hard to clear his sight as he stared at the dead woman.

'Fuck off out the way, gaffer,' a voice warned.

'You can't leave your work like this,' George Landser protested.

'Oh, can't we?'

'Just watch us!'

'Gerrout the way, you drunken bleeder!'

Liddy went to run to her father's side but strong hands grasped her shoulders and she looked into the gnarled features of an elderly man.

'Leave well alone, missy,' he told her firmly. 'Let us take that poor wench and get her ready for her grave.'

Liddy could hear her father blustering, 'Now look here, you can't go. The fires need tending and there are pans to be cleared. If production stops now we'll all be ruined.'

Howls of raucous laughter greeted his words.

'We'em already ruined, gaffer, that's why we works here.'

'What about poor Susie, aren't she ruined enough for you yet?'

The laughter became fury.

'Fuck off out on it, you drunken bastard!'

148

The crowd surged on, fists thudding into George Landser's face and body and he was sent sprawling on to the dirt, clogged feet trampling him as he bellowed in shock and pain.

Liddy shouted angrily and fought to pull free, but was unable to break the grip which held her.

'Leave them go. Your dad aren't hurt bad. Leave them go.'

Only when the crowd had passed through the gates did the man release her, and she ran to George Landser's sprawled body.

He was bleeding from the nose and lips, his face dirtied, his clothing torn, his porcelain teeth protruding grotesquely from his mouth.

He peered dazedly up at her and pushed his teeth back into his mouth, then to her amazement grinned.

'This is a rum go, ain't it, Liddy? I think I'll take more water with my gin in future.'

Liddy burst into tears of relief.

'Cummon, missy.' The gnarled-featured man bent to lift George Landser up on to his feet. 'Let's get your dad home, shall we. He's all right, you see. Only a bit shook up, that's all.'

Between them they half carried George Landser to the house and laid him comfortably on the settle in the overfurnished parlour.

'I'll leave you now, missy. The gaffer's all right, don't you fret.'

For the first time Liddy was able to think clearly enough to thank the man for his help, and then ask him, 'Who are you? Do you work here?'

He shook his grizzled head. 'No, missy, I'm a boatman. Me barge is in the cutting there. I'm come here to visit kinfolk. Me name is Jesse Beech.'

'Beech?' A terrible foreboding dawned in Liddy's mind.

'Yes, missy. Beech is me name.' He nodded sadly. 'I'm Susie's feyther.'

Before she could recover from the shock of his information, Jesse Beech had gone.

'I need a drink, Liddy.' George Landser was gingerly ex-

149

ploring his wounds. 'What got into them, leaving their work for no good reason? Have they all gone mad?'

She stared at him in astonishment. 'No good reason? How can you say such a thing, Pa?'

'I need a drink,' he groaned. 'My God, they've broken my face you know. It hurts like the devil. Fetch me some gin, there's a good girl.'

She remained staring at him, then challenged, 'Don't you know what happened to that poor girl?'

His bleared eyes displayed no comprehension. 'What girl? Had she hurt herself or something?'

Utter dismay flooded through Liddy's mind. 'Oh, Pa, what are you doing to yourself? Are you so saturated with drink that you don't see what is happening before you?' she murmured, then stepped to him and taking his face between her hands she bent close and told him, 'Susie Beech fell into the boiling pan. She's dead, Pa. She's dead! Can you understand that? The poor girl is dead!'

Shock and distress spasmed across his features. 'I didn't know! I thought that she'd only hurt herself.'

He pulled Liddy's hands down and sat shaking his head. 'I need a drink. I didn't know. I need a drink.'

A terrible disgust for her father shuddered through Liddy, and she recoiled from her own emotion in horror.

He's my pa, and I love him . . . She fought to overcome that unbidden disgust but she was powerless against its strength. But he does disgust me, she told herself, what he has become disgusts me.

Anger smouldered, and she fetched a bottle of gin, uncorked it and thrust it into his clutching hands.

'Here, take it. And drink yourself to death,' she hissed, and in that moment would gladly have seen him dead.

Twenty

S eptimus Nairn and James Kerr came early in the morning to make a call upon Mrs Landser.

The salt works were seemingly deserted, only thin plumes of smoke coming from some of the chimneys, none from others as the fires burned out.

'I wonder what's happened here, Jamie?' Nairn stared about him in puzzlement. 'Where is everybody?'

James felt concern when he saw Lydia's wan features as she opened the door to their knocking.

She quickly related the events of the previous afternoon.

'Where is your father? I'd better take a look at his injuries.' Nairn frowned. 'Whoever assaulted him should be brought before the magistrates.'

She smiled mirthlessly. 'He was too drunk to know who it was, Dr Nairn. And I couldn't see because of the crowd around him. But he's not been hurt badly. Only a few bruises and a split lip and bloody nose.'

'Nevertheless I'd best see him,' Nairn insisted.

'If you wish.' Again the mirthless smile touched her lips. 'He's sleeping in the room next to my mother's. Pa always sleeps very soundly no matter what occurs.'

'And you, my dear – are you feeling perfectly well?' he asked her. 'You're very pale and drawn.'

'I'm very well, I thank you. Merely a little tired.'

'Then you rest, while I attend to your mother and father,' Nairn instructed firmly. 'James will keep you company.'

Alone with Liddy, James felt tongue-tied and sought desperately for something light and easy to say to her.

'Will you take some refreshment?' she invited. 'I can make some tea, or perhaps you would prefer cider or beer?'

'Tea would be most satisfactory, thank you,' he mumbled, and was furious with himself for behaving so gauchely.

He felt even more embarrassingly gauche as he scalded his lips and tongue on the hot liquid, and jerking with the shock of the pain spilt some of the tea on to the carpet.

'I'm so sorry! I do apologise,' he blurted, and to his mortification felt the warmth of a blush spreading up from his throat.

Liddy softened towards him, finding his awkwardness and obvious embarrassment both charming and endearing.

'There's no harm done.' She couldn't help giggling. 'And please, let us put aside this formality. We are friends, are we not?'

He suddenly felt relaxed and confident. 'Of course we are.'

Now they chatted with ease and fluency, enjoying each other's company, and for a brief time Liddy was able to forget the troubles that beset her and become a carefree young girl again. On his part James took immense pleasure from the bright eyes and sweet face of this girl before him.

When his uncle returned James experienced a momentarily fierce resentment at the curtailment of his pleasure.

As they said goodbye and his uncle turned away, James obeyed a sudden impulse and whispered to Liddy, 'I'd like to become more than a friend, Liddy. May I call upon you? I'll ask your father's permission to do so, of course.'

Liddy opened her mouth to give a happy assent, then abruptly remembered her sick mother and drunken father. Her newfound happiness fled, her smile faded and she shook her head sadly.

'It's not possible, Jamie.'

His face fell, and tears stung her eyes as she quickly stepped back inside the house and closed the door.

Although disappointed at Lydia Landser's reaction to his request, James's instincts told him that her refusal was not because she didn't reciprocate his feelings. He knew the present

152

difficulties she was facing, and resolved that he would try again at some future date.

As they remounted, Nairn told James, 'We'll take a look at the dead woman while we're here. Such cases don't come along very often. It would be a pity for you to miss the chance of seeing one. They're quite rare, you know.'

James's enthusiasm instantly kindled at this prospect of seeing such a rare case.

'Lead on, Uncle,' he said gaily, and Nairn regarded him knowingly, and smiled secretly.

Susie Beech had lived in one of the terraced cottages that stretched along the side of the highway, and curious eyes studied the two horsemen as they passed along the grimy red-brick rows.

A group of poorly clad men were standing outside one cottage, drinking from jugs which they passed among them.

'That'll be the place,' Nairn observed grimly. 'And they're all getting swinish drunk as usual.' Then he shrugged. 'And who can blame them for that, Nephew. They have little enough encouragement to do otherwise.'

'Who the fuck are you?' a scarred-faced man challenged aggressively as Nairn and James reined in before the group.

'Hold your rattle, it's Dr Nairn,' another man ordered, and turned to shout in through the open doorway, 'Jesse, here's the doctor come.'

Jesse Beech came out of the cottage. 'Who has sent for you, Doctor? There's nothing you can do here.'

His tone was civil.

'Who are you, my man?' Nairn demanded.

'My name is Jesse Beech. I'm Susie's feyther. I'm dealing with the burial. Her mam's too distressed to think straight.'

'I am Dr Nairn, the medical officer of this parish. There will have to be a death certificate issued and I must sign it. So I must view the body and ascertain the cause of death.'

'She was fuckin' well boiled alive,' the scar-faced man spat

153

out. 'And if there was any justice to be had in this fuckin' country the bloody masters 'ud be boiled alive as well. Grinding, robbing bastards that they are.'

There came a concerted growl of agreement from the glowering faces around them, and James felt a frisson of apprehension as he sensed the violence simmering in these people's hearts.

Nairn showed no reaction; he only dismounted and told the nearest man, 'Hold my horse. Come, Mr Kerr.'

James handed his reins to the same man, who accepted them without demur, and followed his uncle into the cottage.

The tiny front room was packed with women clustering around the planked trestles on which Susie Beech lay, covered with a grimy, much-patched sheet. The air was so foul that James tried to breathe shallowly until he became accustomed to it, fearing he would gag if he filled his lungs too soon.

'I must ask you all to leave while I examine this woman,' Nairn requested firmly.

Resentful scowls greeted his words but Jesse Beech told them, 'Do as the doctor says.'

The women reluctantly filed outside, and Nairn told Beech, 'Would you leave us also, and close the door.'

'It'll make the room dark,' Jesse Beech pointed out.

'No matter. I'll light the candle.'

As the door closed, the room was instantly plunged into gloom, and Nairn struck a lucifer and lit the stub of tallow candle. Then he removed the covering sheet from the corpse.

'This is a rare one,' he remarked appreciatively. 'It's only the second time I've seen such a specimen where the entire body has been scalded like this. Do you see, Jamie, how scalding and burning have similar effects as regards the blistering and the stripping of the skin layers. Scalds are merely burns, the difference being that they are produced by moist heat, and burns are produced by dry heat.'

The dead woman presented a gruesome spectacle, but James was sufficiently hardened to his profession to be able to look at her dispassionately and take a clinical interest in her injuries.

154

'If she had survived could anything have been done for her?' he asked.

'Nothing, she would have died quickly. It was God's mercy that she didn't survive only to suffer longer.'

'If the scalding had not been so widespread could we have helped her?'

'We could apply a lime-water and oil mixture, or a saturate of carbonate of soda. Even immerse her in a warm bath for several days. But depending on the severity and extent of the scalding she would still have ended up a cripple to a lesser or greater degree.'

They spent several minutes more making a detailed examination and then Nairn covered her up again, and they left the cottage.

As they remounted the women trooped back inside.

'Does she have other children?' Nairn asked Jesse Beech casually.

'Three, all still nippers, and her mam is too feeble to care for them,' Beech informed them. 'Her man has gone on the tramp. When he got laid off from the salt works he could find no other employment here.'

'I can give you a letter to take to the Guardians if you need to put them into the workhouse,' Nairn offered.

The gnarled features frowned. 'Thank you, Doctor, but I'll try and see what else can be done for them.'

'As you wish.' Nairn kneed his horse into motion.

James was disturbed by the hostility emanating from the crowd of men and as soon as they were out of earshot remarked, 'You would think that we were their enemies, the way they looked at us.'

'They mostly regard us as such, Nephew. When I was a young man I thought them to be like dogs who bite the hands that feed them.' Nairn's grim features were reflective. 'But as I've become older, I've come to believe that their hatred of the gentry who rule over them can at times be fully justified.'

James grinned wryly, and not for the first time thought, My uncle is a true Radical, is he not.

155

Twenty-One

T he news of the stoppage at the salt works came to Edward Harcourt's ears just before noon when he was sipping a brandy and water in the best saloon bar of the Golden Cross Hotel, the favourite meeting place of the town's influential citizens.

'Boiled alive, the wench was.' The raconteur was entertaining a group of cronies with a much-embellished account of the tragedy. 'She tried to swim to the walkway and was screaming for help, but no one could get a line to her.'

'Why couldn't she walk out of it? Those pans aren't deep. She wouldn't have to swim,' one of his listeners objected.

The raconteur looked down his long nose at the interrupter. 'Tell me, William, have you ever tried to walk through boiling brine? I don't think that you'd be able to manage many steps.'

'He would if there was a chest full of money at the end of it. William would walk through Hell's fires for tuppence profit, wouldn't you, William?' a second listener quipped, and there was a shout of laughter from the others in the group.

'Anyway, the story is that the whole of the workhands went storming out of the gates carrying the dead wench with them . . .' the raconteur hastened to reclaim his audience. '. . . and Landser tried to stop them. He told them to get back to their work and take her with them.'

Exclamations of disgust greeted this statement.

'The cruel sod!'

'That was a bad thing to do.'

'. . . Well, they just kept on going and Landser got very roughly handled. Apparently, they used the dead wench like a battering ram, and broke Landser's head for him and he was left for dead.'

'Good for them!'

'Serves the hard-hearted bugger right!'

'. . . And now the works have come to a standstill and the fires are out. It just goes to show, gentlemen, God strikes down those who don't show the proper respect towards the dead, no matter how low in rank them dead are.' The raconteur brought his story to a triumphant conclusion.

Edward Harcourt had listened impassively. Now he quietly finished his drink, and bidding the company a polite farewell walked slowly from the bar.

Within half an hour he was riding along the turnpike road towards Stoke village.

The news of the stoppage did not disturb him. He had intended to get rid of George Landser sooner or later, and now he had the perfect excuse to make it sooner. George Landser was finished at the salt works. What was giving him pause for thought, however, was how to handle Lydia Landser.

Despite his ambition to marry Mercedes Wybergh and her money, Harcourt still wanted Lydia Landser as his mistress, and he saw no reason why he should not be able to achieve both of those ambitions. Harcourt was a patient man, always ready to take the long view of any situation, and now after brief consideration he dismissed the notion of making Lydia Landser any quick offer of his protection in return for her sexual favours. He prided himself on his knowledge and understanding of human nature, and he was certain that she would reject him at this present time. Another all-important necessity was that until he had succeeded in his pursuit of Mercedes Wybergh he must be seen to behave with the utmost probity. Any suspicion that he was interested in another woman would most definitely wreck any chance of matrimony with the wealthy widow.

No, he decided, I'll have to find some other method of snaring little Lydia. I'll have to keep an influence over her in

157

such a way that will not arouse any gossip. But it will have to be carefully done.

A plan was already germinating in his mind.

He turned off the turnpike road and descended the hill towards the canal along which Stoke village stood.

'I wish to speak with your father, Miss Lydia.'

'It's not possible at present, Mr Harcourt. He is unwell.'

'The matter is urgent.'

Liddy remained standing in the house doorway, and repeated stubbornly, 'I'm sorry, Mr Harcourt, but my father is unwell. He's not able to discuss any matters of business.'

Harcourt hid his irritation and persisted politely, 'Miss Lydia, I have to insist that you allow me to come in and speak with your father.'

Liddy was beginning to feel desperate. George Landser was lying upstairs in a drunken stupor.

'But my father is most unwell, Mr Harcourt. He has taken a sleeping draught.'

Harcourt shook his head with a show of regret. 'You force me to speak bluntly. I know what type of sleeping draught your father has taken. I know that he is drunk yet again. But I beg you to believe me when I tell you that I am come here solely to see how best we can resolve the present situation. I have the best interests of your family at heart. Now, may I come in and discuss matters with you? Or would you prefer to continue in your refusal and see your father utterly ruined?'

Realising the futility of further argument, Liddy reluctantly acquiesced.

Once inside Harcourt became brisk and businesslike.

'I'll explain what the present situation is, Miss Lydia. When I took over this salt works I risked keeping your father as manager, even though I knew of his propensity for drink. I've also invested further large amounts of money to sink shafts so that we could increase production. I'm happy to say that those endeavours have at last proven successful, and within a short time production will expand rapidly. That expansion will need

158

vigorous and wise management. I trusted your father when he promised me that he would stop drinking to excess, but he has broken that promise. He is too sodden in drink to be allowed to remain in any position of trust. I can therefore see no other option but to dismiss him from his present post as manager.'

Dismay struck through Liddy, and she protested, 'But it wasn't my father's fault that the woman was killed! And how can you dismiss him? He once owned these works!'

But even as she protested she knew deep down that her father in his present state of mind was not capable of working competently.

'Miss Lydia, as a banker I have shareholders to answer to. It was bank money that was loaned to your father and he has not fulfilled his contractual obligations on those loans. I have had to resist the demands of certain of my own major shareholders that I should have your father committed to the debtors' prison, since he has broken his contract with the bank to repay the outstanding interest charges on his loans.'

With a sickening despair Liddy recognised the ring of truth in Harcourt's voice. She sought for further arguments but could find none, and remained silent.

'However, Miss Lydia, because of the high regard I have always had for your family, I am prepared to do whatever I can to help you in this time of your need. That is, of course, if you will permit me to do so.'

At this moment, Liddy could see no other way out and she nodded. 'I would be most appreciative of any help that you could give to my family, Mr Harcourt.'

Harcourt smiled inwardly with satisfaction. The situation was developing very promisingly. She had been brought to heel more easily than he had anticipated. So much so in fact that he wondered if he should now offer to take her under his protection and set her up in a lodging in Birmingham or Worcester. Then he dismissed the notion. He must keep to his priorities, and Mercedes Wybergh was number one priority at this moment.

He had been giving much thought to how he might simulta-

159

neously place Lydia Landser under an obligation to him, and keep her enmeshed within his power. And now he put a plan into motion.

'I have a proposal for you which although it may sound harsh at first hearing, is nevertheless a solution for the worst of your family's immediate problems.'

He paused, inviting response.

Liddy swallowed her pride. 'I am grateful, Mr Harcourt.'

He became avuncular. 'I can arrange for your father and mother to become tenants of a small cottage which the bank owns. Until their situation improves I can also arrange for them to receive parish outdoor relief.'

A spasm of dismay struck through Liddy at the prospect of such degradation. But she made no reply, knowing that nothing could be said which would make any difference to her predicament.

'As for yourself, I believe it necessary that you should be enabled to earn your own living. Would you be agreeable to accepting some type of employment, suited to your own tastes?'

'I would,' she confirmed quietly.

'Good. I propose then that you should be trained as a schoolteacher. Because of recent legislation by the government, the Board of Guardians has become obligated to employ a female schoolteacher in the Bromsgrove Workhouse.'

'But I know nothing of teaching!' Liddy pointed out. 'How could I be employed as a teacher?'

'You will be sent to London, to the British and Foreign Society's School for Young Women, to be trained in the Lancastrian principles and methods of teaching. I shall advance you sufficient money to pay the fees.'

He noted her doubtful frown and hastened to allay any suspicions she might be harbouring as to his motives for offering her money.

'That advance of fees will be brought to the attention of the Guardians. It will be interest free and deducted in instalments from your salary as a teacher until repaid. What do you say to

160

my proposal?' He stopped speaking and regarded her downcast head closely.

Liddy was thinking hard. She could not help but be suspicious of his motives in offering his help. Yet she accepted that he had not even hinted at any strings being attached to this offer. It all appeared to be perfectly straightforward. At least if she became a schoolteacher she would be enabled to earn some money with which to help her family. She shrugged mentally – Why do I hesitate? What choice do I really have?

She lifted her head and looked fully at him, searching his features for any expression of ulterior motivation. But she could discern nothing more than impassivity.

'When would I be expected to begin this training, Mr Harcourt?'

He pursed his lips judiciously. 'I will have to place your candidature for the post of schoolmistress before the Board. Subject to their acceptance, I will then write to the school principal and ascertain when you can enter upon the training. I would think that you should be prepared to leave for London within the month. That being the case then you will have ample time to help your parents settle into their new home.'

A wave of depression whelmed over her at how low her family had been brought.

Harcourt affected a display of unconcern which he was far from feeling.

'Anyway, Miss Landser, give my proposal some further thought. But I would appreciate your letting me know of your decision as soon as possible. Because if you do not wish to take up the offer, there are several other young women who are eager to do so. I'll wish you good day.'

He moved to the door, then halted as if another thought had just occurred to him.

'Perhaps it might be kinder if you inform your father of his dismissal from here, Miss Landser, rather than I return to do so. Send him to see me if he needs further confirmation.

'I will arrange for a cart to remove his furniture to the cottage, and a carriage for your mother. That is of course if

161

he accepts my offer of accommodation. But whatever he should decide, he must vacate this house before the end of this week.'

He made as if to leave, and Liddy felt impelled to tell him, 'Wait for a moment, please, Mr Harcourt. I wish to accept the post of schoolmistress, and I thank you for your help.'

He nodded brusquely. 'You have made a wise decision. Good day to you.'

Outside he allowed himself to smile broadly.

Liddy remained standing by the fireside for some time. Despite all her worries for the future and her dismay at what she must tell her father, she was experiencing an escalating excitement of anticipation.

London! I'm going to London! What an adventure that will be.

Twenty-Two

W idowhood, or rather the period of secluded mourning that respectable society demanded from the bereaved wife, was proving irksome to Mercedes Wybergh. Married at twelve years of age she had passed from the strict repression of her father into the strict repression of her husband. Her entire life had been spent under male dominance, against which she had mentally rebelled, but physically had been powerless to resist. Her husband's death had come as a happy release for her and now she wanted to enjoy her freedom. But conditioned from birth to obey the mores of respectable society she found it difficult to break free of its binding conventions. Full mourning would last for two years during which she would not be expected to be seen in public enjoying herself. She would wear black crêpe for a year and nine months together with the widow's cap and veil, and for a year after that would wear nothing showy or brightly coloured.

Sitting in her drawing room, she grimaced ruefully. Women were even discriminated against in mourning. A widower was only expected to wear black for a year and could re-enter society after a mere three months.

And a widower can always take his pleasures as he chooses, she thought enviously.

Mercedes Wybergh had endured a lifetime of sexual frustration. She was a hot-blooded woman with a strong sexual appetite, and her much older husband had been a man who sublimated his sexual passions in the pursuit of wealth. Julius

163

Wybergh had only used her body to beget an heir, and after Carlos had been born he had virtually ceased from any sexual relationship with his young wife. But he had continued to rule over her with an iron hand, restricting her liberty and allowing her no opportunity to take any illicit sexual pleasures.

A maidservant came into the room to announce, 'Mr Harcourt wants to know if you're receiving, madam.'

Mercedes briefly considered. Edward Harcourt had called at the house frequently since the funeral, ostensibly to offer his condolences and to discuss certain ongoing financial arrangements that her husband had made with Harcourt's bank. But Mercedes had quickly realised that the banker had another motivation for his visits. She smiled secretly to herself. She had no intention of ever becoming imprisoned by marriage again. And although she hoped to indulge herself with a love affair, it would not be with a man who was primarily interested in getting his hands on her money. She wanted a passionate romance, not a business arrangement. She wanted a vibrant lover who desired her for herself alone. She wanted a young fresh body and a young fresh mind over which she could hold sway. She wanted someone like James Kerr.

'What shall I tell Mr Harcourt, madam?' The maidservant interrupted the reverie.

'Give him my regrets. Tell him that I am indisposed and unable to receive any visitors today. Then come back to me. I have an errand for you.'

Mercedes was acting on impulse. She quickly wrote a note and sealed it, and when the maidservant returned she instructed, 'Take this note to Dr Nairn's house in Tardebigge.'

James stared at the note and told Sean Fitzgerald, 'It's from Mrs Wybergh, asking me to call on her this evening.'

'Does she say what she wants?'

'No. Just asks me to call on her.'

The Irishman winked roguishly. 'Perhaps she wants a bit of the other, my boy. Aren't you the lucky one, if that's the case.'

The vivid recollection of how powerfully she had affected

164

him on the day of the funeral created a frisson of excitement in James's mind, and for a brief instant he wondered if she had been affected likewise. He thrust the thought away, jeering, You're reacting like a dirty-minded little schoolboy, you damned fool. She's old enough to be your mother.

But even as he told himself this another voice whispered, No matter how old she is, she excited you sexually more than any other woman you've ever met.

As he refolded the note he detected a faint scent of perfume from it and again the visual image of Mercedes Wybergh's face and body came into his mind, and excitement stirred.

Fitzgerald was slyly watching him, and chuckled lewdly. 'You young dog, you. I can read what's in your mind and it doesn't bear being published it's so indecent.'

James felt himself reddening and laughed shamefacedly, and to avoid further embarrassing conversation on the topic suggested, 'Hadn't we'd best get started on mixing the physic?'

He put pieces of chalk and charcoal into a large stone mortar and began to pulverise them into a fine powder with the pestle. Next he added water and stirred, then emptied a bottle of laudanum into the watery paste. They ladled the resultant mixture into small flasks and stoppered them.

'What are we calling it this week?' James enquired amusedly.

'Elixir of Minoan calcium.' Fitzgerald chuckled. 'And because we've doubled the amount of laudanum I reckon we can double the price.'

When James had first watched Fitzgerald creating worthless mixtures to be sold as medicines to their patients he had regarded the process very dubiously, thinking it fraudulent practice. But since then he had come to know that their patients demanded medicines no matter whether their ailments warranted them or not. And unlike some of the more poisonous concoctions peddled by quacks and cheapjacks the mixtures made up by Sean Fitzgerald could do no harm to their consumers and, to James's astonishment, in some cases the mixtures appeared to have a definite beneficial effect.

It was as his uncle repeatedly told him: 'The power of

suggestion upon the human mind is a wondrous thing, Nephew, and a mystery which passes all understanding . . .'

'Perhaps you should take a flask of this for Mercedes Wybergh. It might well act as a powerful aphrodisiac,' Fitzgerald teased. 'And if it does then you can take another flask for your own use.'

'If that's the case, then I'm sure that you're in more need of it than I,' James returned the banter.

'Not me,' the Irishman roared. 'I'll have you know, you young dog, that my fame resounds throughout the country. People call me the Irish Stallion. I could repopulate the whole of China with the abundance of my seed. Beautiful women beg me for my favours.'

The image of the beautiful Mercedes Wybergh rose yet once more in James's mind, and he found himself wishing that the intervening hours before the evening might pass with lightning speed.

He still thought of Lydia Landser at times, but when he did so he always felt a stirring of angry resentment edging into the nostalgic regret. He had believed that she felt the same strong attraction towards him as he felt for her. Yet she had gone to London without even a word or note of farewell to him. When he added this to the way she had rejected his request to call on her as a suitor, he was forced to face the fact that she obviously did not want him. Both his heart and his pride had been hurt.

'Would you come this way, sir.' The maidservant led James to the drawing room.

Now that he had arrived at the Wybergh mansion he was feeling increasingly nervous, and was mentally castigating himself for his earlier fevered imaginings: She will have a perfectly respectable reason for wanting me to call on her. I must be the stupidest man in creation to have allowed myself to think what I did.

Mercedes Wybergh was seated in the armchair by the fireside and the soft glow of candlelight made her face look very young.

'Good evening, Mr Kerr. Thank you for coming to see me.'

166

She also was feeling extremely nervous and was half-regretting her surrender to impulse. Now that the young man had come, she didn't know what she was going to say to him in explanation of her note.

James bowed and took her proffered hand. As he bent low towards her the fragrance of her perfume filled his nostrils and he experienced the powerful lure of her sexuality.

'Good evening, ma'am. How can I be of service to you?'

To give herself time to think she gestured towards the facing chair.

'Please, sit down, Mr Kerr, and take a glass of wine.' She rose and went to the sideboard where the decanter and glasses were standing on a huge silver salver. James thought how gracefully she moved.

'This wine is from my own country, made from the grapes of Andalusia. Have you ever visited Spain, Mr Kerr?'

'No, ma'am. I've never travelled abroad. But I wish to do so at some future date.'

He took the glass of golden wine from her, and to his dismay found that his hand was trembling slightly from tension.

Mercedes sensed his nervousness and found it immensely endearing. To find that this young man was vulnerable filled her with a sudden confidence which banished her own nervousness.

She was delighted that her initial strong attraction towards him was being quickly reinforced by this present close proximity, and all regret at having surrendered to impulse was now supplanted by a determination to make him her lover.

She reseated herself facing him and smiled. 'If you should ever visit Spain, Mr Kerr, then you must permit me to act as your guide. My country has so much to offer and I can ensure that you will discover its hidden treasures.'

'That is most kind of you, ma'am.' The warmth of her manner was rapidly rekindling James's amorous hopes.

He sipped the wine and its rich taste was sheer pleasure.

'Some say that this wine is liquid sunshine,' she told him. 'Do you think that to be an apt description?'

'Indeed I do, ma'am,' he agreed enthusiastically. 'It's wonderful.'

She refilled his glass, and again her fragrance enveloped him. He found himself wanting to take her in his arms, and thinking that she was the most sexually exciting and desirable woman he had ever met. The fact that she was so much older than him was of no consequence, and unbidden a scrap of poetry that he had once read came into his memory.

Age and youth doth fly away,
Come then, love then
while ye may.

Oh yes, he told himself, I could fall in love with this woman.

She gestured towards a chessboard which was set up ready for play on a small table.

'My son and I used to play chess every evening when he was here at home. But now that he's gone travelling abroad I have no opponent. Do you play chess, Mr Kerr?'

'I do, ma'am, but not very well I fear.'

'Then I must find out if you are being modest.' She smiled. 'We shall play now.'

She rose and came to take his hand and lead him to the chessboard.

Her small hand nestling warmly in his fingers aroused a sudden protective urge in James. She's so small and delicate. So very feminine, he thought.

As they played she pressed more wine on him, and he began to feel slightly tipsy, and utterly happy.

The hours passed and with each hour James became more and more charmed by this dark-eyed, exotically beautiful woman. The copious amount of wine that he drank went to his head and his world became solely this candlelit room and the woman before him.

After a while the chessmen stayed untouched as they talked of their lives and dreams, their heads close, their fingers touching. Mercedes felt like a young girl again and all her repressed romantic longings surfaced and centred on this young

168

man, while for his part James was already becoming infatuated with her.

The clock struck one and brought James to an awareness of the lateness of the hour.

'I ought to go,' he said reluctantly.

Mercedes' hunger for him was now overwhelming her. She was harbouring an irrational fear that if she let him go from her now, he would never return.

She cupped his face between her hands and kissed him on his mouth.

'Stay with me,' she invited huskily.

James had the peculiar sensation that he had somehow become two entities in one body. One of those entities was eager to make love to her, but the other entity protested protectively.

'It will compromise you if I stay.'

'No,' she whispered. 'No one will know.'

'But the servants?'

'They are in bed and asleep. You can leave before they rise.'

Again her moist lips sought his, and he surrendered to his own fierce desire.

In the bedroom a shaft of moonlight illumined their bodies as they stood facing each other and shed their clothes. James knelt before her kissing the soft warmth of her rounded belly and thighs, burying his face in the triangle of hair, breathing in the fecund heat of her body. She drew breath in a long drawn-out hiss of pleasure, and he carried her to the bed and laid her upon it, taking the dark erect nipples in his mouth, nuzzling his lips over the satin smooth globes of her breasts. She cried out when he entered her. Her nails dug into the muscles of his back, and as his strong thrusts quickened she abandoned herself completely to the ecstasies of this virile loving.

Twenty-Three

D awn was greying the eastern horizon when James left the bed he had shared with Mercedes Wybergh. She stirred and whispered his name, and he bent to kiss and caress her. The night-time's lovemaking had been the most exciting and pleasurable experience of his life and he felt very tender towards her.

For Mercedes the virility of her young lover had been a revelation. She had never dreamed that such ecstatic delight could be experienced. But she was already feeling undercurrents of doubt that she would be able to hold him in her thrall. While the darkness of night had hidden the flaws of her ageing flesh from his eyes she knew that daylight would cruelly reveal that her breasts had begun to droop, her hips to thicken, her throat to ravel.

She pushed him away and drew the coverlet over her breasts.

'You must go now,' she urged. 'The servants will be getting up. Go quickly.'

'When shall I see you again?' he wanted to know.

'Soon,' she told him. 'I will be in touch with you soon.'

Sean Fitzgerald was eagerly awaiting James's return to Tardebigge.

His bulbous blue eyes glistened with lascivious anticipation as he demanded, 'Well?'

James was irritated by the question. He didn't want to talk about what had happened between himself and Mercedes Wybergh. He wanted to savour the memory of the night, and to examine his feelings towards her. He was already

170

emotionally involved but was as yet unsure of the depth and strength of that involvement.

'Well what?' he questioned curtly.

'What happened? Did you have her?' Fitzgerald urged impatiently. 'Come on now, I'm bursting to hear all about it. Is she a good fuck?'

The sudden flaring of James's anger surprised himself. 'I've no wish to talk of it. So let the subject lie.'

Sean Fitzgerald stared hard at the younger man's reddening features and surmised shrewdly, 'Have you become besotted, boy? Did the succulent widow make you fall in love with her?'

James drew a long breath in effort to control his rampaging emotions.

'Listen, Sean, I've no wish to lose your friendship, but I will tell you frankly that I've no wish to talk about what happened between Mrs Wybergh and myself. If you persist in badgering me about it, then we shall quarrel. So for the sake of our friendship I ask you now to let the subject drop and not to refer to it again. It is a private matter between myself and Mrs Wybergh, and I'll thank you to speak of her respectfully.'

He stared levelly into the bulbous blue eyes, and felt that if the other man persisted he would hit him.

The worldly wise Irishman recognised that the young man's simmering rage could erupt into physical violence.

'I'm sorry if I've offended you, Jamie, because there was no offence intended,' he apologised placatingly. 'But as a friend, let me offer you one piece of advice.'

'What is that?' James was still aggressively tense.

'I've seen more of life than you, Jamie, and I know how a woman can sometimes affect a man's wits so that he loses all sense of proportion. My advice is that you tread the road you've now taken with great care.'

'What do you mean by that?' Jamie demanded forcefully.

'Exactly what I say. Older and wiser heads than yours have been addled into madness by a woman. Love is a hot fever at its onset, but fevers cool and men recover from them, and then sometimes curse themselves for the eejits they were. I've no wish

171

to see you make an eejit of yourself, and perhaps do harm to your future prospects. And you'd best hope that your uncle doesn't come to know of this, because I don't think that he'll take the news of you and Mrs Wybergh's connection kindly.'

In his heart James knew that the other man was advising him with the best of motives, and his rage subsided as quickly as it had arisen.

'I tell you truly, Sean, I'm not yet fully understanding of my own feelings about Mrs Wybergh. You're right when you say that I'm suffering from a hot fever. But it's a fever that I've no wish to be cured of.'

'Then let us hope that it will bring you only happiness.' Fitzgerald grinned. 'And we'll speak no more of it until you want to yourself.'

James nodded gratefully.

Mrs Biddle came to tell them, 'There's a man come asking for the doctors. What am I to tell him?'

'Did he say what the problem is?' Fitzgerald questioned.

Her motherly features abruptly soured. 'I didn't ask him. He's one of the "leggers" from the tunnel. I don't talk with such low scum as them.' Her tone became indignant. 'The saucy devil came to the front door, would you believe. I soon give him a piece of my mind and sent him round the back. The cheek of it, a low scum of a "legger" coming to our front door!'

The 'leggers' were a notorious gang of drunken ne'er-do-wells who lived rough in turf shanties at each end of the long canal tunnel. The gang was widely despised and feared throughout the parish and believed to be responsible for much of the thieving and poaching that occurred in the surrounding countryside. They earned their drink money mainly by 'legging' the barges through the tunnel which had no towpath. A plank was placed athwart the bows of the barge and a 'legger' would lie precariously on each end of the plank and propel the vessel forwards by thrusting their feet against the tunnel walls. Because of their constant drunkenness accidents were frequent and drownings also. They would exert uneven strength and rhythm sending the barges crashing against the walls, smashing

172

the planks aside and toppling the leggers down between the barge and the brickwork.

Wanting to make some amends for his previous ill-temper James said, 'I'll go and see what he wants, Sean.'

The legger was a young, long-haired, raggedly dressed man, filthy and unshaven. Although it was still only eight o'clock in the morning he was bleary-eyed and half-drunk, breath stinking of rough cider.

'What do you want here?' James regarded him suspiciously.

The legger regarded James with an equal suspicion. 'It's the doctor I wants.'

'I'm a doctor.'

'You looks too young to be a fuckin' doctor,' the legger doubted surlily.

James had no patience with men of this type and now he reacted sharply. 'State your business or go. I've no time to waste on you.'

'Me brother's been hurt. Can you come and tend him?'

'Have you the money to pay us with?' Sean Fitzgerald spoke from behind James.

'Yeah.'

'Let's see it then.' The Irishman shared the general opinion of contempt regarding the leggers.

The man fumbled among his layers of rags and produced some coins.

'Theer it is.'

Fitzgerald stepped towards him. 'Hand it over.'

'You'll get paid when youse done the job,' the legger growled aggressively.

'We'll get paid now or we'll do no job,' Fitzgerald growled back with equal aggression. 'So hand it over or bugger off.'

The legger's brown-stained teeth bared in a savage snarl, but after a moment he placed the coins in Fitzgerald's cupped palm.

The Irishman quickly counted and frowned. 'There's only four shillings and fivepence here. Our fee for an emergency call out is seven shillings and sixpence. These bastards always try and cheat us. So we don't move until we get the full amount.'

'But that's all the money we could collect,' the legger asserted. 'There's only been a few boats come through last night and this morning.'

Fitzgerald shook his head. 'You're lying.'

'I'm not.'

'You are.'

'I'm not. I swear on me mam's grave, I'm telling you the truth.'

'You never even knew who your ma was, never mind where her grave is,' Fitzgerald scoffed.

The legger's filthy face glowered at the Irishman, who glowered back.

'Cough up the rest or bugger off.'

Scowling fiercely, mumbling curses, the legger fumbled through his layers of rags and produced more coins which he reluctantly handed over.

Fitzgerald checked the amount. 'That's better. Now where's your brother?'

'At the Navigation wharf.'

'What's he done to himself?'

'He's done his hip in by the looks on it. His leg is all twisted up and he's out of his yed with hurting.'

'When did it happen?'

'A few days since.'

'And you've only come to us now?' James couldn't believe what he was hearing.

'I been busy,' the legger muttered sullenly.

'All right. We'll come presently.' Fitzgerald told him.

The legger made no move and Fitzgerald shouted angrily, 'Get off with you, man. Go and care for your brother until we come.'

As the man shambled away Fitzgerald said, 'I think it best that we wait for your uncle to return. It could be a fracture or a dislocation. In the meantime we'll prepare the pulleys and laque in case they're needed.'

He grinned and winked. 'This could prove an earner for us, Jamie. If the man's got "Settlement" in the parish we can bill the Guardians, because we'll more than likely be able to have him admitted to the Workhouse Infirmary.'

'But we've already been paid.' James was puzzled.

'We've only been paid for the call-out, not the bloody treatment.' The Irishman chuckled. 'That's another kettle of fish entirely.'

The naked man lay on his back upon a low wooden pallet placed against the brick wall of the small warehouse. Septimus Nairn stood by him and talked to James and Fitzgerald as if he were giving a lecture.

'Now that I have established that there is no fracture present, gentlemen, I shall explain my diagnosis. See how the left leg is bent and shortened, and the knee is inverted to touch the inner side of the opposing knee, and see this posterior projection. Note also that the limb is fixed at this angle and we are unable to move the femur from the innominatum . . .' As he spoke he took hold of the man's left knee and forced it down.

The man's spine arched and he bellowed in pain.

Nairn ignored him and calmly continued his lecture. '. . . What we have here is undoubtedly a dislocation of the head of the femur into the ischiatic notch. If it were a dislocation on to the dorsum of the ilium the deformity would be much greater and the swelling of the trochanter much more visible.'

A group of leggers among whom was the injured man's brother were standing watching and Nairn turned to ask them, 'What's this man's name?'

'It's Will Powell, sir. And I'm his brother, John Powell.' The long-haired young man spoke to Nairn with a noticeably more civil tone than he had used earlier towards James and Fitzgerald.

'Has he got a "Settlement" in this Union?'

'Yes, sir. We was both born and bred in Bromsgrove itself.'

Nairn looked at his two assistants and nodded with satisfaction. 'Our fee for treatment being thus assured then, gentlemen,

175

we will attempt to reduce this luxation. It will prove difficult, I fear, since it is a primary dislocation.'

He beckoned to the leggers.

'You men, move him into the centre of the floor. Mr Fitzgerald, kindly demonstrate to Mr Kerr how the pulleys are placed and the laque positioned. Use that beam there to anchor the pulleys. And when you pass the restraining rope around his upper body tie it to that upright beyond his head. We shall also use a couple of these people to help hold him still.'

The injured man was rigid with fear, his face grey, his body wet with clammy sweat.

His brother knelt down by him and put a bottle to his lips. 'Take a good swallow o' this, our kid. It'll deaden the hurt.'

Nairn scowled and knocked the bottle away with a swipe of his hand.

'That won't help him, you ignorant fool.'

James looked up in surprise from his task of securing the long broad leather band called the laque around the lower left thigh.

Nairn explained to him. 'For this procedure the muscles need to be as relaxed as possible. Alcohol or opium serves no purpose because the muscles will still tense involuntarily against the pain and that makes the reduction of the dislocation more difficult.'

The rope was passed around Powell's upper torso and lashed around the upright, and two men gripped him under his arms.

The pulley hook was fastened to the laque on his outer thigh and the laque's long tail was passed down the inner thigh and over the hip for another man to apply a counter extension. James and Fitzgerald took the pulley rope and Nairn laid his hands on the patient's knee and hip, and ordered, 'All pull together now. Smoothly. Pull smoothly.'

The pulley blocks squeaked as they turned, the rope and laque tightened, tautened and strained, Powell's mouth gaped wide, and he emitted a bellowing scream of agony.

'Harder. Pull harder!' Nairn ordered curtly, and his fingers whitened from pressure as he twisted the limb.

Powell's screams volleyed, and with a shock James became

176

conscious that for the first time the shrieks of a patient were not lancing through his own head.

'Hold steady! Hold steady! Maintain the pull,' Nairn shouted. He was panting, face red and sweaty with the effort he was making to force the displaced femur head back into its rightful position.

The minutes passed and James's muscles began to ache with the strain of maintaining the tension on the rope. Five minutes became ten minutes which became fifteen minutes, and finally Nairn accepted defeat and ordered disgruntedly, 'Slacken off!'

And Powell's screams lessened to a high-pitched keening.

James was marvelling at his own state of mind. He was feeling calm, and totally indifferent to the sufferings of the man on the pallet.

'Pull again,' Nairn ordered. 'Slow and smooth. Slow and smooth.'

The pulley blocks squeaked, the rope and laque tautened, strained, quivered. Powell's screams filled the air, and James gloried in his new-found indifference, keeping his eyes fixed upon his uncle struggling to repair this damaged human body. Exerting every ounce of his strength and skill and experience not to hurt, but to cure . . .

It's a great calling that we follow, James exulted silently, a great and noble calling. Thank God, I've hardened to the business at long last.

He met the bright bulbous eyes of Fitzgerald, and grinned at how heavily the Irishman was breathing.

'You're making hard work of this, Sean,' he teased. 'You'll be needing a few tots of brandy after it, I shouldn't wonder.'

'Jasus! I can keep this up all day and night if needs be,' the Irishman panted in riposte. 'My only fear is that you'll faint on me.'

Laughter bubbled in James's throat. It was as if a curse had been lifted from him. He was becoming a true surgeon. Resolute and strong. Able to bear the sufferings of the patient because he was inflicting those sufferings for the patient's own good.

Another fifteen minutes had passed before Nairn once more ordered, 'Slack off,' and grumbled to James and Fitzgerald, 'The trouble with these damned leggers is that they develop tremendous strength in their leg muscles. When the musculature goes into spasm as this man's has done, the only way to overcome the resistance is to virtually tear them apart.'

The patient was panting weakly, his eyes closed, his face livid.

'Pull together now. Smoothly. Smoothly. Maintain the pull. Maintain it.'

Now the patient's screams were metamorphosing into strangled moans.

'What the fuck am you doing to him?' John Powell demanded. 'Youm killing him!'

Nairn turned on him furiously. 'Hold your tongue, blast you!'

'But youm killing him, you cruel bastard!'

For a moment it seemed that the legger was ready to spring at Nairn's throat, and James tensed to intervene.

Nairn betrayed no sign of fear and warned curtly, 'I tell you now, John Powell, that if you do not go from my sight this instant it will be the worse for you.'

The two men stood toe to toe, eyes locked in silent conflict, but it was John Powell who finally broke off the battle of wills and shambled out of the building.

'Slack off.' Nairn scowled with frustration.

James asked his uncle curiously, 'Why were you so hard with him, when you always sympathise with the poor and make excuses for poachers?'

'And I still do, Nephew,' Nairn told him in a low voice. 'But these leggers are worthless scum who prey mercilessly on those poorer and weaker than themselves.' He smiled bleakly. 'Just as some of our local gentry do.'

He stood looking speculatively down at the moaning patient for some time, then asked Sean Fitzgerald, 'Do you have any cheroots with you, Mr Fitzgerald?'

'I do.'

'Let me have them, if you please. And will you turn the patient on to his front, Mr Kerr.'

James gaped in utter astonishment as he watched his uncle bend and thrust several of the cheroots deep into William Powell's anal passage.

Nairn straightened and smiled at James's expression.

'This may serve some purpose. Nicotine poisons and relaxes the musculature. A Yankee surgeon showed me this dodge many years ago when I was walking the wards in London. He used a cigar. We could have made a distillate of nicotine, but time is too pressing.' He chuckled amusedly. 'Remind me to extract these cheroots when I've done with this man. To leave them inside him might have serious consequences.'

He grimaced with contempt as he glanced down at Powell's pain-wracked features.

'Not that the loss of such as this one would be of any serious consequence to the world. Turn him on to his back again, if you please. We'll allow some time for the nicotine to take effect, and then recommence. So let's have a smoke while we wait.'

He took a flat silver case from his pocket and offered Sean Fitzgerald a cheroot.

The Irishman accepted, complaining good-humouredly, 'Why couldn't you have shoved these up his arse, instead of commandeering mine?'

'Because these are a more expensive manufacture than your own.' Nairn chuckled. 'They're the finest Cubanos and too good to be wasted on the likes of Powell. My sacrifices in the service of humanity have their limits, you know.'

James went to stand at the door and look out across the wharf yard to the canal. In the distance he saw a horse-drawn barge approaching and momentarily wondered what cargo it carried and where it was bound for. Perhaps it was on its way to the salt works. His thoughts turned to Lydia Landser. I hope all goes well for little Liddy, he thought with some concern.

Then a smile of satisfaction touched his lips. Fresh and pretty though Lydia Landser was, she couldn't compare with exotic, passionate Mercedes Wybergh. Desire smouldered as he savoured the memory of the night he had just spent with her. She was wonderful! He couldn't wait to hold her in his arms again, feel her mouth on his, thrill to her vibrant, greedily demanding body.

'Come. We'll try again.' Septimus Nairn had to repeat his call so engrossed was James in his reveries.

William Powell appeared almost comatose, and when James, at his uncle's direction, felt the man's heartbeat he found it shallow and very rapid.

'The nicotine has taken effect,' Nairn confirmed. 'Let us begin.'

Powell jerked violently and screamed when the rope and laque tautened, but then sagged into a faint and this time Nairn succeeded in reducing the dislocation.

'That's it, gentlemen,' he announced with deep satisfaction.

'Well done, sir!' Fitzgerald applauded.

'Yes indeed, well done.' James's admiration knew no bounds. He truly believed that his uncle was the finest surgeon in the kingdom.

This opinion was echoed by Sean Fitzgerald. 'There's not another man in this country could have reduced this dislocation, I'll bet my life on it.'

He shouted at the unconscious Powell. 'You're a lucky scut, so you are, to have a brilliant man like Dr Nairn here to treat you.'

Nairn issued a string of brisk orders.

'Tie his legs together. Put pads between his knees and ankles. Secure a roller bandage around his pelvis and make it tight and secure. The parts must be kept perfectly quiet for some time to allow the capsular ligament to unite. He is to be taken into the Workhouse Infirmary, opiate fomentations to be applied daily around the area of the joint.'

'When will he be able to use his legs again?' James asked.

'Within four to six weeks, if all goes well. But then he must take it slowly until the musculature recovers its full utility.'

Nairn replaced his top hat and gloves. 'And now I must leave you, gentlemen. We shall meet at dinner.'

When Nairn had left Fitzgerald said wistfully, 'I wish I was half the surgeon your uncle is.'

'I wish that I was one tenth the surgeon he is,' James echoed fervently.

Twenty-Four

Southwark, London
December 1842

R obert Landser cursed beneath his breath and pulled the collar of his coat closer around his throat. The night air was cold, drizzling rain hissed against the hot globes of the gas lamps and the young man's anxious eyes searched the murky grimy street before him. A cab rattled past and a group of noisy revellers spilled out from the gin palace on the corner. Then Robert Landser saw his sister hurrying towards him and went to meet her beneath the lamp.

'Why are you so late in coming? I sent the note in for you hours since.'

'I'm sorry, Rob. I couldn't get out until my roommate had gone to sleep. What's happened to you?' In the dull light Liddy's face was pale and anxious.

'Never mind that now,' he told her impatiently. 'Have you got the money?'

'This is all I have.' She handed him some coins.

'God dammit, Liddy. There's less than two shillings here,' he complained loudly. 'What use is that to me?'

'It's all I have, Rob.' Liddy couldn't restrain the note of resentment at his attitude in her own voice.

'But I must have more money, Liddy. My situation is desperate.'

'Then you must ask your employer for an advance against your wages.'

He shook his head. 'I can't. They sacked me a week ago.'

Self-pity entered his tone as he added, 'They put me out of my rooms as well. I've been sleeping in low lodging houses since. And damned pigsties they are as well.'

'Sacked you?' she exclaimed in shocked dismay. 'Why did they sack you?'

He averted his face and told her sullenly, 'There was a discrepancy in the petty cash. And I was blamed for it. Even though there was no proof that I'd taken it.'

'Had you taken it, Rob?' she demanded. 'Don't lie to me now!'

'I didn't steal it. I only borrowed it, that's all. And if the damned horse had run the way it should have done, then I would have put the money back and no one would have been any the wiser. I just had the most foul luck, that's all. I did nothing wrong.'

'Nothing wrong?' she challenged incredulously. 'How can you steal money from your employers and then tell me that you did nothing wrong? You're lucky they didn't lay charges against you.'

'How could they?' he demanded petulantly. 'I've already told you that there was no proof that it was me.'

Worry battled with anger in Liddy's mind.

'What will you do now?'

'What can I do without money?'

'You must seek for other work!'

His temper flared. 'Dammit all, Liddy, I'm not cut out to be a menial! I've been educated as a gentleman. This is all Pa's fault. Damn him! He's ruined my life.'

'Don't blame Pa for your own faults.' Liddy defended her beloved father. 'You've brought this misfortune down on your own head.'

Robert ignored her and cursed sibilantly.

'Damn him to hell! Here I am near to starvation and he couldn't care less, could he. He's a cruel heartless bastard.'

'He's no such thing. And if he knew the trouble you're in he would help you if he could,' she protested heatedly. 'But what can Pa do anyway? He's a broken man, and has nothing left to give.'

Robert's shoulders slumped and he sighed dispiritedly. 'There's nothing else for it now if you can't help me. I'll have to join the army I suppose. At least I'll get fed there.'

Shock widened her eyes. 'Join the army? But only drunkards and ruffians join the army. And if you were to go for a soldier I'd never see you again. You'd be sent to India and be killed there or die of some dreadful disease. You mustn't do that, Rob. You mustn't go for a Redcoat.'

'What other choice do I have?'

'Listen, I still have some trinkets and a couple of pieces of jewellery that Grandma left me. You can sell them for enough money to live on for a week or so. That will give you time to find some sort of employment.'

He was genuinely moved, and he touched her cheek and told her gently, 'You put me to shame, Liddy. I don't deserve such a good sister. But I've sponged off you too much already. I've no choice but to enlist and have done with it.'

'Oh no, Rob!' she muttered in dismay. 'You can't do that. Sell the jewellery and try to find work. Please, for my sake. I can't bear it for you to go for a soldier.'

She clutched him, burying her face against his chest.

He held her back and carefully straightened her bonnet.

'You'd better get back. You'll get into trouble if you're caught out at this hour, won't you? I don't want that on my conscience. Go on now.'

'Don't enlist, Rob. Please don't go for a soldier.' She was near to tears. 'Promise me that you'll sell the jewellery and try to find work.'

'All right then. Meet me here tomorrow morning.'

'I can't come in the day at all. It will have to be tomorrow night at this same hour.' She was smiling with relief.

'Very well then. Tomorrow night.' He kissed her tenderly and turned and walked swiftly away towards the bridge.

She watched him disappear into the murky night.

Robert Landser was racked with shame as he left his sister. I should be supporting Liddy, he thought, not her me. I'm just a useless bastard, no good to myself or anyone else, least of all to

Liddy. I curse Father for being a feckless drunkard, yet I'm as bad as him. All I do is sponge off my sister. Take everything from her and give nothing.

He looked at the black waters of the river and for a brief instant thought how easy it would be to throw himself into their depths and end his miserable life. But in the next instant castigated himself.

And what would that do to Liddy? he asked himself. Her only brother a suicide. It would break her heart. But what am I to do? What can I do?

Twenty-Five

The British and Foreign Society's School for
Young Women, Borough Road, Southwark, London

T he small bleakly austere room held two narrow iron cots.
A tall chest of drawers with a crock washbasin and jug set
upon it and two wooden footlockers were the only other
furnishings. The white-washed walls were plain but for the
black-lettered motto above the window: GOD SEES ALL.

The jangling of the six o'clock Rising Bell brought Liddy to
reluctant wakefulness and the sharply piercing recollection of
the meeting with her brother. She fought back the panic that
threatened to whelm over her telling herself forcefully, Rob will
find something to do other than enlist. God won't take him
from me.

'If you don't get up soon the day will be over and done with,'
a nasal voice scolded.

She opened her eyes to see in the candle's glow the disap-
proving frown of her roommate, Abigail Tucker, who was
sitting fully dressed on the opposite cot with a large open Bible
on her lap.

'I've been up for hours,' the bespectacled sallow-faced young
woman informed smugly. 'And I've already prepared my group
and gallery lesson. I doubt that you'll have time enough to
prepare any of yours . . .'

Liddy sighed wearily and sat up yawning, arms stretching
wide, full breasts straining against her thin nightshift. Then she
shook her head to clear the dullness of sleep, her long fiery-red
hair tumbling across her freckled face.

'. . . You know how Miss Drew impressed upon us the necessity of making thorough preparation. You have only yourself to blame if you get into trouble again today. You shouldn't be so lazy, lying in bed until the last moment as you do . . .'

Abigail Tucker's spiteful satisfaction provoked Liddy to interrupt sharply. 'Listen, Goody Two Shoes, if I get into trouble again, then so be it. But for now would you kindly keep quiet. Your voice is like a corncrake's, and it's far too early in the morning for me to be able to bear listening to it.'

The sallow features reddened with fury. 'Well, we shall see if Miss Drew is able to bear listening to my voice when I tell her about what you did last night. When I tell her that you left this room after lights-out and didn't come back until long past midnight. We shall see how Miss Drew regards your deliberate rule breaking, shan't we, Miss Landser?'

'Shan't we, Miss Landser,' Liddy mimicked, and stuck her tongue out.

She left her bed and taking the jug went out on to the landing, lit by a solitary flaring gas jet, to the stone trough at the far end where she filled the jug with icily cold water.

'Morning, Liddy.' Another nightshift-clad young girl came to join her.

'Morning, Maddy.' Liddy smiled ironically. 'And so another happy day in the nunnery begins as our novitiates eagerly prepare for their ongoing ordeals.'

'Did it all go well last night?' the young girl whispered. 'Did you meet with your brother?'

'Yes.' Liddy's expressive features betrayed her concern. 'He's lost his employment, and says that if he can't find another position shortly he might well be forced to join the army.'

'Oh no!' her companion uttered in horror. 'But that's terrible, Liddy. How can you bear the disgrace if he goes for a common soldier?'

Liddy shrugged her shapely shoulders. 'It's not the disgrace that troubles me, Maddy. It's the thought of him being sent to

187

foreign countries and being killed in a battle or dying from disease that frightens me.'

Abigail Tucker passed them and went down the stairs.

'That's another thing I have to worry about,' Liddy said pensively. 'Goody Two Shoes is threatening to tell Miss Drew about me not being in my room after lights-out.'

'Surely she wouldn't be so spiteful!' Maddy protested. 'She knows that you'll get into trouble if she does that. You could even be expelled.'

Liddy smiled wryly. 'I believe that for Abigail Tucker, my expulsion is an event to be most devoutly wished for. And to be perfectly honest when it's a choice between expulsion or spending another two months here as Abigail Tucker's room mate, I could almost consider expulsion to be the lesser evil.'

'Don't make jokes about it.' Maddy's genuine concern prompted her to speak sharply. 'I would hate to see you go, Liddy, and so would most of the other girls. And where would you go anyway, and what would you do?'

'I'd become a barmaid in a gin palace,' Liddy joked. 'Or perhaps open a bordello in the Ratcliffe Highway.'

Maddy was forced to giggle, and then said, 'Listen, Liddy. If Old Drew wants to know where you were last night, tell her that you came to my room because I was feeling unwell, and you stayed with me for some hours until I felt better. I shall tell little Janet to say the same.'

'Thanks, Maddy.' Liddy kissed her friend on the cheek, then went back to her own room.

The icy water made her gasp as she splashed it on her face and neck. With a wetted flannel she sponged her underarms, private parts and feet, dried herself on the rough towel and cleaned her teeth using the same water.

She stripped her bedding and folded it neatly, then plaited her hair and bound it around her head. While doing this she read from a book of poetry trying hard to commit the turgid stanzas to memory. She lost all track of time and suddenly became aware of boots clattering on the landing.

'Oh, damn it! I'll be late.'

She hastily dressed in crinoline, petticoat, a simple dark grey gown, pulled on cotton stockings and high-laced boots, then hurried downstairs.

In the small classroom which adjoined the great schoolroom thirty-nine young women were ranged in silent rows in front of the raised platform from which a trio of elder women gazed sternly at them.

'You are late, Landser.' The tallest of the women on the platform glowered.

'I'm sorry, Miss Drew,' Liddy apologised.

'To be sorry is not enough, Landser. You will write out five hundred times, "Tardiness is the proof of a grave fault in character", and bring them to me at supper time.'

For a brief instant rebellion flared in Liddy, but she could not afford to voice defiance.

'Very well, Miss Drew.'

She slipped into the rear line beside her friend Maddy.

'Let us pray.' From Miss Drew's rat-trap mouth this was command, not invitation.

Liddy had not been solely joking when she called this establishment a nunnery. For the young women who entered here as candidate teachers surrendered all personal freedom and were subject to rigid discipline. Their every waking hour from six o'clock in the morning to ten o'clock at night was regimented. They could not leave the premises without written permission from their instructors, and were expected to conduct themselves at all times with the utmost decorum. A Code of Rules governed their lives and any infringement of that code usually meant instant expulsion. Turnover of candidate numbers were high. Some girls could not accept the harsh regime and withdrew within a short time after entry; many more others were deemed unsuitable and expelled.

The vast majority of candidates were here because of grim necessity. They had to earn their daily bread and for those who stayed for the six, nine or twelve months necessary to obtain qualifications of varying grades there was at least the prospect of steady employment as teachers in one of the British Schools

189

which were established all across the country and in the colonies to teach the children of the poor.

'Our Father which art in Heaven hallowed be thy name. Thy Kingdom come . . .' the voices chorused and Liddy begged silently, 'Please God, keep my Rob safe and help him to find a respectable position.'

After prayers the next hour was spent in practising readings in poetry and prose, being monitored and closely questioned on the work by Miss Drew and her fellow instructors.

The breakfast bell rang, and in orderly silence the candidates filed to the dining room where tin bowls of salted porridge had been ranged on the long bare wooden table.

'For what we are about to receive, we thank you, Lord.'

'We thank you, Lord.'

'You may be seated.'

Forty hungry young women quickly sat down on the wooden benches.

'You may eat.'

Spoons rattled against tin bowls as the porridge was eagerly devoured.

A wickerwork basket of bread was passed along the table and each woman took one thick slice. A tray of lumps of hard cheese followed, and again each woman took one portion. A woman carried in a large jug of cold water and poured some into the empty bowls of those who wished to drink.

There was little noise beyond that of masticating jaws; Miss Drew did not approve of any superfluous conversation at mealtimes.

Liddy was deeply immersed in her own thoughts, chewing without tasting the meagre rations, determinedly forcing herself to be optimistic that all would be well in the end, that her beloved brother would not be forced into joining the army.

By nine o'clock the huge schoolroom adjoining the smaller classroom was filled with nearly four hundred girls aged from six to twelve years. The majority were drawn from the mean

190

streets of the Borough, children of the underclass, shabbily clad, undernourished, unclean in body.

Now the candidates became monitors instructing small groups of pupils in slate writing, elementary arithmetic, reading from Holy Scripture, recitation of the Short Catechism, and simple needlework. A few chosen candidates moved to the blackboarding surrounding the huge room and took turns at teaching a hundred pupils simultaneously. Beyond the separating wall of the huge school buildings 700 boys were undergoing the same process under the direction of 60 male candidate teachers in the adjoining School for Young Men.

Although so many different activities were taking place in the hall, the noise was not overwhelming, the only loudly raised voice being that of the candidate conducting the gallery lesson, the candidates teaching the small groups able to instruct in low tones.

Miss Drew and her assistants separated, moving constantly from group to group, evaluating the work of the candidates, intervening and sharply correcting when they considered that the candidates were making errors.

Liddy was instructing a group of the elder girls in the Short Catechism when she sensed the presence of Miss Drew behind her.

'Why was the Sacrament of the Lord's Supper ordained?'

'For the continual remembrance of the Sacrifice of the death of Our Lord, Jesus Christ, and of the benefits which we receive thereby,' the row of small grimy faces chanted listlessly.

'What is the outward part or sign of the Lord's Supper?'

'Bread and wine which the Lord hath commanded to be received.'

'Landser!' Miss Drew interrupted. 'That girl there, standing second from the right, is merely moving her lips. She is not giving the correct reponses.'

Liddy suppressed a sigh of exasperation. She knew only too well that the girl in question was merely moving her lips, because the girl was a virtual half-wit, who could understand

191

hardly anything that was said to her, let alone memorise and repeat the answers to the Catechism.

Miss Drew stepped close to the girl.

'You will give the next response. The rest of you remain silent. Now, girl, at the Lord's Supper, what is the inward part, or thing signified?'

The grubby features stared blankly up into the gaunt face of the questioner.

Miss Drew snorted contemptuously and turned to frown at Liddy.

'How has it escaped your notice that this girl does not know the Catechism?'

'It hasn't escaped my notice, Miss Drew. But the poor child is somewhat backward mentally and cannot be taught what she is not able to comprehend.'

'How are you qualified to judge what, or what not, this child may be taught to comprehend? How long have you been here yourself? Do you have an insight that I am deficient in?' The thin-lipped mouth rapped out the questions, and Liddy felt her own indignation burgeoning at the other woman's overbearing manner.

'Which question would you like me to answer first, Miss Drew?' she challenged heatedly.

The thin lips tightened ominously. 'You need not reply to any of these questions, Landser. At least, not at this present moment. Let it suffice for me to tell you that I do not regard you as a suitable candidate for the practice of teaching. You appear to be lacking the proper diligence, and also in the respect you should be displaying towards we who are your superiors here.'

The woman stalked away and sudden foreboding struck at Liddy. She thought, the miserable old cow would like to get me thrown out of school.

'Please, miss?' A small girl raised her arm.

With an effort Liddy forced a smile. 'Yes, Edith, what is it?'

'I need to pee, miss.'

'Very well. But don't be long. Now, the rest of you, repeat the

192

Articles of our Christian belief. Repeat after me . . . I believe in God the Father Almighty, Maker of Heaven and Earth . . .'

'I believe in God the Father Almighty . . .'

The children's chanting response filled Liddy's ears, but her thoughts were not in this huge room.

Where are you now, Rob? Have you found work I wonder?

Twenty-Six

Charles Street, Westminster, London

T he sergeant of Light Dragoons was resplendent in full regimentals of blue and silver, the hanging white plume of his shako swinging from side to side as he swaggered, one hand on the hilt of a slung sabre, silver spurs jingling musically on his gleaming black boots. Two corporals from the same regiment followed him, but instead of shakos they wore round pillbox forage caps to the sides of which were pinned long streamers of bright-coloured ribbons.

The squalid narrow street was overhung with the smoke pouring from the chimneys. On the corner was the garishly painted public house, the Horn and Trumpet, which served as a rendezvous for recruiting parties and men wishing to enlist.

Several men in ragged clothing, broken boots, shapeless greasy hats and caps lounged against the pub walls, and Sergeant Henry Keating's practised eyes scanned them as he approached, seeking likely prospects for recruitment.

Unwashed, unshaven faces turned towards the soldiers, and a couple of the men straightened their hunched shoulders and stood erect.

Keating halted directly in front of these two and grinned bluffly.

'You look to be strong, bright lads. I'll wager that you're thinking of taking the Shilling? It's two guineas' bounty when you takes the oath, you know. Just think of the good times you could have with that amount of rhino in your pockets.'

194

'The thought had crossed me mind, sor,' one of them answered in a soft Irish brogue.

'Then you'd best step inside, Paddy, and take a glass with me. And we'll have a talk,' Keating invited.

'Oi was thinking of 'listing as well, sor,' the other man told him.

'Then you're welcome to join us.' Keating pointed to the door. 'Go on before, lads.'

He nodded meaningfully to the corporals and they followed the two Irishmen into the tavern. But Keating held back, his attention fixed on a tall red-haired young man who was standing some distance away, staring down at the ground, hands thrust deep into his coat pockets.

Sensing that he was being studied, Rob Landser looked up and met the sergeant's gaze with a defiant glare.

Keating briefly evaluated the young man, noting that his clothing was of good quality. You'll be one of them young wasters who's broke their old ma's heart, you will, he thought. You'll be thinking of 'listing because you're no use for anything else, now that your old pa and ma aren't got no money left to give you.

He moved closer and asked, 'What brings you to this rendezvous, my friend?'

Rob inwardly pondered the soldier's question. What does bring me here? Well, that's easy answered. I've nowhere else to go.

Keating frowned at the other man's silent regard. 'Don't you understand what I'm asking?'

Rob nodded. 'Oh yes, Sergeant, I understand perfectly.'

The educated accent was confirmation to Keating that his judgement had been correct.

'You look like a man who's owned his own horses. Have you thought of joining the cavalry? A man like yourself would do better joining the cavalry rather than some other corps. It's no fun marching when you've been used to riding.'

The fresh features displayed sardonic amusement. 'And what makes you surmise that I've been used to riding, Sergeant?'

195

'You've got the stamp of a horseman, my friend. And if you enter into my regiment you'll be riding the finest horseflesh that money can buy. Our colonel won't have anything else other than pedigree thoroughbreds. We're mounted on as good bloodstock as the highest nobleman in the land. Will you step inside and take a glass or two with me?'

'I'm not really sure that I want to enlist, Sergeant,' Rob told him.

'No matter,' Keating assured bluffly. 'We'll have a drink for friendship's sake.'

'But you and I are not friends. I've never had a common soldier for a friend,' Rob sneered.

Keating replied with a broad grin.

'I reckon that we could become so. I like the cut of you. Come now, join me?'

Rob shrugged his shoulders. 'I cannot resist your blandishments any longer, Sergeant.' The sardonic smile still curved his lips. 'But I repeat, I've no real wish to enlist.'

But you will 'list, you arrogant bastard, Keating promised silently as he ushered the younger man into the tavern. I'll guarantee that. And then you'll get the shit kicked out of you in short order, or my name ain't Henry Keating.

'How many do you have for me, Sergeant?' The plump little magistrate peered short-sightedly through his pince-nez at the ramrod straight soldier.

'Three, sir.'

'Are they sober enough to understand what they're doing?'

'Yes, sir. They've taken a glass or two, but they know what's what.'

In the front room of the police station the two Irishmen were leaning against each other for support, while Rob Landser was slumped comatose upon a bench against the wall.

When the sergeant came into the room with the magistrate close behind, the corporals hastened to drag Rob upright and hold him in a tight grip.

The sergeant thrust small battered Bibles into the Irishmen's hands, and one of the corporals held another Bible close to Rob's lips.

With utter indifference the magistrate mumbled the oath of allegiance and his words were all but unintelligible. 'All of you here to make oath that you will be faithful and bear true allegiance to Our Sovereign Lady, Her Majesty Queen Victoria, her heirs and successors . . . defend her crown and dignity against all enemies . . . all orders of Her Majesty . . . officers set over you . . . So help you, God.'

'Kiss the Book,' the sergeant barked and as the magistrate departed grinned, 'Right then. You're the property of Her Majesty now, my lucky lads. Let's get you looked at by the doctor and then we'll be taking you to your new home sweet home.'

The soldiers chivvied the new recruits to a house in a neighbouring street and made them strip naked.

The doctor stank of gin and peppermint, and he gave only a cursory examination to each man. As they were getting dressed again one of the corporals produced some printed forms, a pen and bottle of ink and barked a series of questions, which the recruits were too drunk to answer with any real comprehension. But the leathery-faced corporal only grinned and entered his own inventions upon the forms.

'Sign here, Paddy,' he ordered, and as the Irishman blinked owlishly, told him, 'Don't bother.' He then scratched a spidery cross and wrote underneath 'Sean Shea, his true mark' and signed his own name beneath.

Drunk as he was Rob was still able to sign his own name in fine copperplate.

'You'll go far in the army, my cocker, writing a neat hand like this,' the corporal chaffed. 'They'll make you a bleedin' general in no time at all.'

Rob, swaying erratically and with drunken haughtiness, declared, 'If that should be so, then I will not be the first of my name to hold high rank in the army.'

'The only rank you'll hold is captain of the shithouse,' Keating growled. 'I'll make sure of that.'

Rob lifted his eyebrows in exaggerated mute interrogation, and Keating hissed threateningly, 'Mind I don't have you for dumb insolence, my bucko.'

'Come on now, Sarge,' the corporal intervened. 'Give him a chance. He aren't even got to the bleedin' barricks yet, has he?'

Keating scowled at the man. 'If there's one type of man that I can't stand, Corporal Jarvis, it's a bastard of a "gentleman ranker". And if there's another type of man that I can't stand, it's them who sucks up to fuckin' gentleman rankers.'

The corporal wisely did not answer, and abruptly found the forms before him of engrossing interest.

'Right then, come on. The train won't wait,' Keating shouted.

He led the way through the bustling streets towards Paddington Station, and the three recruits flanked by the watchful corporals shambled drunkenly after him.

The windy ride in the open rail carriage and the periodic showers of painful red-hot smuts from the smoke belching from the funnel of the engine began to sober Rob. His head throbbed from the effects of the rotgut spirits he had been plied with and his stomach twisted nauseatingly.

Only the leathery-faced corporal was travelling with the three recruits.

The Irishmen were both snoring, and the corporal grinned at Rob and nodded towards them.

'They've got the right idea. Get as much kip as they can afore the fun starts.'

The city was left behind and the train travelled through fields and huge market gardens interspersed with small clusters of buildings.

'We'll soon be at Hounslow,' the corporal informed.

'What will happen then?' Rob enquired.

'I'll deliver you to the barracks. You'll get a bedspace allotted to you, and then tomorrow you'll have your kit issued and start your drills. The best thing you can do is to try and get as much kip as you can. Reveille's at quarter to five. Make sure that you

198

keeps your rhino and valuables next to your balls, you'll lose it else.'

'My new comrades are not to be trusted not to rob me then. You surprise me, Corporal. I thought that we were all a band of brothers in arms,' Rob observed sarcastically.

The corporal chuckled grimly. 'Listen, my buck, you're a Johnny Raw, you aren't got neither brothers nor comrades in the regiment. You're everybody's chopping block, and they'll steal you blind if you gives 'um the chance.'

'Well, I've neither money or valuables, so there's nothing for them to steal.'

The other man roared with laughter. 'Don't you believe it, Johnny Raw, you've still got your eye teeth, and they'll take them if they're give half a chance.'

The train switched on to a branch line at the end of which was a small station. Rob saw two carbine-carrying Light Dragoons patrolling the platform, and the corporal told him, 'They're to stop any runners taking the train from here.'

'Is there much desertion from the regiment?'

'There's enough. Come on then, my sleeping beauties, let's be having you.'

The corporal roused the sleepers and then led the three recruits through the mean narrow streets of the small town to the complex of the cavalry barracks which stood on the edge of the vast gorse-strewn Hounslow Heath. They passed the sentry at the barrack gates who glanced at the newcomers without curiosity then once more stared blankly before him.

Another corporal took delivery of the newcomers and chivied them towards the long two-storeyed red-brick block that was to be their quarters.

The barracks appeared strangely deserted in the gathering dusk and the only lights were those glittering from the windows of the big three-storeyed officers' mess at the far end of the huge parade ground.

Their conductor was a sour-looking, taciturn man who said nothing until they reached their destination block. The ground floor was composed of stables, and the men's rooms were in the

199

loft above reached by an outside stairway which led on to a frontal veranda.

'You get in there.' The corporal pushed Rob through a door.

He stood for a moment accustoming his eyes to the gloom, and depression whelmed over him. The long narrow low-ceilinged room stank of stale cooking, unwashed flesh, and the acrid reek of the stables below. Two rows of close-set wooden cots lined the walls, and each of the corners were shielded from sight by blankets hung over ropes.

The blanket in the corner to his left was suddenly pushed aside and a woman's head appeared from behind it.

'Who the fuck are you?' she demanded fiercely. 'Just try pinching anything from here and I'll shove a fuckin' blade through you.'

Rob sighed wearily. 'I've no intention of stealing anything. I've been allotted a bed in this room.'

At the sound of his accent the woman's aggressive attitude metamorphosed into eager curiosity. She stepped out from behind the curtain to come and examine him closely.

'You're a Johnny Raw, ain't you? You talks posh. Was you a gennulman before you 'listed?'

Now Rob could see her clearly. She was young, with a gamine prettiness, slender body and a mass of tousled hair which hung down around her shoulders.

'No, I'm not a gentleman.' He felt suddenly desperate to lay his aching head down and sleep, and looked about him. 'Which bed can I use?'

'Any of 'um for tonight. The troop's doing the guard at Hampton Court Palace. They won't be back till tomorrow night. What's your name?'

'Robert Landser.'

'Pleased to meet yer, I'm sure, Mr Robert Landser.' She grinned and for a moment resembled a cheeky urchin. 'And I'm Gabey Patterson. Me husband is Corporal Thomas Patterson, who's the cock of the walk in this quarter. I ain't got any nippers to introduce to you yet, but it ain't for lack of Corporal Thomas Patterson giving me the necessary, if you knows what I mean.'

'Charmed to make your acquaintance, Mrs Patterson.' Rob bowed slightly, and she crowed with delighted laughter.

'Oh, you're a real toff, ain't you. Wait till the rest o' the girls meets you. They'll think you're a real swell, they will.'

Rob's head was spinning with tiredness. 'If you'll excuse me, Mrs Patterson, I really must get some rest. I haven't slept for some considerable time.'

'All right, Gingernut, you get some shut-eye. There'll only be me and the rest of the women and kids in here tonight, so you'll be able to sleep like a daisy. Take that bed there. It's Frankie Jones's. He ain't lousy like some of the bastards in this place. So you won't pick up any little six-legged lodgers, if you know what I mean.'

Still fully clothed Rob lay down on the straw-filled canvas palliase and within moments had collapsed into exhausted sleep. Gabey Patterson stood looking down at him for a while.

'You're a good-looking boy, Gingernut.' She grinned. 'And I always has liked gennulmen better than the roughs and scruffs. Who knows what might happen between us?'

She fetched a ragged dirty brown blanket from her corner and laid it over him, and he twitched and cried out in troubling dreams in which he saw his sister reaching out towards him, her face wet with tears.

The first bleak grey light of dawn had entered the fetid gloom of the barrackroom when the shrieking of excited children woke Rob. For brief moments he blinked dazedly up at the stained plaster of the ceiling wondering where he was, and then full recollection returned, and he grimaced in disgust.

'How are you feeling today, Gingernut?' Gabey Patterson grinned down at him.

He pushed himself upright, and groaned softly as pain throbbed in his skull.

'Drink this.' She handed him a small basin filled with steaming liquid.

He gulped the gritty unsweetened coffee, and as it moistened his parched mouth and throat he began to feel a little better.

'Come and meet the girls,' Gabey invited, and Rob turned his attention to the other people in the room.

Three women were sitting at a trestle table which had been set up between the rows of beds, and a swarm of noisy, grimy children of varying ages fought and scuffled about them.

Rob rose and followed behind Gabey Patterson, and the women stared at him with calculating expressions.

'This is Abigail, Dorcas and Martha, and this is Mr Robert Landser,' Gabey grinned.

'How do you do, ladies.' Rob bowed slightly, and the women chortled delightedly.

'It's right what you told us, Gabey. He's a real swell, ain't he?'

'And good-looking as well.'

'A proper gent!'

There was a half-eaten piece of greyish-looking bread on the table and Dorcas Murphy, a greasy-haired, broken-nosed, middle-aged woman, picked it up. 'Ere, 'andsome, have summat to ate.'

His stomach was queasy from the effects of the previous day's rotgut spirits, and he had no appetite.

'Thank you, no,' he refused politely. 'I'm not hungry.'

Dorcas grinned and offered with a lascivious wink, 'Well, maybe you've the hunger for summat else, 'andsome. I might be sweet-talked into giving you a bit o' that, if you plays your cards right.'

'Oh, Dorcas, you're a bloody caution!'

Her companions laughed raucously.

'Leave the poor bugger be,' Gabey Patterson chided laughingly. 'He'll be thinking that he's come to a bawdy house else.'

'I wasn't thinking o' charging him for it,' Dorcas quipped, her broken decayed teeth bared in a grotesque parody of a seductive smile, and she ran her hands down over her huge flaccid breasts. 'He can 'ave all this for love.'

The door slammed open and a stentorian voice bellowed, 'Get outside, Johnny Raw. Jump to it, you bastard, or I'll roast you!'

'Best look sharp and do what the corporal tells you, or you'll be meeting the "Drummer's Daughter" afore you're much older,' Gabey Patterson advised. With a sinking heart Rob rose and hurried to answer the summons.

Twenty-Seven

Mrs Ellen Macrae, Superintendent of the British and Foreign Society's School for Young Women, gazed sternly at the young woman who stood before her desk.

'Even if I accept your explanation that your reason for leaving the school without permission was an urgent meeting with your brother, Landser, I still cannot pardon such a gross breach of our rules. You will therefore be expelled forthwith.'

Liddy uttered a muted exclamation of distress.

Ellen Macrae was not unsympathetic towards Liddy and she told her, 'Left to myself I would not have expelled you, Landser. But I am bound by the rules laid down by our Board of Directors.'

She lifted a large leather-bound ledger from the desk drawer and opened it.

'When Mr Edward Harcourt approached me concerning your admittance for training at this establishment, Landser, he was informed that board payment was to be six shillings weekly paid entirely in advance. The total sum for the six months training period being seven pounds and ten shillings. This was duly paid. You have completed three months two weeks of training here; I shall reimburse you the two months two weeks board payments which remain: a sum totalling three pounds and two shillings and sixpence.

'As regarding any future employment as a teacher, your grades here have been satisfactory, but obviously you cannot be recommended to teach in a superior school. However, I am prepared to recommend you for teaching in a workhouse.'

Ellen Macrae awaited Lydia's reaction with some interest,

appreciating as she did that for any student the suggestion that they should go and teach in a workhouse was regarded as an insult to their intelligence and capabilities. A workhouse teacher was considered by any other teacher to be the lowest of the low.

She was surprised to see a fleeting smile touch the young woman's lips.

'Do you find amusement in what I have told you, Landser?' she questioned sternly.

'I do, ma'am,' Liddy answered forthrightly. 'Because a workhouse teacher is precisely what I was going to become. Mr Harcourt intended me to be the schoolmistress at the Union Workhouse in Bromsgrove, at a salary of ten pounds per annum with board and lodgings provided.'

She couldn't help but smile broadly now.

'I confess that I am much relieved, ma'am, to discover that I have qualified for that position after all.'

'You may go, Landser.' Ellen Macrae did not return her smile. 'The college secretary will give you your reimbursement. I would advise you to return to Bromsgrove as soon as possible and find out if Mr Harcourt will still allow you to take up the position at the workhouse.'

As Liddy closed the door behind her, the full implications of her expulsion hit home. What if Harcourt won't give me the position because I've been expelled? What shall I do then? And Rob? What has happened to Rob?

Momentarily anxiety whelmed over her, but she stubbornly fought it back, forcing herself to reason that he had most probably carried out his threat to enlist in the army. He must have done so, she thought. He must. Otherwise he would have come to meet me. He must have enlisted. Anyway, I'll leave a letter for him at the porter's lodge here. Then if he comes in search of me he'll know that I've returned to Bromsgrove. I'll sell the jewels and trinkets and leave the money in the letter for him.'

She prayed silently, Please, God, help Rob. Please keep him safe, I beg you. Please keep him safe . . .

*   *   *

205

'And you're leaving here for good, are you, missy?' The kindly old porter grinned at Liddy's sad expression. 'Now why look so down in the mouth, missy? Most o' the young women who leaves here am only too happy to be going.'

'I'm worried for my brother,' Liddy explained. 'You will keep this packet safe for him, won't you?'

'Don't you bother your head about that, missy. This packet 'ull be as safe with me as if it was in the Bank of England.' He winked as his fingers felt the coins inside the cloth wrapping. 'And so 'ull this money be safe as well, missy. If your brother leaves a message or sends a letter here to you, I'll make sure that it's forwarded on to the Post Office in Bromsgrove. And if by any chance your brother don't come for the packet, then I shall forward it to the Post Office in Bromsgrove for you to collect it from there.'

'Thank you for your kindness,' Liddy told him gratefully. 'Here's some money to pay for the forwarding. And if my brother does collect the packet, then have a drink with the post money.'

The porter grinned happily. 'Oh, I'll do that all right, missy. Don't you bother your head over that.'

Twenty-Eight

L iddy journeyed from London to Birmingham by train, arriving late at night. To husband her scant money she sat by the fire in the Ladies Waiting Room at the station, snatching a brief fitful sleep before setting out in the very early morning to walk the further ten miles to Bromsgrove. It was nearly mid-morning when, travel-grimed and footsore, she wearily carried her carpet bag up the muddy narrow lane towards the isolated cottage where her parents lived.

Her father smiled as he opened the door to her knocking.

'Liddy, my dear, this is a wonderful surprise. Are you come home for a holiday? It's nearing Christmas Day, isn't it? Come in, come in. This is a wonderful surprise.'

She looked at him with concern. His face was haggard and unshaven, his hair unkempt, his linen black with dirt. The stench inside the cottage was foul and dust lay thick on every surface.

George Landser's hands were shaking visibly as he gestured towards a chair by the side of the rusty grate where a small fire flickered.

'Sit down, my dear, and warm yourself.'

She could smell the reek of stale sweat and gin emanating from him.

'Where's Mamma?' she asked.

'She's in bed, my dear. She's not well. Not well at all. I think it best that you do not see her.'

She stared at her once dapper-dandified father and tears filled her eyes as she muttered brokenly, 'Oh, Pa, what's happened to you?'

He seated himself on the opposite chair to face her. A muscle in his cheek was twitching violently, and he clasped his hands in front of him as if in prayer.

'It's my nerves, Liddy. My nerves are at breaking point. The only thing that helps me is gin.' A wheedling note entered his quavering voice. 'Did you happen to bring a bottle with you, my dear? I'm in sore need of a drink. It's the only thing that helps me now. It steadies me, d'you see.'

Suddenly a high-pitched wailing sounded from the next room, and Liddy started in shock.

'It's only your mamma, my dear. You needn't concern yourself. It's only your mamma.' George Landser's stained porcelain teeth bared in a grotesque caricature of a reassuring smile. 'Did you happen to bring a bottle with you?'

Grief and anger battled for mastery in Liddy's mind, and anger momentarily prevailed.

'No, Pa, I didn't bring any drink with me. And it's not more drink you need, judging by the state of you.'

He frowned and exclaimed petulantly, 'I'm the best judge of what I need, Liddy. I'm the best judge of that.'

The high-pitched wailing trailed into silence as Liddy used both hands to rub away the tears that were blurring her sight.

'I'm going to see Mamma.'

She rose, and her father rose also in quick alarm.

'No, my dear. It will only cause you distress. I've already told you, she isn't well. But I'm caring for her. You've no need to concern yourself about her. I'm caring for her.'

'It's plain to see that you're not even capable of caring for yourself, Pa,' she snapped curtly, and pushed past him to fling open the door of the adjoining room.

Inside it was so dark that she was forced to stand still until her eyes were accustomed to the gloom. The stench here was equally foul, and intermingled with it was an added peculiarly feral rankness.

She crossed the room and pulled back the thick curtains which veiled the small window, then turned to look at the bed.

The sight of her badly emaciated, half-naked mother caused

her to gasp in horror. Beatrice Landser's features resembled a living skull, her visible skin was caked thick with filth, her hair was a tangled greasy mass upon which the tiny pallid specks of lice could be seen moving. But more terrible than all this were her eyes: huge, red-rimmed, and gleaming with madness.

'Oh my God!' Liddy felt sick and faint, and was suddenly overcome by the desperate need to escape from this room, from this cottage, from the sight and sound and stench of her parents.

She ran from the cottage and down the lane, and behind her she could hear her father shouting plaintively, 'Will you bring a bottle back for me, Liddy? Bring a bottle back, won't you?'

Liddy ran until she was gasping for breath and a sharp stitch tore at her side. She slowed to a walk, her thoughts a tormented maelstrom, grief and despair tearing at her.

What am I to do? she asked herself over and over again. What am I to do? Tears fell from her eyes. Oh, Rob, where are you? I wish you were here to help me.

She came to hump-backed bridge and leaned on its parapet, staring down at the dark water of the canal. The air was cold and dank, the skies as grey and forlorn as her mood. Lost in her own sadness, cheeks wet with tears, she was unaware of the approaching barge, and unhearing of the sharp echoes of the barge-horse's steel-shod hooves upon the metalled towpath.

The barge passed beneath her but she was hardly conscious of its passage.

Some yards further and the barge slowed and halted, and the ageing, grizzled-haired bargee walked back along the towpath and on to the bridge.

'It is you, aren't it, Miss Landser?'

At the sound of her name Liddy wiped the blurring tears from her eyes and fought for self-control. Then she turned to the stranger. As she looked at his gnarled features recognition gradually dawned.

'It's Mr Beech, isn't it? Susan's father.'

He seemed pleased by her remembrance. 'It is, missy. Jesse Beech in the flesh. I'm on my way to the salt works to pick up a cargo. It's a busy place now that the new brine beds have come into production.'

'And your grandchildren, are they well and happy?'

'Oh yes. They've got a new mam now. Their dad married a young widow-woman, and she's a good soul and treats them like they was her own.'

'I'm very pleased to hear that, Mr Beech,' Liddy told him sincerely.

His eyes dwelt on her tear-wet face for some moments, then he questioned hesitantly, 'I know it's not my place to ask a young gentlewoman like yourself such things, but is everything all right with you? Only you look very down with yourself. And to be standing here in this lonely spot in this cold weather and all, well, is there anything grieving you, missy? Is there any way I can help?'

His simple kindliness shattered her hard-won self-control, and suddenly she couldn't stop herself sobbing. She felt his arms round her, her face pressed against his tarry coat, and she heard his comforting voice.

'That's it, missy. You have a good cry. Let it all come out from you. Have a good cry. You'll feel all the better for it. I'll help you if I can. I'll help you. Have a good cry.'

And cry she did, until all her tears were spent. Then she dried her eyes and drew a long, deep breath. As the cold air filled her lungs it brought with it the rapidly strengthening resolve that she would not allow herself to be defeated by her present troubles.

'Thank you, Mr Beech. I must go now.'

He stared closely at her. 'Are you sure that you're all right, missy? Is there anything I can do to help you?'

She smiled gratefully at him. 'You've already helped me more than you can ever know, and I thank you for it.'

She walked hurriedly back into Bromsgrove and bought a wooden pail, carbolic soap, broom, scrubbing brush and clean rags, bread, bacon, potatoes, tea and a cone of sugar, then, heavily laden, set out again for the cottage.

There was no answer to her knocking so she opened the door and went in, calling, 'Pa, are you here?'

The small living room was deserted, the fire almost dead in the rusty grate, an empty gin bottle upon the table. She was suddenly assailed with an irrational fear that her parents might be lying dead in the other room. She could not bring herself to open its door, and stood for several minutes mustering her courage.

Her heart pounding, racked with the dread of what she might find, she opened the bedroom door.

The wailing cry made her jump, and relief shuddered through her when she saw her mother's skull-like features and red-rimmed eyes.

'Thank God you're alive, Mamma. Where's Pa?'

Beatrice Landser gave no indication of understanding the question, or of recognising Liddy. She lay in her filthy bed of rags, hands held up as if to ward off a danger, mouth agape, emitting the eerie-sounding wailing cry.

'I'm not going to hurt you.' Liddy felt pity stirring for this pathetic creature, yet strangely no sense of any kinship. It was as if her mother was a stranger.

She went outside and searched the immediate environs of the cottage, but found no trace of her father.

'He's most probably gone to buy more drink,' she surmised.

The cottage water supply was a small streamlet running past its rear, and Liddy filled her pail with its clear cold water and set to work.

She accepted that it was pointless to try to wash her mother's bedding or clothing, since a search of the cottage revealed that there were no replacements for any of those articles. But she could wash the woman's face and body.

When she went towards her mother, however, Beatrice Landser screamed piteously and burrowed beneath the rag coverings like a terrified animal seeking the safety of its lair. Liddy wasted little time in trying to coax her mother.

To tell the truth I don't really wish to touch her, she admitted guiltily to herself, and tried to assuage that guilt by setting to and furiously scrubbing the floors, walls and meagre wooden furnishings. The task took a long time and it was growing dark before she had finished.

She washed her face and hands in the streamlet, and dried herself on a piece of clean rag.

'Liddy? Is that you, Liddy?'

She heard her father's voice and turned to find him standing some yards away. She examined him anxiously and to her dismay saw almost instantly that he was drunk.

'Why have you made the cottage all wet?' he challenged querulously. 'We shall catch our deaths of cold.'

Liddy was torn with a mingling of anger and grief at how her once loving, intelligent, dandified father had metamorphosed into this filthy human wreck. But she didn't want to quarrel with him now if it could be avoided.

'I'll make a fire for you, Pa.'

'What with? I've no coals,' he growled.

'I'll look for some wood in the hedgerows.'

He swung about and went into the cottage.

Liddy walked to a copse some distance down the lane and rummaged in the undergrowth for dead fallen branches. She made several trips with her arms full, piling the wood by the side of the door, then broke it into smaller pieces and busied herself laying a fresh fire upon the few glowing embers in the rusty grate.

Her father sat at the table, taking swigs from a fresh bottle of gin, eyeing her morosely.

'Can't you stop drinking for a single hour, Pa?' She could not help the hardness in her voice.

'Don't take that tone with me, missy,' he warned. 'I'm still your father, and you'll show me respect.'

'How can I respect you when I see what you've become?' she demanded.

'Get out!' He came to his feet, bellowing in fury. 'Get out before I kick you out!'

She faced him unafraid.

'What about Mamma? What has she had to eat today?'

'I'll care for your Mamma, just as I've cared for her ever since you deserted us.'

'You know very well that I didn't desert you, Pa,' she said indignantly.

'You did! You and that worthless brother of yours. You both deserted me! When I needed you most, you turned from me! You abandoned me!'

'I didn't abandon you,' she reiterated angrily.

'Yes, you did. You went gallivanting off to London, just when I most needed you. It's your fault that Mamma is like this. It's all your fault.'

She could stand it no longer, and snatching up her shawl and bag, she went to leave. She lifted the latch of the door.

'Nooo!' He wailed in anguish. 'Don't go, Liddy. Don't leave me again. Please. I'll be good, Liddy. I promise. If you stay I'll be good.' He sounded like a small frightened child. 'Please don't leave me. Please.'

In that instant Liddy knew with absolute conviction that if she did not leave now, she would carry the burden of her parents until either they or she died. That she would become the parent and they the helpless children. That she would never be free to live her life as she might want to live it.

She sighed with heartfelt despair, her hand fell from the latch, and she turned back to her father.

'Don't distress yourself, Pa. I'll stay.'

Twenty-Nine

January 1843

E dward Harcourt sat with his fingers steepled before his chest, head bent, listening intently to the words of the shabbily dressed, insignificant man standing in front of his desk with his hat clasped in both hands.

When the man finally finished speaking, Harcourt looked up and told him, 'You've done well, Jenks.'

He opened his desk drawer and took out some gold sovereigns which he passed across to the man.

'Does you want me to continue to watch, sir?' Jenks asked.

Harcourt shook his head. 'No, that won't be necessary. You can go back to the other task I set you.'

Jenks tugged his greasy forelock, and then replaced his battered hat on his head.

'Thank you, sir. Thank you.'

When Jenks had gone, Harcourt smiled grimly. 'So, that's the way of it. That's why she is always so cool towards me, he thought. The rumours that Widow Wybergh has a secret lover are true. And it's young James Kerr no less. I'll wager that that young bastard will end by wedding her. He'd be a damned fool not to.

An intense feeling of rancour coursed through him, and he promised himself, That's a score I'll have to settle with you one day, James Kerr.

Edward Harcourt took no heed of the fact that in all likelihood James Kerr knew nothing of his own intentions towards Mercedes Wybergh. The fact that the young man had thwarted

214

him, no matter unknowingly, was enough to make him an enemy. But Harcourt had no intention of trying to settle the score immediately. He was a firm believer in the ancient Spanish adage, that revenge is a dish best eaten cold.

Liddy halted at the street door of the bank to allow the shabby man coming out of the door to pass. She was dreading meeting Edward Harcourt again, dreading the prospect that she would be told that no position was available to her now that she had come back in disgrace, dreading whatever humiliations she must undergo from his tongue.

For a few moments she waited, summoning her courage, then drew a deep breath and entered the bank.

The clerk tapped the door and opened it.

'There's a young woman here who wants to speak with you, sir. She gives her name as Miss Lydia Landser.'

Harcourt smiled grimly. 'So, she's dared to show her face at last. Bring her in.'

As Liddy was ushered through the door he rose and came round the desk to greet her.

'Miss Lydia, please be seated.'

He returned to his own chair and stared closely at her, noting now the wan features and the drawn expression. He was perceptive enough to sense that she was under a considerable mental strain, and decided to move cautiously and see what advantage he might gain from that fact. He decided also that he would not tell her of the letter already sent to him by the principal of the Battersea school detailing the facts of Lydia Landser's expulsion.

'You seem tired, Miss Lydia. May I offer you some refreshment?'

Despite her dislike of the man Liddy was touched by this display of consideration.

'I thank you, sir, but no. There is something I must tell you of, which I fear may greatly displease you.'

Now that he was close to her again, Harcourt was once more experiencing the powerful sexual attraction she exerted over him, and he told himself, Now that the Widow Wybergh is presently beyond my reach, I can concentrate fully on this one, can't I?

Aloud he invited, 'Then tell me.'

He sat listening impassively while Liddy related truthfully what had happened in London. She made no attempt to hide anything or to make excuses for what she had done.

Behind the impassive mask Harcourt's devious mind was racing, and when she fell silent he asked her sternly, 'If this happened in December, why have you waited until three weeks into January to come and see me?'

'I was too embarrassed to do so before, sir,' she admitted.

'Your expulsion is most regrettable. Your concern for your brother gives you credit. But it has to be said that he has proven to be a worthless wastrel and I am sorry that I ever recommended him for any position. He has disgraced his family's good name.'

Shame flooded through Liddy, and it was all she could do to keep her head held high and meet the man's eyes. She readied herself to bear with dignity the rejection which she was convinced was coming.

Harcourt sighed and shook his head, and in a gentler tone continued, 'However, I am inclined to the belief that in this case you are more sinned against than sinner. Will Mrs Macrae confirm all that you have told me? Will she also confirm that you are sufficiently qualified to teach in a workhouse school?'

Liddy felt a stirring of hope. 'I'm sure she will, sir.'

Harcourt steepled his fingers before his chest and pursed his lips judiciously as if he were pondering deeply.

Liddy's tension increased almost unbearably, and her breathing quickened.

Harcourt was also racked with tension, but his tension was sexual. He was fighting against the urge to savour the sight of her firm high breasts pulsing against the bodice of her gown. He knew instinctively that even in her present desperate situation, any wrong move now on his part would drive her from him for

216

ever. But he was confident that the right move now would inevitably in the course of time bring her to his bed.

'Well, Miss Lydia, I have the fullest confidence that you have told me the truth about these unhappy events. Therefore I shall give you a letter to take to the workhouse instructing the Master that you are to take up your position there, and commence upon your duties immediately.'

Her relief was so intense that she expelled her breath in an audible gust and her tensed muscles momentarily slackened. She was hardly conscious of his continuing words.

'. . . of course I shall have to seek Mrs Macrae's confirmation for all that you have told me. The board will demand no less. But I feel sure that she will so confirm.'

He paused, as if awaiting reply, and she told him with real gratitude, 'I thank you, sir. I thank you most gratefully.'

He waved her thanks away with a fleeting gesture of his hand.

'If you will wait outside, I'll pen the letter for the Master. His name is Melen. How you address him will be decided between yourselves.'

He reached for his steel-nibbed pen and a sheet of notepaper.

Liddy did not rise immediately. She wanted to ask him for another favour, but was hesitant to do so.

He looked questioningly at her. 'Is there something more?'

Her white teeth briefly caught her lower lip. 'There is something that is troubling me, sir.' She could not easily find the words she wanted.

For the first time in the interview he allowed a smile of encouragement to touch his mouth.

'Please, Miss Lydia, if I can be of any further service, then ask it of me. I know that our past relationship has never been that of friendship. But I hope that you have now been given some indication of my regard for yourself, and of my hope that we may at some future date each regard the other as a friend.'

Liddy was experiencing embarrassment that she had so misjudged this man in the past, and had been so eager to think badly of him.

The emotion caused her to flush, and Harcourt saw that flush

217

and imagined how she would look in the throes of lovemaking, and he felt his manhood harden involuntarily.

Fearing his reaction would show in his expression he pretended a sudden fit of coughing, hiding his face behind his large handkerchief until he had regained control of his rampaging lust.

'I do apologise. I'm beset with a cold at this time. Now, what is it that is troubling you?'

Liddy found, much to her own astonishment, that she was willing to trust and confide in him.

'It's my family, sir. I've no notion of where my brother is at present or what has become of him. And my parents . . .' She went on to tell him of their physical and mental conditions and forced herself to be completely truthful about her own feelings for them. 'I will speak frankly, sir. There is no affection between my mother and myself, and there has been none for many years. I may appear to be unnaturally callous, but I cannot help my feelings. However, I still owe to her the duty of a child towards its parent and intend to fulfill that duty.'

Harcourt was momentarily taken aback by her harsh candour, and thought to himself, There's a hardness in you, girl, which I hadn't realised you possessed.

Aloud he said in a bluff tone, 'You are a very forthright and honest young woman, Miss Lydia. There is nothing of the hypocrite about you. Therefore I shall be equally honest and forthright.

'It is a sadness for me to see the deterioration in your father's physical and mental condition, because I cannot help but feel that perhaps inadvertently I have contributed towards that deterioration. I should have insisted that he continue to seek some sort of employment, instead of having him granted outdoor relief. By allowing him to live rent-free in my property and ensuring that he and your mother have been receiving an adequate allowance for their subsistence I have enabled him to live in idleness. And, as we all know, idleness leads to boredom and boredom leads to vice. Your father's vice is drunkenness, which I fear has now destroyed his capacity to perform any useful work.

'However, no matter how much the board badgers me to cast your parents off, I intend to ensure that they can stay in the cottage for as long as they wish to, and continue to receive the parish relief.'

Shame welled up again in Liddy. She hadn't known that her parents were living rent-free in his property, or that the Board of Guardians wanted them taken off the outdoor relief. She felt impelled to tell him, 'Sir, I've sorely misjudged you in the past. I can only hope that you will forgive me for it.'

He waved her words away. 'Please, let us say no more of this. There is nothing to forgive. Now, may I offer you some advice?'

'Of course, sir.'

His manner became avuncular. 'Go to the workhouse directly and get settled into your duties there. When you are so settled, then you can give some thought as to how you may best help your parents. If you feel the need to discuss the matter with me, then don't hesitate to call on me.'

Liddy could harden herself against injustice and aggression, but kindness made her vulnerable and now she felt tears stinging her eyes.

'I can only thank you again,' she muttered.

Harcourt had his head bent while he began to pen the letter, but a fleeting sly glance at her face told him what he needed to know, and he smiled secretly with satisfaction.

He completed the brief note, scattered drying powder on the wet ink, and blew the excess away. Then he folded and sealed the sheet of paper and handed it to Liddy.

His manner was now brisk and businesslike.

'I wish you good fortune in your new position, Miss Lydia. And now I must bid you a good day.'

He busied himself with a ledger and, saying her own good day, Liddy went from the office, feeling warmed by his kindness.

Outside in the street the air was fresh and crisp, and she breathed deeply of it. Invigoration swept through her and her confidence expanded.

'Everything will be all right. No matter how bleak it might look, everything will start to come right from now on.'

She walked briskly down the long High Street and out of the town until she came in sight of the grim building with its high spiked walls, then halted and stood staring at it.

'There it is, my new lodgings. Ah well, "Bastille" it might be, but it's got to be better than sleeping under a hedge, and that's my only alternative at this point in my life.'

Smiling wryly she walked on towards the great iron gates.

The story of James Kerr and Lydia Landser will be continued in *The Workhouse Doctor,* **to be published soon by Severn House.**